"I meant what I said earlier, Beth. Come hell or Falcone's hitmen, I'm with you for as long as you need me. Or want me."

Beth clenched her fists even as her body swayed toward Brendan. Oh, how she ached to take what he so freely offered, but though he didn't know it, she was fighting for his very life. The life he'd all but laid at her feet just now. And she wouldn't—couldn't—risk his life. "Just get out, McCall."

As if her words hadn't affected him, he strolled to the door. "Lock it after me, babe. I'll be watching from outside—got to keep the princess safe."

She'd done what she could to save him. Now he had a chance of staying safe and alive... and she couldn't allow herself to want any more than that.

Dear Reader,

Welcome to another month of excitement and romance. Start your reading by letting Ruth Langan be your guide to DEVIL'S COVE in *Cover-Up*, the first title in her new miniseries set in a small town where secrets, scandal and seduction go hand in hand. The next three books will be coming out back to back, so be sure to catch every one of them.

Virginia Kantra tells a tale of *Guilty Secrets* as opposites Joe Reilly, a cynical reporter, and Nell Dolan, a softhearted do-gooder, can't help but attract each other—with wonderfully romantic results. Jenna Mills will send *Shock Waves* through you as psychic Brenna Scott tries to convince federal prosecutor Ethan Carrington that he's in danger. If she can't get him to listen to her, his life—and her heart—will be lost.

Finish the month with a trip to the lands down under, Australia and New Zealand, as three of your favorite writers mix romance and suspense in equal—and irresistible—portions. Melissa James features another of her tough (and wonderful!) Nighthawk heroes in *Dangerous Illusion*, while Frances Housden's heroine has to face down the *Shadows of the Past* in order to find her happily-ever-after. Finally, get set for high-seas adventure as Sienna Rivers meets *Her Passionate Protector* in Laurey Bright's latest.

Don't miss a single one—and be sure to come back next month for more of the best and most exciting romantic reading around, right here in Silhouette Intimate Moments.

Yours,

Leslie J. Wainger
Executive Editor

Please address questions and book requests to:
Silhouette Reader Service
U.S.: 3010 Walden Ave., P.O. Box 1325, Buffalo, NY 14269
Canadian: P.O. Box 609, Fort Erie, Ont. L2A 5X3

Dangerous Illusion
MELISSA JAMES

Published by Silhouette Books
America's Publisher of Contemporary Romance

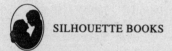 SILHOUETTE BOOKS

ISBN 0-373-27358-4

DANGEROUS ILLUSION

Visit Silhouette at www.eHarlequin.com

Printed in U.S.A.

MELISSA JAMES

is a mother of three living in a beach suburb in county New South Wales. A former nurse, waitress, store assistant, perfume and chocolate (yum!) demonstrator among other things, she believes in taking on new jobs for the fun experience. She'll try almost anything at least once to see what it feels like—a fact that scares her family on regular occasions. She fell into writing by accident when her husband brought home an article stating how much a famous romance author earned, and she thought, "I can do that!" Years later, she found her niche at Silhouette Intimate Moments. Currently writing a pilot/spy series set in the South Pacific, she can be found most mornings walking and swimming at her local beach with her husband, or every afternoon running around to her kids' sporting hobbies, while dreaming of flying, scuba diving, belaying down a cave or over a cliff—anywhere her characters are at the time!

For my dad, who loved James Bond and spy books and movies. He would have loved to be tall, dark and dangerous, like McCall—well, you were dark, anyway. You would have liked this book, Dad.

My deepest thanks goes to Marg Riseley, who stepped into the breach to read this one for me, and reminded me of points I'd forgotten; and to Olga Mitsialos, thanks once again for being reader and suggestion person extraordinaire. To both ladies, your constant support was invaluable— especially when I needed help cutting this book down. And my undying gratitude goes to my editor, Susan Litman, for helping make this book what it is now, by fabulous revision suggestions and always being there to plotstorm with me. These Nighthawks wouldn't be the people they are without you!

Chapter 1

Renegade River, Bay of Islands, New Zealand

It was her.

Oh, yeah, it had to be. No other woman had ever roused that knife-edged core, gut-gnawing hunger, scraped with a burning need to hold and protect. Scraped, not mixed. It never blended, like something meek or tame. Nothing about his reaction to her was *tame*. One look and his veneer of social graces shed like molted skin to reveal the raw male animal beneath, hungry and hot, savage and needing.

Instant obsession.

McCall stood five feet from the round, cross-beamed window beneath an intricate and beautiful sign like something straight out of Middle Earth, proclaiming her to be:

Elizabeth Silver, Potter of Excellence.

He watched her working at her wheel, her face—that unforgettable blend of lush South American exotic and haunting English-rose beauty—filled with gentle concentration.

He'd loved her trademark auburn curls, but the new, almost

boyish style, a cropped mop of raven hair, only intensified her surreal loveliness. The haunting star-queen—everything else faded away, submerged beneath the power of the dark azure eyes in that amazing face.

Even in quiet repose without a trace of makeup, it was definitely her face. The unique light and dark, serenity and turbulence, so-intense-it-slammed-you-in-the-guts beauty that had launched a million magazines and spawned male fantasies beyond count from the time she was fourteen. The unsmiling waif.

She'd smiled for *him.*

They'd met while shooting promo pics for a navy recruitment drive, and he'd immediately seen the wistful, shy girl inside the haughty model. And within hours, he was in so deep he'd never really found his way out.

He could still see her lying beneath him, drugged by his kisses, her swollen mouth smiling with innocent desire…driving him, the guy his SEAL team called *The Untouchable,* to his knees. All he knew was, he had to have her—but he couldn't make love to her while they met in secret. She'd asked him to wait until they revealed their relationship to her wealthy parents. Touching and kissing, making promises during stolen meetings. *I can't tell my parents about us yet, Brendan…but I will soon, I promise…I promise.*

That damn word still yanked his chain. Yeah, she'd gone *slumming* with him all right. She'd wanted a holiday from the jet set, and he'd made it clear he was happy to be her slave for as long as she wanted him.

But within six months she'd returned to her uptown life, hit the high-class party circuit—and then more dubious gatherings. Hanging on the arms of the rich and infamous with men of evil reputation. Yet she'd still seemed so damn innocent, above it, or beyond it all. Always, she seemed apart from the angst and lusts of life, as if she'd fallen from a star.

Until the day she'd married arms and drugs dealer Robert Falcone, she'd still been *his.* Though his world was her exact opposite—a world peopled by pimps, black-market traders of weapons and human flesh, while he infiltrated and busted their filthy deals with his trained undercover teams—he'd been fool enough to believe she'd come back to him.

But he couldn't forget her. She was Helen of Troy, Cleopatra, Aphrodite—but she was *his.* He'd staked his claim, and one day he'd mark her, brand her to the world. McCall's woman.

That objective hadn't changed in ten years. He wanted her even more now that the big-eyed elfin-child had become golden, lissome woman. The flames of desire still licked at his soul. They were always there, burning alive all they touched in sudden conflagration.

McCall dragged in a breath that felt like the center of a firestorm—blasting hot, scorching him from the inside out. Yet it was April in New Zealand, mid-autumn, and the lush, green coolness of the air couldn't be milder. She sat at her potter's wheel in a quiet house amid the emerald hills, a long-lost dream of wistful beauty, and he felt like a caveman wanting to drag her off by the hair. *My woman.*

Hold it in, or she'll run again.

If the boss knew of their past, he'd take him off this assignment for sure. But Delia de Souza Falcone was his one lapse in a perfect career, his own private ghost—the haunting immortal who walked with him by day, her sweet whisper in his ears by night—but when he awoke, she was never *there.*

Yet here she was in the Bay of Islands, in quiet, semirural New Zealand, of all places. The country right next door, yet it was the one place he hadn't thought of looking.

He thought he'd known her better than anyone living; but he'd been forced to reassess that half-assed belief when Anson, his superior in the information-and-rescue group known to the upper brass only as the Nighthawks, had told him there was a strong probable hiding out in northern New Zealand.

So she made a fool of you again. What's new about that?

Yet he couldn't help but admire her guts. Damn smart of her, coming here, setting up a business like a bona fide ordinary citizen. If he hadn't thought of it, neither would Robert Falcone—and it appeared to be so. Falcone had seemingly forgotten his wife and spent five years chasing another woman,

Verity West, a fellow Nighthawk, code name Songbird. Her cover as an international singer nicknamed ''The Iceberg'' had made her irresistible bait for a man like Falcone, who saw women only as trophies to show off, or for breeding children for him. Songbird played her part in bringing Falcone's networks down, until he escaped from custody with the help of corrupt police on his payroll.

But a week ago the Nighthawks received positive confirmation that Falcone's hunt for his supposedly dead wife and son had intensified after five years on the back burner, and he was concentrating on the South Pacific. Anson had again gone through all the Delia possibles, coming up with this woman, and only by sheer luck had he, McCall, beaten Falcone's men here. He had about two days to get her out of here, though how the hell he could do that with the orders he'd been given was beyond him.

Keep all information pertaining to who you represent or what we want from her confidential until you get a positive ID, and proof that she has the tape of Falcone ordering a hit on Senator Colsten. If she goes to the press, she'd prejudice the case in court and he'd go free…and more innocent people will die. This woman is either Delia de Souza or her cousin, Ana. We have positive confirmation that Ana de Souza flew in to Amalza five days before the accident that killed one of them—and the other had to have taken the child, and the tapes. Getting the proof we suspect Delia holds, and taking down the rogue Nighthawk in league with Falcone, are our number-one priorities.

Damn it! He knew Anson was right, but how the hell was he supposed to gain her trust without giving her the truth?

It's what you've done the past ten years with every other mission. Just get on with it.

He pushed open the rounded door beside the round, cross-beamed window—a savvy move on her behalf, making the half-hidden house vaguely resemble a hobbit hole—and the bell above tinkled. He stood in the doorway, framed by the glow of early morning, and waited. *Look at me, Delia.*

''I'll be with you in a moment. Please feel free to look

around." Her voice, with a perfect New Zealand soft burr, was cool as spring water, gentle as the pitter-pat of new rainfall, and though it was miles from the husky Rio accent he remembered, it still hit him with a fission-blast of heat. He didn't move, didn't speak. Her beauty was gently mellowed in the simple jeans and soft lavender woolen sweater she wore, covered with a clay-smeared smock. Her once perfect, soft, long-fingered hands were grubby from her work, with chipped, short nails and cracked, rough skin. But it *was* her. He knew it.

Look at me, Delia....

Finally she looked up, her dark blue eyes fixed on his face, half smiling in professional inquiry. "May I help you?"

No start, no shock, not even a hint of recognition. She sat as serene as Raphael's Madonna, calm and lovely as Botticelli's Venus. One look at her, and she'd knocked him off his feet; she looked at him and obviously felt—nothing.

Could she have forgotten? Was she the actress of the century, or could Elizabeth Silver be her real name? Was this a simple case of a freak coincidence of looks and age?

And in being an illegal immigrant? an inner voice jeered.

Jerked back to reality, he ran his gaze over her again, watching more than her face. *Read her body language.*

Hell no! She knew him all right. Her eyes and face remained calm, but her fingers were scrambling in a hasty attempt to cover the sudden hole in the wet clay she'd made with a jabbing finger.

He wanted to get her out of here and fast, before Falcone's hit men found her. And he would, even if it killed him. Even if he weren't committed body and soul to taking her filth of a husband down as part of his Nighthawk mission, he'd do it—for her.

"Sir? Are you all right?"

He shook himself. "Yes. Sorry. I was expecting—" *you to recognize me* "—someone older."

She didn't smile. "Elizabeth Silver does sound like someone's maiden aunt." She remained as far off as Delia had always been, until a magical summer day when a young SEAL lieutenant's outrageous comments had made her giggle, getting them both in trouble with the irate photographer… "I guess I could change it by deed poll if I wanted to."

Not in this lifetime, baby. The only living woman who could legally change her name from Elizabeth Silver in New Zealand was fifty-four years old, a mother and grandmother who lived five hundred miles away on the South Island, near Christchurch.

"Yeah," he agreed with an easy returned smile, leaning on the doorpost. "But it suits you."

She lifted her eyebrows. "I'm nobody's aunt that I know of."

You're no maiden either, you're Mrs. Falcone. His jaw tightened. *Get that through your head, McCall; she's another man's wife. She hasn't been yours for years.* He forced words from his half-frozen lips. "I beg your pardon. I don't know you, do I? Your face reminds me of someone I used to know…"

Not a twitch or start, no telltale flush or paling of her golden oval cheek. But—her fingers…were they shaking? "I seem to remind a lot of people of someone. People always ask me that." She lifted clay-smeared hands in inquiry. "May I help you, or are you just browsing? You're welcome to look around all you like."

"Just looking. I saw your house and sign, and I couldn't resist having a look in here."

"That was its design." She smiled, this time with a little genuine feeling. "Please feel free."

Slammed in the solar plexus. Just one smile and he was winded, scrambled, foolish and fooled. Part of him wanting like hell to believe she was Delia, the other half so bloody naive it was laughable, all wishing and wistful. A dumb-ass jerk wanting her to be genuine—just Elizabeth Silver, Potter of Excellence. A legal identity to smile at, think about, take dancing or to dinner and make love with, like any other woman…as if she weren't the runaway wife of a billionaire black-market arms and drugs dealer whose men were reported to be hot on his tail right this minute, bent on kidnap and revenge of said runaway wife.

Both halves of him so fierce in their driving male need, so finely balanced on a hot knifepoint he felt as if he walked an electric tightrope, and he was nobody's gymnast. This mission could all fall apart because he couldn't change the way he felt any more than he could stop the sun rising tomorrow.

Tomorrow. One day closer to Falcone getting her. Yet he stood here like a teenager in his first burst of lust. Lost in the same old need, its ache undiluted. He had two days max to gain her trust, while from half a world away Falcone sat smack between them, pulling his strings and smiling like an obscene demigod, holding a high-caliber automatic to her head.

She's in danger. Just do your job.

She was watching him. Checking him out…and not in a sexual manner. Beneath her ultrafeminine, gentle exterior, her eyes acted like a computer, seeking out his secrets. Finding what he wanted to hide. Working out his agenda.

He made himself nod, still watching her. ''Thanks. I'll look around. Did you paint that sign yourself?''

''Yes.'' Her words were cool and distant, a step back, a mile above. The star-being, the haughty Brazilian princess. She'd retreated behind barriers he couldn't navigate, jamming his prelim-data radar like an EA 6B Prowler at night.

He couldn't blame her. The intensity of his briefest gaze on her almost blistered his own skin.

Get a grip on yourself!

He wandered around the studio. *The bell above the door's connected by wire to an intercom system too high-tech for a business this small. Window onto the main road looks double-glazed—bulletproof. Both the doors to the outside, and the door leading into the private house, look at least two inches thick, with a one-sided quadruple locking system protecting the house.*

She's watching every move I make. Her eyes are calm, but she just dented the pot on the wheel again, her fingers are gripping its base so hard. It's already twisted out of shape with her foot jerking the wheel pedal.

Yeah. Way too tense for a woman with nothing to hide.

At random he picked up a vase. It was flute-shaped, thin as the most delicate glass, of a blue so clear he could almost see through it, like a wash of oceanic beauty. A woman's face superimposed, like a hologram for its fineness, its sweet lost-soul effect. "This is amazing."

She nodded with regal carelessness. "Thank you."

"How much?" Nothing in the whole studio had a price on it that he could see.

She told him, her cool, clear voice almost a shrug. As if she'd picked a price off the top of her head.

His mental alarm started shrieking. Everything she said and did was way too casual for the levels of tension he felt radiating from her. Oh, yeah, she knew him, remembered him. Was she fighting the same grinning demons he was? Wanting, aching for a touch, playing the fiddle of imperative danger while they burned with need....

She apparently misinterpreted his silence. "That's in New Zealand dollars, not American." He guessed she was speaking in reference to his California accent, still strong after living for a decade in Canberra, Australia's capital.

"Very reasonable." With almost two NZ dollars to each American dollar, the vase was almost indecently cheap. "I'll take it." And he wanted it. Even if it hadn't been a piece of such clear-water, haunting beauty, he'd want it. He wanted a permanent part of her to stay with him even after she'd gone.

Yeah, he'd hit the jackpot at last. No other woman had ever set his body on fire with such white-hot, furious need. Only Delia. She'd scorched him with every smile, every laugh at his jokes, every secret she'd told him—and she'd drugged his very soul with kisses so sweet, shy and desperate, his lips still burned with their imprint ten years later. In five months, she'd dragged his heart from its place of deep, dark hiding...and she'd slipped some intrinsic part of his *self* inside that incredible aura of hers, and taking it back had never been an option.

Gut, heart, body and soul, all screaming, *I've found her.*

Yet if she was Delia, she was another man's wife, even if

that man was a slime-bucket criminal who got rid of his en-
emies with his army of contract killers.

And still McCall wanted her, his desire raging and unstoppable.

Had he ever really known her? The Falcone case had long
ago forced him to reassess everything he thought he knew.
She'd been an eighteen-year-old girl when they'd met in secret
for five beautiful months—then she was gone. Within a year
she'd married Robert Falcone, a smiling demon who left the
hearts of brave men slamming against their ribs and their guts
knotted. What had life with Falcone done to the woman-child
who'd been so pure, so protected and innocent to McCall's
world-weary eyes?

Seeming oblivious to his turmoil, Elizabeth Silver, Potter of
Excellence, wrapped the vase in tissue paper and placed it in
a bag with her amazing design on its silvery folds. "Here you
are, sir." Her hands trembled slightly as she handed the pack-
age to him.

On instinct, he zeroed in on her eyes, and saw unmasked
terror…and haunting recognition. Then it was gone, so swift
it felt like the passing of an F/A-18. He had to force himself
not to blink. Was this an Oscar-winning performance, or was
he wishing, hoping so damn hard for her to be Delia he'd
gone catatonic?

Right. You can do this. He handed her a credit card with
his real name, watching her as she took it. Would she react?
Not likely, if she didn't react to my face or voice. But it was
a risk he had to take, with only two days to gain her trust.

Her eyes flicked over the name with detached profession-
alism as she made up the bill, then she handed him the slip
to sign. "Thank you, Mr. McCall. Please come back." Not a
single sign of recognition, just a courteous dismissal.

He didn't believe it—didn't believe *her.* She'd had a decade
to perfect her act. He wasn't going anywhere. Not when every
screaming instinct told him he'd found her at last. "My mom
has a set of pottery at home in a similar blue to this vase, but
she broke her teapot. A tall one, in a classic design. Do you
think you could make a replacement? I'd love to surprise her

with a new one.'' Since his mom had run off when he was eight, taking his sister, Meg, and leaving him alone with his drunken dad, she sure as hell would be surprised—surprised he'd bothered to find her. But it made him sound like an all-round nice guy, and women liked that kind of man. He had to gain her trust fast—it meant her life—and his long-absent mom may as well be useful to him for once.

It worked. He got another smile, a fluttering of her fingers. ''Of course I can. Does the piece have any particular design on it?''

''Daisies.'' A spur-of-the-moment decision. ''You know, like that old china pattern? Flannel daisy, wasn't it?''

Her cheeks flushed, her eyes glowed from within, like far-off stars warmed by sunlight. He didn't know what, but he'd said something to bring her to life, one way or another. ''I can make something similar, but please bear in mind that the design and china are classic. I can never hope to create anything that perfect.'' She went on, neither needing nor wanting his reassurance on her talent. ''I could have it finished in twelve days. Perhaps I can send it on to wherever you're going?''

''I've got two more weeks here.'' He watched her in what he hoped was a strong-male-interest-without-interrogation manner. Hell, the best he could hope right now was that he didn't look like a psychotic stalker. When it came to Delia, his feelings were so screwed he didn't know what he looked like or what he felt.

One of her eyebrows lifted. ''Two weeks in the Bay, in autumn? You're not touring the whole North Island?''

Okay, that was weird. It was fixable. ''I'm on long service leave. I've been here a month, with Auckland as my base, doing the beaches and wilderness. I've seen from the Harbors to the volcanoes around Rotorua and the ski fields, not that there's snow yet. I checked out the South Island, too. It's a gorgeous place, isn't it? Just like it looks in *Lord of the Rings.*''

Innocuous babble of an American tourist, lifted straight from a tour guide. He'd flown straight into the Bay last night, his security clearance absolute and unquestioned.

This wasn't working. His hatred of the lies he told wouldn't show, he was too good to let it slip—but the people he lied to were the pond scum of the earth, and lying to this pristine princess made him feel as if he'd joined their ranks.

If he kept up the act, she'd bolt. He had to tell her the truth, or the mission would blow up in his face. The consequences to him were immaterial compared to those before the whole Nighthawk team, and especially to this woman and her child.

Because if he didn't get her out of here fast, no matter what her name was, Elizabeth Silver would be a dead woman within days.

Chapter 2

*B*rendan?

It took every scrap of self-control not to cry out his name, but she'd done it. She'd waited in silence for him to show a sign, to show her that he knew her, for him to tell her why he was here, and she'd received—nothing.

Nothing but lies.

McCall—she couldn't think of this big, dark half stranger as Brendan, not *her* Brendan—was lying through his teeth; but Beth nodded at his tourist patter. Seeming to accept him at face value was the only way she could buy time to *think*— think about why he was really here, what he wanted from her. It was obvious, from his nonidentification, that he didn't have positive ID on her, and he wasn't going to recognize her.

He should have known better.

She'd been on the alert since the whispered phone call this morning, warning her that a man was casing all the potters' studios, buying nothing but asking lots of questions.

But she'd never expected *this*. Not *him*.

Even after ten years she'd known him. Leaner, tougher, with deep scars hiding inside his forest-green eyes, and his black hair long and gypsy-wild instead of military-short—but it was still him. Her heart hit her throat and hammered, making her quiver with one look at him. No longer in the immaculate dress whites in which she'd met him, or the self-conscious suits he'd bought for their dates—no, he was dark as the storm clouds gathering outside in jeans the shade of night, boots and an ankle-length black leather coat over a thick deep gray woolen sweater.

He didn't say her name. He didn't show any recognition, and he didn't say a word to reassure her about why he was here. He'd treated her as a stranger, asking odd questions, watching her, handing her his damn credit card.

A word kept floating around in her head, keeping her cool and in control under the words straining to fly from her lips.

Orders.

She'd stake her business on the fact that McCall was under orders to keep her under surveillance, to stay close and not spook her. But she wouldn't risk her life—or that of her son.

Betrayal.

This wasn't her Brendan McCall, the young, intense, *wonderful* navy poster-boy with whom she'd spent the five most magical, stolen months of her life. Escaping from the bodyguards Papa set on her when she could, paying them off when they'd found her with him. Doing anything she could to be with him.

Keep focused. One mistake and Danny won't see his next birthday.

Right. Focus. She flicked a glance at him, and she could see the honed instincts of a professional beneath the veneer of intense male interest. The tourist patter didn't fit the searing glances, the tense, unable-to-relax stance of his tall, super-muscular frame, the way he was taking everything in with mathematical precision, taking mental notes. If he was a tourist, *she* was a native resident of Antarctica.

So McCall had finally found her…but obviously he hadn't come out of love—and whether he was on the side of the angels or the devils didn't matter. If he'd found her, Danny's father couldn't be far behind. Just by showing up here, McCall could bring the force of eternal night down on her little boy.

She repressed a shudder. Danny's father wanted his son, and if he knew who she really was…

He didn't want me, Deedee—he wants Delia de Souza. Even after I bore him a son, he kept saying that I didn't match up to his expectations of Delia. I got so mad I told him I was Ana—and I told him the real Delia is hiding in England. I didn't know how obsessed he was with you, or that he'd come send his men after you. I thought he loved me, but as usual, it's you he wants….

She jumped into speech. "That's what I love about New Zealand—you get every weather and place, all in two islands. I love the beaches here, and I head down to the ski fields in winter. It's always quiet here then, and I can close up shop for a week. I can't ski, but jumping on a toboggan is fun." *That's it, play the tour guide, the friendly businesswoman. Even if he knows who I am, he can't get any confirmation unless I give it.*

And she wouldn't give him a thing, not even knowledge of the magnet-to-polar effect he was having on her.

He was even more incredible than he'd been when they first met. In his dress whites, he'd been sexy in an immaculate, awe-inspiring, bad-boy-in-hiding style. Now he was strong and weathered, taut and hot and intensely masculine. Dark as night, rugged and turbulent, like a living storm inside a cloud—a jagged-edged force about to unleash. He was discordant poetry, unchained symphony and all man.

He didn't have a *go-to-hell* face—more like *come-to-hell*. He was already there, burning inside his own heat, the inferno beckoning her, irresistible, insatiable—and the moth's wings were already on fire.

And I'm a fool. He's not here for himself. Someone sent him.

She watched him smile and nod, but inside those deep forest eyes, he was adding up every word she'd said, and breaking it down. "You don't ski? I thought most New Zealanders would."

Delia had been an enthusiastic skier. There were hundreds of photos of her as the unsmiling snow queen. "Not after knee surgery. I don't have the flexibility for it anymore." *Not bad, for a spur-of-the-moment story.*

"Did you have an accident?"

He was on the hunt, and if he were in Falcone's pay she was up that wild Renegade River outside, without a paddle.

*Don't think of him as Brendan…don't…*but he'd haunted her too long, his long-ago love for her was her only balm in a world gone insane—and she felt a piece of her, the innocent girl, dying with the need to pretend. *To lie to him.*

"I was a mad netballer as a kid. Dad and Mum—" she forced the New Zealand pronunciation through an aching throat "—took me all over the country. When I was fifteen I lost my cruciate ligament twisting to throw the ball. I took up pottery while I recuperated, and was hooked. I need my leg in good working order for the wheel pedal. I won't risk another operation just for the sake of skiing. Toboggans are great fun."

Doubts. Shadows. A web of confusion spun at a moment's notice, born of fear and the scent of danger surrounding her—the danger emanating from him, this dark stranger with eyes like the Amazon rain forest, taut whipcord muscle beneath his snug jeans, and specters of fire and shadows stalking his heart. He made her hot and cold all at once, filling her with memories of tender starlit magic.

As if he was remembering, too, his eyes grew lush and hot. "Have dinner with me tonight, Elizabeth Silver."

Well, that was a curve ball out of left field she should have expected, yet she felt her cheeks heating and her breath freeze in her lungs. Just as well, since she'd almost blurted, *Your employer wouldn't appreciate that, would he?*

And damn it, he was already tempting her too much. Oh, to be a normal woman again, free to be with this forbidden fruit of a man….

The man who sold his country's secrets to the highest bidder, and only got out of treason charges because he disappeared from America and never went back.

She reined in her thoughts. *Control, control!* The mantra had been her best friend over the past six years, and she grabbed at it with all the fevered intensity of a woman hit by a wallop of terror—and unwanted desire. "I prefer Beth." *Why did I say that? I'm talking too much.* "Sorry, but I'm busy." *Much better.*

He took a step closer. She could feel the heat inside him, the wildness he kept under tight leash. The hidden lightning in his soul called to her long-forgotten heart and spirit—the promise of a breaking storm on a deep summer's night. And oh, the woman in her screamed to run into the uncontrolled tempest inside him, and get absolutely soaking wet.... "Tomorrow night...Beth."

She managed to hold in the strange, delicious quiver of feminine need and met his eyes, willing a veneer of calm to cover the tangled emotions within. "You're not my type."

He didn't flinch, didn't even move. The only indication of his feelings at her lie registered in the slight hardening of his fine-chiseled mouth, the deep grooves of his dimples slashing downward. "Do you have a *type,* Elizabeth Silver?" he asked in his deep, rough voice—a creature of the night, a gypsy spirit hiding beneath the tourist's mask.

"Teddy bears," she said blandly. "I like the boy next door. A guy who takes his kids and wife to games and the movies."

He took a step closer. "I think you're lying." His voice, dark and wild as the night, vibrated into her soul, stripping its layers of defense. "I think you've got a weakness for bad boys."

Ana. Not me! Ana! Ana had been the one who liked bad boys, and she had made it known internationally.

Beth closed her eyes and dragged in a harsh breath, sucking air in till her lungs felt ready to explode. The gentle jasmine scent in the burner, meant to uplift her customers, felt obscene in her nostrils as she waited for the words to come. So it had come back again, the reap-what-she'd-sown consequences of one stupid decision—the reason she'd left her life behind. The foolish mistake she'd made when she was all of nineteen, yet it still dragged behind her like a chain gang's weight. In tearing grief for her parents' deaths, she'd allowed the cousin who'd been like a sister to her walk in her shoes for a month. Poor little Ana, with the near-identical face to hers, brought up by Delia's parents after hers died—but with such a different life. So sheltered and cosseted and *lonely,* spending most of her childhood and teen years in hospitals or in grueling physical therapy for a bent back from severe scoliosis. Finally healed, she'd wanted to know how it felt to be Delia de Souza, supermodel, beautiful and admired and worldly—*just for a little while, Deedee...a few weeks? It would be fun for me...and you'll get a chance to rest for once....*

She'd been paying the price for allowing the charade ever since. Years and years of running, paying for Ana's innocent, foolish mistakes—and her penchant for dangerous men.

What was she saying? Ana was the one who'd paid. She'd *lived* with her mistakes—Ana had died for hers.

"You're wrong," she said now, with the conviction of utter truth. "Bad boys have bad hearts. I want a nice guy, the nice house, picket fence and all that."

"And based on ten minutes' acquaintance you know I don't fit the mold?" His lifted eyebrow and a slow, knowing smile emanated an aura, a feeling of currents too deep and strong, and she was flailing in waters too uncharted for her to swim in safety.

Breathe, her mind whispered.

Smiling with would-be blandness, she lifted a tourist guide from the counter. "You quoted the guide verbatim. You've never been south of this part of New Zealand, have you?"

"No." His mouth twitched into a full-bodied grin. With the rumbling chuckle, a lock of dark hair flopped over his forehead, as if to hide his eyes. "So one lie—a white one at that, meant to impress you with my wealth and ability to be idle for long periods of time, excludes me from the teddy bears' picnic?"

It was so hard to keep a straight face with him moving closer, wearing that lazy grin. She'd almost forgotten how his rumbling, self-mocking humor always made her laugh. McCall had *bad boy* written all over him, yet he was *good*—too good.

A man who made her want to smile, tease and flirt just as her life had exploded in her face was way too dangerous to play with. She had neither the experience nor the ammunition for it.

She moved back to gain perspective, which she couldn't do with his taut, jaguarlike body leaning close to her, just close enough to be screaming *male interest*. "Afraid so."

His eyebrows lifted. "You can tell I'm not a boy next door?"

"I'm sure the mamas next door were warning their daughters to bolt rather than trusting them to your care," she retorted.

He burst out laughing, warm and musical and fascinating as the sea on a deep summer's night. "I'm sure you're right...as sure as I am about the fact that teddy bears aren't really your thing. Some instinct tells me you're a 'bad boy' kind of girl."

No. Not anymore. She'd been cured of that girlish fantasy forever, thanks to Ana. "My instinct says that your instincts don't always work to your good." She held out the bag containing his vase. "Have a nice stay in the Bay, Mr. McCall."

"What if I don't give up?" he muttered, low and urgent, moving closer as she backed off, his eyes shifting from calm forest to stormy crystalline. "What if I come here every day until you change your mind?"

He'll keep coming anyway, if Danny's father sent him here. And that was the only real option—it wasn't as if Interpol would send a man who'd already betrayed his country for cash.

The truth of it tore at her wistful wish that he could have come here for her, and ripped it into bloodied shreds. "I'd say, don't annoy my customers."

He rocked back on his feet, the deep intensity lightening as he chuckled again. His smile lit his whole face, including the fascinating cleft chin and left dimple, with male strength and beauty. "Lady, you don't give much away, do you?"

Not when my son's life depends on it. She smiled, hoping to look bland, uninterested, but her needs and fears were already submerged beneath the long-dormant woman, leaving her in hopeless, needing confusion. Within ten minutes of meeting McCall again, her emotions were so skewed she barely knew what she said or did. Her heart had been iced over so long she'd thought it in permafrost to anyone but Danny; now it was melting so fast she felt as if McCall had jet-streamed it to the equator by one of the Hornet planes he'd once loved so much. "What did you expect on ten minutes' acquaintance?" Her voice sounded husky, deeper and huskier than her practiced, gentle New Zealand accent.

She watched those amazing rain-forest eyes of his register the sound of her voice, and take the information in. *Click. Lock.* Another piece in place. Another bullet in the barrel of the gun of exposure—and she was facing it down in hopeless defiance.

"Well, a guy can always hope." He shrugged and picked up his bag. "I'll be back."

He meant it. He'd be back. She closed her eyes for a moment; then she fixed her gaze on him. "Why? Why me?"

His deep, compelling eyes on hers, he closed the gap between them. With infinite gentleness, he tipped up her chin with a finger. "Why do you think?" It was a whisper of heated sound, coffee-warm breath tiptoeing over her face, his touch tender. His masterful strength leashed...for now, at least. McCall would never hand control to anyone else for long.

Yet, no matter how she fought it, the slow blush filled her cheeks at his touch—a wave of half-shy sensuality, a woman-to-man acknowledgment of his effect on her.

No, no! Any act she put on now would be useless. She'd given it all away with a moment of involuntary feminine need. Her lashes fluttered down; she looked at her trembling fingers in disgust. Yet, how many long, cold years had it been since she'd known the sweet drowning, the yearning for a man's touch?

Not since Brendan.

"If I knew, I wouldn't need to ask," she whispered back.

"Does there have to be a why?" His finger moved over her skin in a slow, subtle caress. She felt the quiver touch her soul, the heat streak straight from her heart to her most feminine core.

Without knowing it, she nodded.

Still holding her chin with a finger, he flicked his other hand toward the large pewter mirror hanging over the counter, designed as much for warning against strangers as it was for beauty and security. "Look in that." He walked to the door, opened it. Then he turned to look in her eyes—a moment's truth flickered in their hidden depths, lush and hot with untold secrets. "Watch out for strangers, Elizabeth Silver."

As the door swung back to close after he'd gone, she felt his veiled warning touch her heart with icy, chilled fingers.

Chapter 3

"Cameras in place, Ghost," he reported into the cell phone to his commander in Canberra. "Covering the entire perimeter every two yards, fences and in the garden. Two on each roof corner, with immediate heat-detector relay to me. Sentinel alarmed so they can't be disabled. A three-second relay to home base, and to me within fifteen. She can't get away."

"Good work, Flipper." Anson used the code name McCall hated with all his usual curtness. It referred to McCall's SEAL background but he always felt like he should make dolphin noises when Anson called him. "Don't leave the subject—24/7 watch. Wildman's stationed two miles south, Braveheart two miles north, Panther the other side of Russell. Heidi's west of the Bay, in the market village. Each has a ten-minute deadline to reach you."

Perimeter covered as always, even in a one-man op—every contingency covered, including his death. The watch over his radial pulse sent satellite updates every ten minutes back to base. If he went down, the team moved in to protect the subject.

"Roger that, boss. I'm good to go."

"Subject update?"

"Sleeping." The heat detectors in the roof cameras flashed two unmoving objects—three if you counted the puppy her kid had sneaked in after his mother went to bed.

McCall grinned. Yeah, he could relate to that. He'd always done the same with the neighborhood stray after his old man fell into a drunken stupor or went out on the boat for night fishing, leaving him alone. Funny how that sour-tempered old mongrel's presence had been so reassuring to his eight-year-old mind, after his mom and Meg disappeared. He'd even grown to love the unwashed stink of the dog. The smell of the docks was familiar, and the pungent odor was a reminder, even in sleep, that he wasn't alone.

So Beth's son was a lonely kid, too, even though his mom had stuck around, and obviously loved him.

Yeah, Beth Silver seemed the original earth mother. Through the silvery radiance of moonlight pouring through her windows, he could see a house filled with mellow redwood furniture, bare flooring and fireplaces, loads of scatter rugs and comfy sofas. Homemade touches like cross-stitch pictures and paintings, scattered pieces of pottery. Pictures of her with her son, the boy now named Danny. The boy who looked enough like Robert Falcone to be his missing son, Robbie.

He sensed Beth Silver would be a tigress when it came to protecting her son. She'd lie, cheat, steal—maybe even kill—to stop anyone taking him from her. He'd probably get the kid only over her dead body.

A good thing he wasn't after the kid. What he did want was that lithe, lissome, feminine body warm and alive—and filled with him. Hearing her cry his name when she—

Yeah, as if you're gonna get that anytime soon, when she refuses to even recognize you. Face facts, McCall, she was slummin' with you ten years ago, and she ain't gonna contaminate herself or her precious son with any down boy again.

The garden outside the house filled the place with the scent of blood roses and ferns, touches of jasmine and gardenia, earth and work and *woman*. This was a modest, lovely home, with a hint of an untamed heart in the rolling hills surrounding the property. Even the old, moss-covered craters of long-dead tiny volcanoes that dotted the whole northern island seemed to fit the deep-hidden, slumbering fire of the woman who lived here.

The rustic beauty of her home suited the picture Delia had told him she wanted one long-ago night—"A pretty little cottage I can do up myself, with a rose garden. My own house I can take care of myself, away from all the people and servants and fuss." Her eyes had glowed with a young girl's simple dreams.

For her wants to be so meager had seemed strange to the point of alien to the half-wild gang-kid from the docks of L.A. Her upbringing, her homes, everything about her was as lofty as a high-ranking Brazilian diplomat's daughter could be— and she deserved every care and luxury. Things he could never have given her back then, and still couldn't now. He could give a woman comfort, but never first class. He'd never be rich.

But they were things she obviously still didn't want. She'd made her simple dream come true.

A blip alerted him before he saw it. A vision passed by the window a moment later, ethereal, ghostlike in her simple white sheath nightgown, barefoot. Silhouetted by the soft light of the glowing coals in the open fireplace, her nightgown became translucent satin, and her golden body and small, high breasts were in sweet shadow…and he ached like hell, watching her. Like a siren, she was there one moment, taking his breath with her otherworldly loveliness, and gone the next.

He'd frozen in midcount, dragging in a breath. Incandescent loveliness in the tender moonlight pouring through the window. The quiet, unsmiling waif returned to her milieu. *Delia.*

Get a grip, McCall! He willed his hormones to subside, but he found himself watching, waiting for her to pass the window once more. Then, his body aching and pounding inside those fire-scorched chains of the wanting he couldn't conquer after a decade, he left the perimeter. Blowing out a mist-heated breath of frustrated *need,* he headed to the doubtful comfort of his bedroll, damp from the rain leaking into his motorbike's pack. The closest to a cold shower he'd get, but standing naked in a glacier wouldn't do a thing to douse the fire burning him alive.

From behind that triple-locked door, behind the peephole, the woman who still felt like a ghost inside her own life after years of hiding sagged against the wall, and breathed again. Beth passed an unsteady hand across her forehead. Why, why had she looked? Why, when she knew she'd only lose herself in the sight of him?

Twice now, he'd done the impossible to her. Last time, she'd loved him in minutes; now, within a day, despite all she knew about him, McCall had gone from her deepest terror to her dark sentinel, fascinating her with all a child's fear of the night—a night he walked in with ease and grace, as if he belonged to it, or the night belonged to him. Even a prosaic task, such as opening his bedroll, took on a life of its own.

For some reason a line of poetry danced through her mind, slightly corrupted: *He walks in beauty like the night.*

Fool. She sighed and returned to her bed. When it came to McCall, a fool was all she'd ever been.

And though the thicker wool of her cushioned bed enfolded her more closely than the thin pallet McCall had rolled himself into, she found no comfort, no rest or release from heated midnight dreams, lush as black silk and just as terrifying.

Her peaceful life here in New Zealand with her son was over. Out of the shadows and into the fire—a fire that would burn her baby alive. All her plots and strategies, all her sacrifices were worth nothing if Falcone got to Danny. And if he got to her—

She shuddered. McCall might suspect, or think he knew, but he couldn't prove a thing. She held the only proofs, just as she held Falcone's life in her hands. A dual-edged sword meaning death, and so Falcone had kept his search low-key, discreet. But if he got her, she knew exactly what Falcone would do—what he'd wanted to do for the past twelve years, since she'd reached the age of consent at sixteen. And he'd take back his son.

It wasn't happening to Danny. Her little boy would live and

grow and play in peace, become a man like his grandfather, and his honorary grandfathers, and if she had to sacrifice her life for that to occur, so be it.

Her sleepless eyes watched dawn break over the tiny harbor across the road, knowing that McCall was doing the same, laying aside his wildness like a folded cloak and slipping into the persona of humanity he shed with the fall of night.

She rubbed her eyes. She *definitely* needed more sleep if she was indulging in dawn fancies, turning McCall into a creature of the twilight. He wasn't after her blood to keep himself alive. He was just a man, about to betray her and her little boy the same way he'd betrayed his country, and for the same reason.

Money. It was as cold and as crude as that.

McCall pushed open the door of her studio and walked in. He didn't question it, didn't wonder if he should keep watching from across the road, as he had all morning. It had nothing to do with the afternoon rain drenching him. The coolness soaking him through was refreshing after hours of his body aching from superheated dreams, waking and sleeping: dreams of slipping that wraithlike sheath from her pearlescent skin, and burning alive with her in the inferno their loving would create.

No, the ache had grown unbearable, and he accepted the simple fact. He needed to see her, talk to her to ease it. As simple and as damn complicated as that.

"Good afternoon, Elizabeth Silver." He had to keep playing the game until she gave him a sign, let him into her world, and hand over the evidence he knew in his gut was here somewhere.

But she barely nodded at him. No politeness today, no sword-thrust to his verbal parries—and he could now see what watching her from across the road didn't show. Her mouth drooped as she worked; her hands were barely steady enough to mold the clay. The defenses she'd erected against him yesterday had come crashing down—for now. "Did you get any sleep last night?"

Or had she stayed behind that window, as caught by him as he was by her? The young Delia hadn't been able to keep her eyes…or hands…from him for long, and whispered between drugging kisses that thoughts of him kept her awake at night.

A no-sleep op was okay for him. Even if he hadn't been SEAL trained, he could get by on two or three fifteen-minute snatches of shut-eye through the night, as he'd done for most of his life. But the stress on her pale face was delicately obvious. Her tiredness made her lovelier than ever, as wraithlike as that slip of silk she'd worn in the night and as haunting, even in her prosaic jeans and woolen jumper outfit.

"Did *you* sleep?" Her soft, cool voice was gravel in her sleepless state, hitting him hard and low and fast with a jolt of hot need. "A sleeping bag on the grass can't be comfortable." Her eyebrow lifted, the challenge seeming stronger for its quiet femininity. "You do realize that stalking me by day and watching me at night, sleeping outside my house, does nothing to reassure me that you're a member of the teddy bear's picnic?"

She had a point. He made himself shrug, thinking fast. "I've run out of money?"

Her chin lifted. Her barriers were coming up, and clicking into place. "I don't think so."

Aiming to charm her, his mouth quirked up. "Um, I *really* want that teapot for my mom?"

"If she exists." She sighed. "Can we stop this, please? If I see you outside my house at night again, I'll call the police."

"And say what?" he growled. "A man's asleep on public ground across the road? That's not a felony in New Zealand."

"I saw you in my yard last night. Touching my house. Trespass with intent, I think that particular felony is called, isn't it? And since you're so well versed in New Zealand law, Mr. Tourist-just-here-for-two-weeks, maybe you can tell me what bylaw it's part of, so I can tell the police when they get here."

McCall swore beneath his breath. He'd well and truly blown his tourist cover by his knowledge of international law, and she was no longer a delicate, hollow-eyed china doll, she was tense and tight-stanced, ready to fight. "Are the police coming now?" he asked in a dark growl. Not that it mattered. With a call from Ghost or a high-ranking police commander, they'd back down fast. But Falcone had paid off people in authority before, and his men were already in the South Pacific. He didn't want to tangle with more authorities than he had to because it put her at risk.

"Not yet." A hand came up from behind the counter: wiped clean of the wet clay, it held a cell phone. "I've punched in the number. You have ten seconds to convince me not to complete the call."

Damn, didn't she know better than that? "You shouldn't give intruders warning of your intentions. Ever. They could disarm you in seconds." It would take him four, tops.

"I wouldn't try it. Your fertility would be in question in seconds." Her other hand lifted, holding a heavy baton. "I also know two different types of martial arts."

He didn't doubt her. It explained her tight, controlled stance, her legs splayed and arms tense, ready to attack. She wasn't a fool, then, just too angry to care—or maybe, beneath her projected fear and mistrust, part of her knew he was here to protect her, so she was giving him a chance to explain himself.

"And if I don't punch a security code into my alarm system every half hour, the police will be here within two minutes, and the security cameras installed into the ceiling have already relayed your image to the firm," she went on, her eyes hard.

"Why would you be telling me all this if you thought I was going to attack you?" he asked softly. "You wouldn't. Not unless you believe in your gut that I'm not here to hurt you. So this whole farce is unnecessary."

She glanced at her watch. "Nine. Eight. Seven."

Damn it! His mission was top secret—

"Six. Five."

He couldn't tell her everything, but he could play one ace. "You already know why I'm here," he murmured, low with masculine tension. "You've known since the moment you saw me, no matter how well you hid it. Even though I had to let you go with them that night, you knew I'd come back for you one day.''

A moment's silence. "It's time for your medication, McCall. Unless you were brought up in Dunedin, or have been here in the past couple of years, I don't know you." When he didn't answer, she shrugged. "Perhaps you should just tell me what it is you really want from me.''

"You know what I want, Delia." He used the name deliberately. "Just like you knew my name before you saw it on my credit card.''

Folding his arms across his chest, he stood silent, waiting.

Was it a trick of the half light of the storm outside, or did her cheeks warm? "I thought that was what it was," she said in a would-be casual voice. Shaking beneath.

He moved closer, all man now, the Nighthawk in him shot to hell at the gentle floral scent of her fresh-washed hair, the glowing golden skin, free of makeup, the aura of *woman* beneath the coolness she projected. "What?" he whispered. "What is *it?*"

She moved her face, as if in denial. Denying his question, or the raw male need straining from his every pore, screaming at him to take her, to find release from this unbearable *need,* this half-crazed tension inside her warm, golden loveliness?

Her answer, when it came, was unsteady. "I'm afraid you've crossed the world on a wild-goose chase, Mr. McCall. I'm not who you're after. I'm Beth Silver." She put down the baton and phone, and moved to her potter's wheel, switching it on and reaching for her clay, kept wet in the double-thickness plastic bag. Finding steadiness inside familiarity? Was she so scared of him?

Not you, fool—you represent her losing her anonymity and freedom, he thought with a flash of insight. *She doesn't know if I'm working here alone, or if Falcone's close behind.* And damn it, he couldn't tell her the truth until he got clearance, or verification of her identity. Lives hinged on his obedience to the Nighthawk mandates. "My mistake," he said slowly, testing her. "You look so much like a girl I once knew.''

But the time was coming—and soon—when he'd have to

force her out of the shadows. Already the credit-card slip she'd given him was being fingerprint tested for any criminal records; the photo he'd taken of her face matched against all recorded shots of Delia. She had hours to hide in her cloak of anonymity.

"So long as you don't believe it." As she kneaded her clay, added water, her face grew calmer; she spoke with that otherworldly calm. "Don't tell me—the model, right? The one who died a few years back in a car crash? People used to mistake me for her all the time. I was even photographed a few times, and put in trash magazines. You know, the 'Elvis is still alive and in South America' stuff, except substitute Delia, and New Zealand." She looked up at McCall, her face filled with cool pity. "If you cared about her, I don't blame you for hoping I'm her—but the body was there, Mr. McCall. Accept facts. Delia de Souza is dead. There won't be a resurrection."

The quiet finality in her words sent a creeping shiver down his spine. What was she telling him—that she was Ana de Souza or that, in her eyes, Delia had died long ago? "I know, but she meant a lot to me, and you're so much like her."

Testing her. Would she react?

She merely shrugged. "I'm sorry, Mr. McCall. Much as I'd like to earn what she did, I'm just Beth Silver, an average single woman bringing up her son alone."

"Never average. You've never known what average is," he murmured huskily. Taking another step, he felt her body respond, and not in fear. Deny it as she would, the current of desire moved back and forth between them from him to her, her to him, with a life of its own, warm and aching and needy.

She gulped. The movement was quiet, intrinsically ladylike, yet her throat still convulsed, as if his words hurt her. "Maybe I want to know. What average is, I mean," she added. As if she'd been thinking of something else she wanted to know.

What they both wanted to know. What they *wanted*, ached for.

Keep your mind on the assignment, or she'll be gone by

nightfall. "Average women don't have a security system to rival Fort Knox," he suggested. Probing.

She kept her face averted, not enough to be interpreted as fearful. More like she was looking over his shoulder. "I have my reasons. None of which should concern a complete stranger."

He couldn't think, couldn't act like a Nighthawk, standing in the warm intimacy of her studio with the woman who drove him out of his rational mind with blood-pounding *want.* "Am I a stranger, Beth?" His voice grew huskier as he gave her the dignity of her chosen name. He couldn't care less what her real name was right now. His body was hard and tight with the flaming brand of aching need that being within three feet of her engendered in him. "Can you look me in the face and tell me I'm a stranger?"

A little shrug. "What's hard about that? We met yesterday. You are a stranger."

Yet she didn't look at him, and her voice held a telltale quiver. As if her heart rebelled against the half lie she told. As if she was fighting for her very life…and if she was Delia or even Ana de Souza, that's exactly what she *was* doing. He knew, understood, even appreciated her spirit and fire and guts, fighting alone to save herself, and her child.

But everything in him, heart and gut and *man,* rose up in equally dark, hot rebellion. Like a tiger crouched in the dry grass ready to pounce on its prey, he took the final steps to her and put his hands on her shoulders. He felt her start, ready to bolt that moment. "Look at me, Beth." He heard his voice, stark and graveled, filled with unbridled need and lust and untold secrets, and he felt her lovely body quiver in response. "Look at me—look in my eyes and tell me you don't know me."

Her fists clenched so hard he could feel her arms shaking beneath his hands. She didn't turn her head.

"We were never strangers," he muttered, rough and hard, yet keeping his hold gentle. Thrilling to the touch of her, even beneath a baggy sweatshirt, to that quiet, feminine scent filling his head, because it came from her. "From the moment we met—no matter when we met—it was there."

She finally turned her face, and her eyes locked on his. She was nothing like that star-being now, just a woman in a desperate quest for truth. "Who are you?" she whispered.

"You know who I am," he growled, wishing, willing her to hear his heart, his gut-deep need.

She shook her head—a tiny movement, yet with plenty of power. Fighting still, but she lay passive beneath his hands, allowing him to touch her. *She may not trust me, but she wants me. I can use that to Nighthawk advantage, to save lives....*

What a crock. He'd never heard such pathetic crap in his life. He almost heard the universe laugh at his self-delusional thought.

"Tell me. Please." Her voice cracked, turned husky, a warm, lingering echo of the throaty alto he'd hungered to hear again for years. "What are you? Why are you here?"

"You tell me," he commanded, using the magnetic pull he knew she felt, to make her answer him. "Tell me who you think I am."

"It's not your name—it's—" Her lovely eyes filled with desire and distress, and a heart-deep terror that made him want to touch her, hold and comfort her. "Why are you here? Who do you work for? Who paid you to find me and to watch over me? Why are they doing this to me? What did I do?"

"Maybe I'm here for me." He moved another half inch, and the current of heat hitched up another notch. Dangerous power, a firestorm waiting to unleash. "I waited for you to call, for you to come to me," he said huskily. "I gave you my private cell number. I didn't change it for six years. I kept the phone for that long, until I gave up on waiting for you to call. Didn't you know I'd have helped you leave him if you needed it?"

"You don't know Danny's father—how could you help me?" Yet her voice held no strength. Her face was pale, her nostrils flared, like a doe about to bolt—the fight-or-flight response he suspected she'd lived on for years. "I don't know you. I don't *want* to know you. I don't believe in anything or *anyone.* I don't trust anyone.'' Yet, as though she lay helpless in a trap, she didn't, or couldn't, move away from under his touch. ''Especially not a man who tells me nothing about himself, yet expects my private confidences in return.''

A flickering, fading defiance that still slammed him in the guts. Someone with her life history couldn't afford to let a man into her world who didn't tell her anything, or give her any reason to take him on, let alone tell her the whole truth.

So give her what you can.

''Ex-Lieutenant Brendan McCall of the U.S. Navy SEALs, at your service, ma'am.'' He made a tiny, self-mocking bow.

Silence for a moment. ''Why ex?''

Oh, man, she knew where to hit…and he had to tread carefully here. If she was Delia, she might know why he was ''ex'' Lieutenant McCall. Her father would've had him investigated for sure.

And the utter truth of that left him speechless and his head spinning. Why hadn't he *thought* of that? The proverbial had hit the fan a decade ago, and it was only now that he finally got it. *Her father had me investigated. That's why she never called me. That's why she's been looking at me as if I'm a monster. She thinks I'm a traitor to my country, in Falcone's pay now.*

Ghost would have his hide for this, and strip him of his commander's rank, but he had no choice. He couldn't wait for clearance now. If he put her off now, she'd slam the emotional door and never open it again. ''I was dismissed.'' A bald, blunt statement that in no way hid the lingering shame. Even though it was a top-brass decision for the greater good, and he'd agreed to it for international security, the sting still whipped him with merciless taunts—*always your father's son, McCall*—especially if he'd lost Delia because of it.

There was no going back: his reputation as a SEAL, one of the white knights of national security, had shattered years ago. He couldn't go back to the States without dismantling a decade of lies, and blowing apart assignments that hinged on his being able to infiltrate illegal rings that accepted him as one of their own. He had to remain a seeming criminal for the sake of international peace and security. He couldn't go home, could never see anyone he knew or cared for again—

Yeah, a little voice jeered. *There're so many of them.* That was why he'd taken the job with the Nighthawks, and accepted the cover that ruined his reputation. He had nobody to hurt. Besides his old SEAL buddies, there was no one to give a toss that he'd apparently sold secrets to the enemy just before a war.

Ten years later, he wondered if the price he'd paid was higher than he knew. The whispers that someone in the SEALs had sold out had been nudging around before he took the op; Ghost had used the story to give his disappearance credence.

Had Eduardo de Souza put two and two together and made an equation that spelled disaster for his heart, and Delia's?

He couldn't tell her. It would clear him in her eyes, yeah, but it would condemn her beloved father as a snob who'd torn his daughter's life apart for the sake of bloodlines. For Eduardo de Souza had been Brazilian ambassador to the U.S.A., with the resources to find the truth. He could've easily verified the stories, discovered that Lieutenant McCall was a man with full military honors and an open offer from his admiral to return to the SEALs anytime he tired of playing international spy.

To clear his name in her eyes, to restore her trust in him, he'd have to destroy her beloved father's memory.

"Touchy subject, I think?" Her soft voice broke through his inner blackness like a half rainbow in a storm cloud. "You don't want me to ask you why you were dismissed."

The unexpected understanding made his hands tighten on her shoulders. "No, I don't. Thank you," he said quietly. Few people in his life had respected his need for privacy and silence.

"So then, are you going to tell me why you were in my garden at two in the morning, terrifying me?" Far from belligerent, her voice was low, musical with feminine huskiness, a siren's song.

He took the final step, putting his body within an inch of hers. "Did I terrify you? *Do* I terrify you?" His heart pounded out a different, insistent rhythm. *Trust me, Beth.* And it gave him a tiny start of surprise that her chosen name sprang to his mind, rather than her real name. Maybe it was because Beth, with its gentle, quiet loveliness, suited her so well.

She looked at him, then away, leaving a flash of incandescent blue behind that burned in his memory. ''Yes, you terrify me…''

But it hadn't been terror in her eyes then. Temptation slammed him in the guts, leaving him under its command. Her face—that unforgettable face, those amazing eyes, filled with desire and need—need for his touch…

She wanted it as bad as he did. Wanted *him*.

It would shoot all the Nighthawk rules to hell, rules he'd followed with the fanaticism of a zealot since joining the spy group ten years ago. If Anson knew, he'd strip him of his rank, turf him out of the Nighthawks, but right now he didn't give a damn. With a low growl he reached for her—

''*No.*'' A quiet word, weak and shaking, but combined with muddy hands that trembled and eyes filled with sudden, doe-like terror, it held all the force of a Mack truck.

He dropped his arms as if she'd used the baton on them. ''Don't be scared of me, Beth,'' he said softly. ''You know I'd never do anything to hurt you.''

She turned away, concentrating on her sodden, shapeless lump of clay as if it held all the secrets of life. ''I don't know anything about you, McCall. Don't tell me anything. I don't want to know. I just want you to leave. Get out of my life.''

He took the blow in silence, still and cold. Well, what had he expected—that she'd actually give a damn if a guy like him lived or died?

Oh, he had friends, the guys on his old SEAL team had never believed the rumors about his treason. To a man, they'd still eat a bullet for him. His navy seniors would return his rank to him, and give him a new team any day he asked. His fellow Nighthawks would jump out of a plane, chopper or ship to save him, but because of the necessity of absolute anonymity in the job, when he went home, he was alone.

Nothing new. It had been that way since he was eight years old. He'd been alone his whole life. Just the way it was.

He thought he'd learned to live with it. Obviously not since he'd returned to Delia's—*Beth Silver's*—life, and the strange thing was, it didn't matter to him right now if she was Delia or not. He needed her with the same gut-burning intensity he'd felt ten years before, and hadn't known since.

"Yeah, sure. I'll go." His voice grated a little, so what? It wouldn't happen again. This wasn't anything he wasn't used to. He'd get over it. Get over *her*.

There was no other choice.

He turned at the door, hoping to God his face didn't mirror the torture inside him. "But I'll be back." He walked out, willing his gut to untwist enough so he could breathe again.

Chapter 4

Come to hell, baby...

Even knowing she was playing with the destructive conflagration of a volcanic eruption, it had taken everything she had to hold out against the pull. The *need.*

Despite the orders she knew he was under, he'd given her the truth, trusting her with a painful piece of his past, and she heard his soul's call in return. *Beth* was his unspoken cry in the perimeter of the shadow-world they both inhabited—and it was the name she heard inside him, the acceptance of who she said she was, that all but undid her.

Almost as much as the man himself.

Oh, *the man.* Even when he'd had the tourist's mask in place, all she saw was the dark-hearted barbarian, the savage heathen pulling her out of her ordered, controlled, hemmed-in life. She heard it, heard all he wanted to say to her in just the air he breathed. The wild singing, like pagan night revels, bursting to life from deep within the tight-leashed male strength of McCall, commanded the long-dormant woman in her soul. *Come to hell...*

Drawing her there irresistibly. A mirror image to the mystery inside herself. McCall had scorch marks on his soul, a deep core of loneliness waiting to be unleashed, and a young boy's dreams lying in scattered shards at his feet.

Yet like a mad, vulnerable boy playing a game beyond his ken, he picked them up and tried again, facing danger down with a grin and a challenge thrown like a gauntlet on a jagged cliff in a lightning storm, daring it to kill him. *Come and get me, baby.*

Temptation flooded her, almost beyond control. Her *no* had been a flickering defiance, all but whispered. He knew—he had to know the desire inside her, even as she tried to deny it—but he'd respected it. Respected her will, her wishes. He'd walked out when she'd asked. The sight of him leaving, his voice guttural and his eyes holding the very soul of darkness and self-hate, had gutted her. If she could have made herself speak, she'd have called him back.

Like a sudden slam in her ribs, she remembered five years ago, and the midnight call that had sent her and Danny on a life-or-death bolt across the world. *Falcone's men shot Dan through the forehead. He's dead, love. Leave the country now, follow the procedure Dan set up for you, or they'll find you within hours.*

She shuddered. Even if she didn't believe McCall was one of Falcone's men, she couldn't tell him. She couldn't give in to the temptation to touch him. She had to get rid of him somehow, before they killed him just for knowing her.

I'll be back.

For his sake, she had to pray he wouldn't.

She started when the bell tinkled, announcing a customer. Looking at the sodden mass beneath her fingers, she groaned to herself. Oh, boy, she was losing it. Sitting here destroying her work, wasting time thinking about McCall when she should be making her plans for escape....

"Here. You need this."

Starting with the rough, gravel-over-velvet voice from in front of her, she glared up at the dark, mysterious and so-very-sexy reason for her turmoil. Well, he said he'd he back...she just didn't expect it so soon, nor had she expected him to be soaking wet and wearing an ankle-length dark leather coat, wrapped around him like the storm outside. "W-what's this?"

His gaze on her was lush heat locked inside savage concern. "A sweet roll, fresh fruit and coffee. You need it."

Unable to face him after he'd met her cruelty with rough kindness and care, she lowered her eyes. The fretful nap she'd fallen into after dawn left her too distracted to think of eating while getting Danny ready for school, and she'd forgotten lunch.

How he knew, she didn't question. She lifted her clay-coated hands. "Can you mind the store while I wash?"

He shrugged off the coat, hanging it on the door hook. Beneath the damp, close-fitting deep green knit sweater, his muscles flexed and rippled with the movement. Danger honed inside dark masculine beauty. "Are you sure you trust me in your precious store? I could have a moving truck around the bend."

She threw him a wry glance. "Somehow I don't think it's my pottery you're after." Even if he looked throughout the store, even broke into the house and ransacked it, he'd find nothing.

Good reminder. The world righted itself again. That big, muscular bronzed body of his was unkickable...and that was as far as she'd trust him, no matter how often he fed her.

She got to her feet, and the world took a sharp turn right— uh, right or left? She blinked to reorient herself, but even half a dozen did nothing to reduce the sudden vertigo.

The low growl shivered into her nerve endings; his arms came around her, keeping her upright. "Come here." A moment later she was in the big, padded wing chair she kept for customers. He crouched down right beside her, putting a morsel of warm sweet roll between her lips. Its rich flavor burst onto her tongue with lush stickiness. "How long has it been since you ate?"

She welcomed the taste of the honey, nuts and fruit inside the roll, like a fruity baklava, with a soft moan of delight. "I haven't been hungry."

He fed her another piece. "Get hungry. You can't get away with erratic eating habits anymore. You're a mother."

His blunt words made her stiffen, but he was right. She couldn't function properly if she allowed the stress of McCall's eruption into her life to disrupt her eating habits. She couldn't escape if she was too weak to run.

How ironic that the one person who should want her weak and needing and afraid was feeding her, taking care of her, keeping her strong.

He's just trying to make me trust him. But she couldn't stop eating the wonderful food, couldn't hold back from looking into his eyes...eyes so tense and filled with commanding, compelling desire, she gave a hot shiver. His taut, muscular frame, masking burning heat and hiding a leashed savagery, made her feel alive and strong—and like a *woman* for the first time in a decade.

"C'mon, Beth, I know you like it. Open your mouth." The low, sensual growl didn't startle her; it had long ago become part of her, waking or sleeping, an internal "on" switch only he knew how to find in her. She opened her mouth for him without even making the conscious decision.

Frozen. She'd been frozen since Papa told her that the man she adored was a traitor to his country. Her emotions encased in a delicate layer of ice, afraid to trust her own judgment. Now the ice was melting. With one look from his forest eyes, fire slammed into ice and kept on burning, hard and bright and remorseless as the sun. Within a day he'd brought her back to life. The ice that had been her protection for a decade was a puddle of warm, slushy water at his feet.

She automatically opened her mouth for more food when he urged her, finishing the roll and fruit salad with yogurt.

"Good girl," he whispered in her ear, making her shiver, warm and sensual. Fear and distrust, sweetness and pain, defiance and trust and need...McCall left her in a perpetual state of confusion. A man absolutely and utterly wrong for her, yet so *right*....

Yes, a hit man in the employ of an arms and drugs dealer would be just right for a woman on the run.

Yet when he held the polystyrene cup to her mouth, she drank, as trusting as a baby, and another taste explosion filled her. Oh, *joy*—her favorite South American blend of mocha coffee! She moaned as the exotic sweetness ran riot on her tongue. With cream and sugar, just as she liked it. Just as he'd brought it for her years ago, complete with hamburger and fries. Nobody else dared give her food that could make her put on a single ounce. But Brendan had known how much she loved rich food and drink; it was her personal ambrosia and nectar, and by the time she'd met him she'd no longer cared if she was super-thin or not, a supermodel or not. And he'd known that, too.

He knew too much…oh, dear God, what had she done? He'd set her the simplest of tests, and she'd failed!

She didn't dare let her gaze fly to his, or let herself stiffen. *Danny, think of Danny!* "Oh, this coffee's good…." Her purr was alive with sensual discovery. "Would you mind telling me what blend it is? I'll have to put it on my shopping list."

"Games can only last so long." He tipped up her chin, making her look at him. "I didn't buy the coffee to trip you up."

Maybe he hadn't, but she had tripped up, and they both knew it. "I'm feeling better now." She got to her feet. "Thank you," she said simply. "I hadn't realized how long I'd gone without."

He shrugged. "It's been a while, but I'm kind of used to doing it." *For you.*

The unspoken words shimmered in the warm, fragrant air inside the studio, the dangerous half light of the storm outside, and she wanted to scream. For years her cover had been impenetrable. Now, within a day, she was giving herself away with every word and act. Even to allowing him to feed her foods he knew his Delia would have loved. Dizzy as she was, her strict upbringing would never have allowed her to trust a real stranger so completely, the stranger she'd claimed McCall to be…and no man would know that fact better than he, who had seen her freeze when any other man even tried to make the slightest move on her.

She'd never allowed any man to touch her but her beloved SEAL, her Brendan, whom she'd brought to life as he had her.

From that first brooding look, she'd been intrigued; but when he didn't try to touch her apart from the demands of the photographer, she'd felt drawn. Then, when he actually made her smile and even laugh amidst the crowd of bodyguards, hangers-on and wanna-bes she'd so hated, she'd tumbled, head over feet, straight into first love. She'd given Brendan her heart and soul, her hopes and dreams. So he'd learned what she couldn't resist, and gave it to her with the smile that made her want to do anything to please him.

Damn it, she'd just revealed another chink in her armor—her unconscious acceptance of the rights she'd once given him to touch her, feed her, care for her. The past she'd tried so hard to lock away in darkness had been brought to light with a stupid cup of coffee and sweet food.

Pull yourself together! Danny's innocence and freedom—and your life—depends upon this. McCall's knowledge of you is stronger than anyone alive. You can't let him see inside, just like he won't let you see inside him.

Denial was not only superfluous at this point; it was ridiculous, beneath her intelligence and his. So she chose to take refuge in deflection. "I need my wheel now, Mr. McCall."

His eyes turned as dark as the crashing clouds outside as he got to his feet. He stood before her with feet splayed and arms folded, aggressively male. "Playing the fiddle while Rome burns? It's too late, too dangerous, to continue to deny what I already know is the truth. We have to talk."

Meeting fire with fire, she lifted her chin in cool challenge, daring him to keep trying to get inside her mind. "We do? *We* do—does that mean you'll give me something beyond your tourist prattle and your former rank and serial number?"

The walls slammed into place before her eyes, bricks and mortar rendered in granite. "I thought not." She nodded toward the door. "Mr. McCall, this is still my property. Watch from across the street. I may not have any customers until after the storm, but you'd scare off any that dared to come out in this weather."

He took a step toward her, two. "That's the intention."

Her eyebrows lifted. "Well, we've come forward—some honesty at last. Maybe soon you'll even tell me what you want from me."

Taking the final step, he touched that high-held chin. His gaze, burning hot and dark as starless midnight, settled on her mouth, and she shuddered in raw desire and hopeless confusion. "Take out the 'what' and 'from,' and you get the picture. *I* want *you,* no matter what your name is."

Aching, she lifted a hand, and the dry clay on her fingers and palm cracked and fell to the floor at the same time as thunder split the sky outside—and his last words penetrated her consciousness. Her hand fell. "More honesty. That's impressive. A shame it all seems to revolve around your delusions of who I am."

He gave a low growl of frustration and cupped his hand around her arm, his touch as tender as his words were uncompromising. "You don't have much time left. They're on the move. He'll come himself this time. And he's not coming to reclaim his wife. You humiliated him in front of his people, his world. He's coming to kill you personally."

On some deeper level she felt the gentle motions of his hand supporting her, but over and above it was the whitening of her cheek, like a gunshot to a vein leeching out her life force. *Control, control...* It took all she had, drawing on strength she didn't know was still inside her after so many years on the run, but she didn't sway into him, or lean on him. "Let go of me."

His hand dropped. He took a step back. Watching her.

Her eyes held his, shattered, pleading. "Let me go. Please. I can make life safe for my son again, if you leave for an hour."

Fingers curled into palms, making tight fists, as his eyes squeezed shut. A breath came from him as if it had been forced, a warm, coffee-scented zephyr from the heart of a man in torture. "I can't. God help us both, Beth, even if you and your son weren't in more danger than you can handle, I can't."

She dragged in air. His scent came inside her like a beloved enemy, and she knew that scent, heat and coffee and rain, ancient pain and pagan need, would haunt her for the rest of her days. "Don't do this to me. Don't destroy my life."

Eyes bleak as midwinter opened. "I don't have a choice. You have a day, two at most. You'll need me when it all goes down."

You don't have much time. They're on the move. The echo of his voice kept resonating back to her, each time more urgent, more imperative. *You humiliated him…he'll kill you personally.*

Given what Ana had told her about Falcone, every word made perfect sense. *Did he know from personal experience?*

"There's an umbrella in the stand behind the door," she said quietly. It wasn't an inference; it was a command. *Go.*

Without a word he tossed the coat over his shoulder and strode out into the rain. Half-wild storm winds swirled around him, soaking him. And from the hill across the road he watched still, tense and strong and with an overwhelmingly masculine beauty. Yet he'd never looked more alone.

She turned from the sight, aching with regret for what couldn't be. Whether he was a good guy or in Falcone's pay, no matter how she felt about him, she didn't have a choice.

You have a day. Two at most.

She'd been responsible for enough deaths. She had to get away—from here, and from McCall—before she killed him, too.

McCall stood across the road, watching her close the store. Though the rain worsened with the close of day, his coat stayed slung over his shoulder; he barely noticed the lashing bite of the hard-hitting needles of water. All his life, from fishing boats to the navy and SEALs, and now with the Nighthawks, he was used to extremes of weather, especially water. He was used to being alone and cold; it didn't bother him.

What got to him was Beth dismissing him. *Take the umbrella and go. Watch me from outside, out in the rain where you belong.*

Even when she'd said she loved him a decade ago, he'd always felt on the outside looking in with her, a guttersnipe daring to look at a duchess. Nothing had changed in ten years, except her address and marital status. The freezing tone of her voice—the dismissal bordering on contempt—left a slightly acrid taste in his mouth, as if he'd inhaled the cordite from a smoking gun.

Yeah, and the gun was from his own pocket. Being near her was a constant game of Russian roulette, yet like a fool he just kept on turning that barrel….

Even when Delia had whispered words of love to him a decade ago, he'd known it wouldn't last. He'd always known the truth—he wasn't classy enough for the ambassador's daughter turned jet-set model. He'd forced himself to finish high school and even got a football scholarship to UCLA, but he'd still ended up working on a fishing boat to pay the bills— just like dear ol' Dad. He'd left that, too—the heavy drinking day and night had reminded him too much of his father. The booze and the fighting was the reason his mother had left. To this day, the smell of gin or beer made him want to heave his guts.

For the life he had now, he'd always bless old Burt Miner, ex-USAF. Burt had caught the nineteen-year-old Brendan hiding out in a corner of a hangar watching a weekend air show. Gruff, foul-mouthed old Burt had correctly interpreted the furious scowl on Brendan's face as frustrated longing, and had given him a friendly chat about how it felt to really fly.

He'd come to the airstrip on all his days off after that, watching in ill-contained anguish as the guys with money took off for the skies, until Burt either got sick of him or took pity on him and finally taught him to fly.

When Burt found out about his talent in the ocean through a newspaper article about his impromptu rescue of a little kid drowning off Long Beach one weekend, Burt pulled in some favors and arranged for a navy officer to see his protégé's skill in the air. After rigorous water skills tests and IQ exams, the navy recruitment officer talked to Brendan about the navy taking over his endangered college scholarship, and joining

NROTC—the Navy Rescue Officers Training Corps. Two years later he'd come out an ensign, with the respect of all who knew him in his new world. Then, as the recruitment officer had prophesied, McCall—*Ensign* McCall—did the Basic Underwater Demolition Training course, survived Hell Week with ease, took the weapons and foreign language courses, learned to work in a team and joined the SEALs.

From there, he hadn't looked back. Raw guts, a willingness to learn, do anything, anywhere, anytime, and 24/7 availability had got him to SEAL lieutenant by age twenty-six, and where he was now, at the ripe old age of thirty-seven—commander of Nighthawk Team One, one of three trusted seconds-in-command in Nighthawk Area 4, South Pacific region. He now ran every op that Pacific Region commander Anson, code name Ghost, or the medical/field Team Two commander, Irish, or Special Infiltration Team Three commander, Nightshift, wasn't personally in on. He was up there with the big guys, on track to running his own Nighthawk region one day.

But none of that would have impressed Delia's socially impeccable, class-conscious parents. If they were still alive they'd look at him and see the snot-nosed punk who played hide-the-booze with his dad's empty beer cans and gin bottles, an ex-gang member of low-class origins.

That was all her incensed papa had seen, when he'd found them together that final night. Without a word Eduardo de Souza, Brazilian Ambassador to the USA, called in his security men. He got kicked out of his own car, landing right on his bad-boy ass. Humiliating punishment for daring to look in Delia's eyes, let alone for touching her, loving her as if she was a normal girl.

What would Mama and Papa have thought of the man who'd become their posthumous son-in-law? Nobody knew who Falcone really was, or how old he really was, not even the CIA. The entry in the Register of Births, Deaths and Marriages in England was dead fake—as dead as the man who'd been paid to enter it for Falcone more than thirty years after he was born God knows where. According to that certificate he was forty-four, but nobody believed that; the guy was fifty at least. But the anonymity of name and age and even nationality let Falcone slide in and out of two worlds, a smooth-spoken phantom menace the authorities couldn't seem to hold on to.

And without hard evidence against him, they were helpless. If they couldn't get him in custody fast, and keep him there this time, Beth's life wasn't worth squat. And her kid—

Time to get back to work. And keep his mind there until Beth and her kid—his *subjects*—were safe. Permanently.

Another night on the grassy hill across the road, taking fifteen-minute catnaps on his bedroll. Hourly reports to Anson proved he was still on the job.

Watching.

Chapter 5

The next morning, McCall woke up before six.

Judging by yesterday's routine, he had ten minutes before she got up. With precise method, he packed up his bedroll and poncho tent, then washed himself as best he could in the near-stinging coolness of the river down the road from her house. Then he snatched a standing breakfast of two high-protein bars, beef jerky, a tetra-brick of juice and a tepid thermos of coffee, keeping an eye on his paraphernalia of gadgetry that gave him fifteen-second updates on Beth and the kid.

He followed at a discreet distance as Beth drove the kid to school, then walked him in, her arm draped around the boy in a gesture of loving, possessive motherhood. Lucky Danny Silver.

At nine-thirty, he pushed open the door of her studio.

"Mr. McCall. Back so soon?"

Her cool, soft voice held only a hint of the exasperation he sensed she was feeling. He knew she'd seen him across the road, seen him follow her to the school and back on the motorbike again. She'd known he'd come in as soon as she opened the door. But she wasn't giving him even polite acceptance of his presence.

This dance of words was intricate, two introverted loners both trying to win at Twenty Questions, outrunning their pasts and memories of love like civilians behind enemy lines. Winning her trust without giving any in return was the hardest assignment Anson had ever given him.

Thirty-six hours left to get a positive ID and get her out of the country.

"I'll always come back," he said quietly. "I'll keep coming back. I'll keep watching. And you know why."

She frowned for a brief second, her eyes shadowed. Then the look vanished. "I won't change my mind, McCall. I don't date complete strangers who wander into my studio one day and—"

He tried to do it gently, but still he threw his bomb. He had to get through to her somehow, and soon. "It's time to stop playing games. You're not the kind of woman to let me feed you without knowing me."

She held her color, and her composure. "All single mothers need help occasionally. I thank you for that, but it doesn't mean I'm going to tell you my life story. I've made mistakes in my life, but I won't take chances with my son's well-being."

"You *have* made mistakes in the past, haven't you?" he asked, dark and compelling. "But compared to Robbie's father, I'm small potatoes." He used the name of Falcone's son with gentle care.

"Do you have trouble hearing? My son's name is Danny, and mine's Beth. You don't know anything about my life, or about Danny's father." She was pale now, but her defiance flamed still. "And nobody in their right mind would discount you, McCall, or think you're small compared to anyone." The whites of her knuckles showed, she was gripping her workbench so hard. "I keep telling you, whoever you think I am, you have the wrong person."

Thirty-five hours fifty-six minutes. This felt more like fencing in darkness, rapier-sharp and buttons off. Shadowboxing with the faceless enemy of suspicion between.

"Have I?" Testing, he touched her cheek with a finger, and he saw the wave of warmth fill her face and throat. No matter what came from that ripe, luscious mouth of hers, her body betrayed her will, telling him this obsession was far from one-sided. She wanted him, maybe even almost as bad as he wanted her. "I don't think so," he murmured. "And your son—Robbie?"

She jerked her face away, as if realizing her mistake too late. "Stop it. I told you his name is Danny. Don't touch me."

He dropped his hand, yet stayed so close that her scent of drenched roses filled his head and curled itself around his libido like a purring kitten, begging to be stroked, caressed. "You tell me when you're ready—to talk, or touch. Your call."

She shivered, her lashes dropping over eyes suddenly cold. "Keep your distance, McCall."

"My name's Brendan," he growled, his hands curled into impotent fists at his sides. If he could be one hundred percent honest with her, it would bring out her natural honesty in return. But with Nighthawk security at risk from the faceless assassin in the ranks, he couldn't do a thing about it. One wrong word, one indiscretion and she'd have the ammo to hit the media rounds. If the Nighthawks were destroyed, more innocents would die in unsanctioned wars that couldn't go into full swing without Falcone's guns and mines and dirty bombs.

He had to keep silent. His career might survive the indiscretion, but others would pay with their lives.

As if she'd read his mind she put her hand out, with a bright smile as fake as her words. "Hello. My name's Beth Silver."

She'd put up another roadblock between them—and it was big as a boulder. It half killed him to laugh as he took her hand, but he did it—and touching her in any form was no hardship, even just the small, work-hardened hand lying in his rough palm.

Then, as he held her hand in his, a haunting sense of undone déjà vu came to him. Doubts. Shadows. Uncertainty. Something fundamental had changed from ten years before....

"It can't be," he muttered beneath his breath. Not *Ana.* He'd never met the cousin Delia claimed to be almost her double, but...*no.* A strong similarity in looks could only do so much for a man. This woman, and this woman alone drove him to the edge of sanity's cliff with slamming, scorching-hot waves below—and he wanted to drown in it, bathe in the liquid fire torching a searing path between them.

She *couldn't* be Ana. Obsession with a woman to the point of exclusion—being lost inside and consumed by *Delia* was his fact of life. Saving her was his mission, whether it was on the Nighthawks' agenda or not. Wanting, needing to lose himself in her was his private hell, the torture he showed no one. If he could have her just once—

"Things must be bad if you've started to talk to yourself."

Roused from the furnace burning his soul, he looked at her. She'd tilted her head, with a little, inquiring smile. A simple thing, sure, but a massive leap forward from the *go-back-to-the-hellhole-you-crawled-out-of* tone she'd kept with him since he'd tried to connect with her yesterday.

A step up in getting her and the kid out of here?

He laughed, going for common ground. "Lady, I'm from L.A.—the home base of actors, directors, plastic surgeons, walking, talking Barbie dolls and therapists. We're all nuts, and believe me, talking to ourselves is the least of our problems."

A little grin peeped out from behind her barriers—a genuine, honest-to-God smile that reached her eyes. Her cheeks flushed a delicate rose, and he ached, seeing the transformation. The star-queen vanished, and another being sat at her potter's wheel. A woman of gentle, big-eyed loveliness, and her sweet shyness socked him in the guts with masculine awareness. She'd become a *normal* woman he could smile at, talk to, and maybe, God help him, touch...not just feed her, but explore the combusting sensuality he knew wasn't one-sided. To have her mouth, her lush body beneath his—

"And which of the above are you?"

Keep going, just keep chipping at her barriers. Thirty-five hours and forty minutes... "Not guilty," he returned with a wink. "I never had designs on Hollywood after living near it half my life. I can't manage the overinflated sense of self-importance."

Her head tilted a little more, her eyes twinkling. "You don't want a hundred-foot trailer on set, imported water and French-milled soap to keep your manly beauty intact?"

He backed off a step, folding his arms as if she'd called his masculinity into question. "Twenty feet's ample, and water from the tap and good old Dial soap will do me just fine. Chlorine and fluoride can't do me any more damage than living in that crazy city did."

She laughed. Oh, man, she laughed as if she meant it, as if she'd spent years needing to laugh again. The husky sweet music of it sucker-punched him, and sent a king hit right to his heart...because if it wasn't quite Delia's laugh, it was close enough. A woman's version of the girl's husky giggle that IDed her with ninety percent accuracy. The knowledge speared him with guilt, pity and the ruthlessness of duty.

It all added up. The food, the coffee; her reaction to hearing Danny's real name; the fear, the security system—her laugh. Her response to him, as white-hot as his was to her. This woman was Delia de Souza, ID virtually positive, unless by some crazy quirk of fate Ana de Souza also had the same laugh, the same tastes in food...and in men.

McCall was no stranger to duty. He had only two choices now—to find solid evidence of her identity, or call Anson and tell him of his past with Delia, and his certainty that Beth Silver and Delia de Souza were one and the same.

The latter would be enough for Anson to move the equipment in tonight. The full show—mikes, cameras—a full regalia of watchers, as much to protect her as to keep her from running. This woman was the only one who could give him the irrefutable proof the Nighthawks needed to give the World Court, the only ones left who might be able to extradite Falcone from Minca bel Sol, his luxurious little bolt-hole in the Pacific—

And because Anson doesn't know her, he'll take me off point. And if she doesn't trust me, how much chance have any of the other Nighthawks got, apart from forcibly abducting her and the kid? Then we'd never get the evidence—and we've got a snowball's chance in a volcano of finding it. She's too smart not to have stashed it where we'd never find it without her cooperation.

God help him, he had to keep silent, both to Beth and to Anson. He had to find physical evidence of her identity by the end of this day, or they could all go down in a hail of bullets.

The bell above the door gave a violent jangle as the door flew inward. McCall wheeled around, reaching for his weapon, training his eye on the target—but his gaze fell by two feet to find the culprit…a kid erupting into the room, a kid with a shock of thick dark hair, a thin build and intense, soulful eyes.

Danny. Maybe—almost definitely—Robbie Falcone. The resemblance to his father was uncanny.

The boy tore in, straight past McCall without noticing him, traipsing mud through the showroom, a football under his thin arm and his dark-eyed face alight with joy. "Mr. Branson says if I practice hard I might get off the reserves bench next week!"

"Oh, sweetie, that's wonderful."

Stuffing his Glock back in his jacket, McCall turned around to see Beth's face, stricken pale—she'd seen the gun, all right—but she infused her voice with a happiness as strong as the boy's, her eyes bright as the Pacific sky. "Do you want to practice again this afternoon? I can close the store early."

The boy's eyes fell, his thick dark lashes covering them. "Mummy, you play like a *girl.* Mr. Richards said I can go over now and play with him and Ethan."

McCall smothered a grin; but any urge to smile faded when he saw the flash of panic that came and went in Beth's eyes, so fast an untrained eye couldn't have seen it. "Sweetie, you know I think Mr. Richards is very nice, but—"

"But we don't know him well enough. We don't know what he might do," Danny said with an adult-sounding weariness that told McCall he'd said this too many times before. Was the poor kid only six? He sounded forty; and suddenly, he wasn't "the kid" anymore. As in smuggling the dog in at night, in this, Danny Silver was a brother in arms, a little kid whose life necessitated that innocence must be shattered for survival.

Poor kid. Poor Danny.

Beth gave a swift, unreadable glance at McCall then turned away. "Exactly. Good boy."

The boy's face turned earnest, pleading. "But, Mummy, we know them. Mrs. Richards is your friend. And Mr. Richards, he's not like the other guys' dads…he goes to church."

"Danny, I'd rather play with you myself. You know, just you and me." Beth's face had a haunted, hunted look to it now.

"No! I don't *wanna!*" The boy stamped his foot, red-faced with fury, lapsing into childish speech. "I wanna play with Mr. Richards and Ethan! I want someone who can really *play!*"

Beth gave another swift glance McCall's way. "Danny, we have a customer here. Can we wait until he's left the showroom to continue the conversation?" *Please leave,* her eyes begged.

What was he doing here? He had no right to listen, not even for their protection. He turned to leave the showroom.

"But, Mummy, they're playing *now,* and you always talk and talk until it's all over and I can't go!" Danny's face was blazing with indignation and pleading combined. "I don't *wanna* talk 'bout it again—we talk all the time. I wanna *go!*"

Beth closed her eyes, but not before McCall, looking over his shoulder, saw a warrior-size guilt spear through the indigo depths, acknowledgment of a six-year-old's unwanted perception. "I said *now,* Daniel." With a swift movement, Beth twitched the curtain to the washstand and drying room.

"But I gotta go to the park right *now* or they'll be gone— and Mr. Richards says he's gonna show me and Ethan how to do a catch an' a pass, and I could get into the team next week—"

"I said *now,* Daniel Silver!"

Oh, boy, Beth was pulling rank on Danny. A decision made in fear, if he knew anything at all—and though she didn't know it, she'd regret this later, with bitter tears. McCall pulled open the door, but couldn't resist another glance, and his heart twisted. Danny's shoulders had slumped; his mouth trembled in silent mutiny, but he went ahead of his mother into the storage space. Obedient, maybe, but McCall would bet his eyes glittered with all the fire of resentment he felt. He knew; he'd been there.

"Mr. McCall."

About to close the door behind him, McCall turned to her.

Her words were innocuous, but somehow filled with meaning when combined with the blazing message in her eyes. "Thank you."

She'd thanked him for leaving? Refusing to show her how much she'd shocked him with that unexpected leap forward in her trust, he nodded. "Sure. But, Beth?"

One eyebrow lifted, but her eyes were softer. Open. She was listening to him.

He dragged in a quick breath, and said what he had to—for Danny's sake. "I understand what you want—better than you know. But Danny will remember today, and whether he thanks you or hates you for it is up to you." He gazed into her eyes and went on, knowing he risked shattering the trust he'd felt from her moments ago. "I was only eight when my mom left, and I still remember her last words to me, the look on her face as she said them."

"And?" she asked, her gaze intent on his face. "Besides the fact that I don't need to keep making that teapot for her."

"No. You don't." He gave her a brief, self-mocking smile of acknowledgment. "What I'm saying is, Danny's trying to find his way in life, and friends and sport are vital to a child's self-esteem. Being called a mama's boy is fatal. He'll be bullied about it all his life, no matter where you go."

Her face closed off. "What do you know about it?"

He shrugged. "Maybe not much. I'm not a father. But I was a boy once, and most boys believe the same credo. If you keep overprotecting him he may make it to twenty-five, but if all he remembers is you stopping him from living the life he wants for himself, he won't thank you, Beth—and you should know that better than anyone. Your parents turned you into a model, their pride all centered on your looks and fame, and you resented them for making you live the life they wanted for you.''

She whitened, her eyes dark and shattered. ''Thank you for your honesty.'' She wheeled about, heading for the curtain where heavy tapping sounds indicated Danny's obedience was wearing thin. ''I'll be right back,'' she said, her voice filled with quiet bitterness. ''You seem to think you know all about me.''

Yeah, that precious moment of trust between them had been just that—a moment; but what choice did he have but to do it? He couldn't gain her confidence at the cost of Danny's happiness. He might be a lowlife, but he hadn't gone that far down yet.

McCall let the door fall to behind him, trying not to listen in as the woman on the run fought with the loving mom, faced with a vivid, passionate boy who just wanted to play—a child's birthright that had become a rare privilege to him.

''It's just *practice,* Mummy. I need to practice so's I can make the team! An' you *know* Mr. Richards is nice!''

Beth said something to Danny, low and pleading. McCall squelched the temptation to use his earpiece to hear better.

''Why can't you be like the other mums?''

Silence for a few moments, then Beth asked something. Even muffled by the curtain, McCall could hear the bewildered hurt in her voice, and he ached for her.

''The kids all make fun of me 'cause of you. I just wanna play football, Mummy. I just wanna *play* with my friends!''

The throb and lilt of anguished passion came so clearly through in Danny's voice, McCall ached for him, too. He'd never realized how hard life must be for them both....

Beth's next words were again muffled and indistinct; but Danny's were not. ''Why?'' he cried, kicking something, and it thudded with the impact. ''I never go anywhere without you but at school. All the other kids get to play, and their mums don't watch them all the time. It's not fair. *It's not fair!*"

Beth's voice, discernible now, throbbed with anguish. "I'm sorry, sweetie," she muttered in a thick tone, obviously fighting tears. "But that's the way it is."

The halting words touched McCall's soul. Why hadn't he ever realized what she'd been through, what she'd sacrificed to have this strange half life of fear? What price had she paid for her son to live untainted by Falcone's corruption?

"I'm almost *seven*, Mummy! I'm big. I wanna play football! An' I'm goin' to play with Ethan an' Mr. Richards!" Danny pulled the curtains open, storming out.

Reacting on instinct, he reached out, snaking an arm around the boy's waist, lifting him off his feet and whirling him around in a playful motion. "Hey, there, big guy. Where are you off to in such a hurry?"

Taken off guard, Danny giggled and squirmed.

"Let him go. Put my son down!"

Chapter 6

McCall turned around in time to see the terror and despair touching those lovely eyes. So he was the bad guy again. He set Danny back on his feet, his eyes never leaving hers.

She flinched at the open challenge. Within seconds she masked her emotions with her curtain of calmness, looking at Danny. What lay behind it hovered between them like a mute aura, haunting him with its utter aloneness, its wistful, never-can-happen effect.

He jumped in with words he didn't know were on his lips until he spoke them. "Hey, buddy, my name's Brendan, and I play a fair game of football myself. I played on my varsity team. We can play right outside the house, so your mom can see us and know you're safe."

Beth's head snapped up at the impulsive offer, her dewy eyes searching his—distant again. Star-being's eyes, filled with suspicion and doubt. Shadows inside her soul, and not giving him an inch of trust.

But Danny's thin, intense face grew eager and alive with a naked longing that overcame his natural timidity. A boy wanting a man who would teach him how to be a man—an instinctive need all boys sought. A mirror for the look he'd felt on his own face too many times to count, until he'd given up believing his dad cared, or would ever play anything with him. "What's varr-city?" he asked with an odd lilt, trying to imitate his accent.

McCall grinned. "Varsity. It's my college team. UCLA."

"What's You-see-ell-ay?"

He mentally adjusted to a six-year-old's level. "UCLA is a really big school in America, in my hometown. It's the University of California, Los Angeles campus. See? UCLA."

The little dark face lit even brighter, grabbing on to the only point vital to him. "He can play football! Mummy? Can I go play? Please? *Pleeeease?* He says you can watch…"

Her glance said it all. Hunted. An animal in a net, trapped between the demons of doubt, wishing to give in to the natural longing of her son, and fearing the resentment of the child she'd sacrificed everything for. "Danny—"

The bell jangled again, a cheery sound cutting the tension like a butter knife: softly does it. A happy-faced man in his mid-thirties poked his head inside the door and grinned at her. "Hey, Beth. Donna said you'd be happier for Danny to train with us if we're in sight?" He pointed to the grassy field before the hill McCall slept on each night.

Strangely, Beth whitened at the words; but within moments she gained control, and smiled. "Thanks, Ken. I appreciate your thoughtfulness." She turned to Danny. "How's that, sweetie?"

But McCall heard her voice quaver. Equilibrium wasn't yet restored. Beth Silver was a woman on the edge of one hell of a precipice, and McCall would be there to catch her when she fell, whether she trusted him to be there or not.

Danny whooped. "All right! Let's go, Brendan!"

"I don't think we need bother Mr. McCall now, Danny."

McCall caught the boy's quick, longing glance as Ken Richards headed across the road, his arm slung across his son's shoulder. "It's no bother," he said, smiling at the boy. "I'd like to play." Yeah, he remembered too well sometimes watching the kids playing with their dads, and wishing his dad could be interested—or sober enough—to play a game with him. But drunk and abusive, ignoring him unless he had to thrash him again for some boy's misdemeanor, he'd still known who his dad was. His dad wasn't the role model he'd longed for, but he had a face to the name. Danny Silver had neither.

Danny's face had lit up like the Sydney Harbour Bridge during the Olympics. "Thanks, Brendan!"

McCall grinned. "High five." They slapped hands.

"That's Mr. McCall to you, Danny. Respect your elders— and strangers," Beth said, cool. Reminding him who he was. *Keep your place.* And in her opinion, his place was nowhere near her son.

He shrugged. "Let him call me Brendan. Doesn't hurt anyone." In fact, it was the first time in years anyone had used his given name. It felt good. Like he was a normal member of the human race, with people who knew him, or liked him.

"It does if he learns to trust everyone who offers to play with him," she hissed, in a fierce undertone. "And remember, Danny, Mr. McCall *is* a stranger. We do know Mr. Richards, and surely he can show you all the moves you need."

"Can't I play with Brendan?" Danny's piping voice thickened with the tears in his eyes as he looked up at McCall with sudden doubt, fear and suspicion. "Don'tcha like Brendan, Mummy? Is he one of those bad guys? The Stranger Danger guys who wanna take me away?" With the words, he shuffled backward toward his mother, his thin body shaking. "Are you gonna hurt me, or my mummy?"

Poor little Danny. Trembling with terror, he was still trying to cover his mother, to protect her....

Beth had done a hell of a number on him. Not that he blamed her, but couldn't she *see* what damage passing on her fears and well-founded paranoia was doing to this child?

McCall squatted on his haunches. "Danny, your mom's right to warn you of the danger—there are a lot of people like that in the world—but I would *never* hurt you, or your mom. I'm here to help you. I'm your friend." He held the boy's gaze unwavering, willing him to see a truth his mother refused to recognize.

If anything, Danny whitened more. "M-Mummy said that bad guys say things like that to make you go with them...."

"Yes. They do," he admitted. "That's one of the things you learn as you grow up, Danny. You learn who to trust. You learn to listen to your instincts—"

Danny sniffed, and wiped his eyes on his school-jumper sleeve. "What's that? In—"

"Instincts," he repeated gently. "They're those things that talk to you, that tell you when something, or someone, is good or bad, nice or scary." He reached out, touching Danny's shoulder. "There's a voice in your head when I touch you, isn't there? It's either saying 'Brendan's a nice guy,' or 'I don't want this creepy guy talking to me. I don't trust him.'"

Danny nodded solemnly. "I hear it."

McCall smiled at him. "You don't have to tell me which it is, but your mom will always need to know when you hear the voice saying the bad-guy thing to you, okay? It's your body's warning system, telling you something bad's gonna happen to you if you don't get away. You should always listen to it."

Danny's tear-wet face broke into a tremulous smile. "My voice likes you, Brendan. My voice says you're a cool guy."

McCall grinned at that. "My voice says you're a cool guy, too, Danny." He winked at the boy, who held up a hand. He slapped it in another high five.

Danny lifted his face to where Beth watched them—her face damp as her son's, and just as pale. "Mummy? I—I don't think Brendan's a bad guy...and—and—" his little face grew so uncertain, so lost "—and, well, Ethan's got his own dad..."

Beth closed her eyes in agony. "Go on, sweetie. Mr. McCall will be with you in a minute." Her voice sounded flinty, filled with the anguish of fear and turmoil hiding inside her eyes.

Danny whooped again, and bolted out, yelling for his friend. The door slammed behind him. McCall stood, waiting.

When she didn't or wouldn't speak, he took the initiative. "You won't have any cause for fear—or regret—in letting me play with Danny."

Her eyes didn't open. "If I see even the smallest reason to worry, McCall, you'll be dead in seconds." She put a trembling hand out to him, her eyes open and filled with a magnificent fire. A vivid-eyed tigress protecting her cub. "Give me your keys and your wallet."

Without a word he handed them over.

"And—and the other thing you had in your hands a few minutes ago. And any others you have hidden on you." A shaking defiance, her nostrils flared and her cheeks white. "You're not playing with my son with that *thing* on you."

McCall swore beneath his breath. Great. The Glock was the easiest weapon to reach in crisis, there to protect her and Danny, but there was no way she'd believe that.

He handed over the semiautomatic, his throwing knife and the small second pistol to satisfy her, but kept the sleeping darts made by the Nighthawks' chemistry department and doctors. He had to have some protection for Danny if—

"You make one move away from that hill and the police will be here in two minutes. I'm friends with the local lieutenant."

He'd expected a threat of some kind. "I'm not going to hurt him or take him from you, Beth," he said quietly. "Listen to your heart. Listen to your instincts. You know me."

She turned away. "My instincts have been wrong before."

He silently cursed Eduardo de Souza for his hatchet job on Beth's innocent love and trust. There was nothing he could say to fix that. "Do you have any more stipulations, or can I go outside and teach Danny some football now?"

She scowled at him. They both knew she was painted into a corner. If he played with her son, she couldn't go anywhere, couldn't run without him knowing, at least during the day, but if she'd said no, Danny would have resented her for years. The good mommy giving her son what he needed, vying with the hunted woman's need to keep her son safe from Falcone's clutches.

Needing to reassure her, he said, "I swear to you, Danny couldn't be in safer hands." If only she understood that—man, he'd lay down his life for the kid. Go down as the last resort, take your targets down with you, but at all costs save your subject, the people you'd sworn to protect. It was standard Nighthawk policy as well as his own personal vow. If you couldn't prove your belief in that credo, you didn't make it past the first round of recruitment. "Your son's safety is sacred to me."

She looked down to the wet clay beneath her fingers, now a half-sodden lump from too much water, and too much unconscious pounding. "Just remember," she said quietly.

"I do," he said softly. Testing her. "I remember everything. Do you remember, too? Do you?"

She turned on her wheel and began shaping the clay with distracted fingers. "Just go. Please." Her voice was weary, gentle and sad. She turned her face and scrubbed at her cheek with clay-smeared hands, smudging her cheek. A dirty angel wiping at tears she was too proud to show him or use to gain sympathy.

He couldn't push her anymore.

But he'd call in the team to move into the local perimeter at least. And Anson had to come in on this as well, with a second team. He had no choice if he wanted to keep Beth and Danny alive.

His gut churning, he followed Danny's path out the door, knowing it wouldn't be long before Beth shut up shop and followed them, watching him as he'd been watching her.

With his Glock in her pocket.

McCall had almost pulled a gun on Danny—and not just any gun. A Glock 18 with a release button for automatic firing...

Whatever McCall did for a living these days, he was a consummate pro. Instincts honed to a razor's edge.

Beth still felt the tremors down her spine. Did he draw to protect her, or himself? And if he was so wired that he'd pull on a little boy, what would happen when the real danger came?

She couldn't let her son be here when it happened.

Trust me, Beth. Do you remember? Do you?

Watching them through the window, she stifled the pang of wistfulness. Oh, she remembered all right—and ached.

After a decade that seemed more like a century, he was back, and he'd made a little boy's dream come true. For the first time, Danny could look at a friend playing with his dad and not feel wistful…and even McCall couldn't be that good an actor. He was having as much fun as Danny, teaching him to pass and catch, kick the ball and take a tackle.

Much as she was terrified to trust him, McCall was acting like a normal dad out there. The kind of dad Danny longed for with his sweet, innocent baby's heart…and she knew that, if McCall's recollection of this day would be hazy in hours, it would shine in Danny's memory for years to come.

McCall was right, damn him. Danny was suffering because of her stifling overprotection. She had to take risks…and though her mind screamed that this one seemed too big to take, her heart and deepest instincts cried out that McCall was here to help her, to help Danny.

Listen to your instincts. You know me.

She stifled a sigh and moved to return to her wheel, when the phone rang. She grabbed the receiver, placing it between her shoulder and ear for balance as she washed her hands. "Hello?"

"Hey, Beth. It's Donna."

The smile on Beth's face came through her voice. Donna Richards was the mother of Danny's best friend Ethan, and the closest thing to a girlfriend she'd ever known. "Hey."

"Did that guy find you? Mr. Tall, Dark and Gorgeous, not to mention Ruggedly Mysterious?"

She sobered immediately. "Yes."

"Do you know him?" Donna whispered as if McCall could hear. "I thought he might be an old lover come to play catch-ups…"

Dear Donna, couching it as "girlfriend" questions, in case he was Danny's father, and there with her now, or listening in. Beth closed her eyes, and offered a silent apology for the lie she had to tell. *For Donna's sake...* "No. But—but, Donna—it's turned personal," she said, keeping her voice light, as if she and McCall were an item. "If I need to leave the Bay suddenly—"

"I'll be thrilled that you've finally decided to get a life, sweetie. Consider the house closed up and the business taken care of for a few weeks, until you contact me." Donna's return voice was teasing, cheerful. "By the way, I found a new piece of technical wizardry to amaze you. I bought one, and organized for yours to come through the mail. It should come today, I think. Enjoy it, okay? And don't even think of paying me. It's a gift."

Beth sighed, both in relief at the information and Donna's careful wording down the phone line. A new, unused cell phone every two months, untraceable to her because it was always in Donna's name and billed to Donna's address, spelt a six-letter word she was addicted to—safety. "Oh, that's so sweet. Thanks, Donna. And..." she hesitated, then said it, "And thanks for sending Ken and Ethan here to play."

"I'd want that, too, in your shoes," Donna said simply. "Beth, I'd like to ask a favor. A big one."

"Name it," she replied without hesitation, rubbing moisturizer into her dry, cracking hands. Donna had given so much through the past two, almost three years.

Unexpectedly, Donna asked, "Do you trust me?"

Beth frowned. "Of course."

"You—you know Ken and I can't have any more kids..."

"Yes." Beth put aside the bottle of hand cream. She knew that for Donna to mention the painful subject after almost losing her life giving birth to Ethan, this had to be serious.

"We're going camping this weekend...and Ethan's decided it's not enough, just having us. He—he wants a friend to come. More specifically, he wants Danny..." Her voice trailed off. "Beth..."

Words sprang to her lips—words she could never say to Donna. Her friend didn't plead for her son, a child as precious to her heart as Danny was to Beth's.

How could she let Danny go, but how could she say no?

Ethan had probably already told Danny…and again, Danny would resent her for years if she didn't let him go. She'd seen it in Danny's eyes—she'd seen it in Ken Richards's face, in Donna's—even in McCall's, bare minutes ago.

Damage.

Scalding tears filled her eyes. The thing she'd worked so hard against—what she'd sacrificed her world for—was happening. She hadn't protected Danny, she'd infected him with her fears. Fears justified in truth, but fears no six-year-old should know about, let alone act upon, or hate his mother for.

She had to let him go.

You have a day, two at most. Dared she risk it? If Falcone's men were as close as McCall hinted—

A sudden, blinding thought hit her. *I can plan our escape while Danny's away.*

As if he could hear the cogs turning in her mind even from a hundred meters away, McCall glanced at her, intense, searing with heat—and knowledge. Yes, he knew she'd run, and he'd be there to stop her.

"I think Danny would love it, Donna. Thank you."

Her friend's voice sounded choked up. "No, Beth—thank *you* for trusting us with Danny."

Beth felt almost sick. At least Danny would have one night with Ethan. It wasn't a proper goodbye, but it was something. "Don't go in too lonely a spot, will you? I'd worry about that."

Donna was an intuitive person, and had already picked up on the unnatural tension. "Of course, Beth. We haven't booked. At this time of year we don't need to. We were just going to drive off into the sunset tomorrow morning."

Perfect. "Sounds good. I'll, ah, need to know, the, ah, exact location when you arrive. If it can be an, um, open kind of place, Donna? Where there's lots of space for him to run?"

To her credit, Donna didn't gasp at Beth's impeccable English suddenly descending into broken um-and-uh speech—their devised signal. "Of course, Beth. I know how Danny likes to run free."

"Sometimes I think he'll, um, take off and fly on his own

if I didn't watch him. Let me know if he's too much, and I'll, um, come and get him," she laughed, feeling a trickle of sweat run down her spine. The code had been practiced so many times; but now that the time had come, neither of them was ready for goodbye.

"Of course. Can you pack his things? Pack a big bag for him—Ken's planning to take the boys fishing, and you know how many times I'll have to make them change out of wet, filthy things. We'll pick him up tomorrow morning, first thing."

"Tonight might be better," she suggested. "Then if he gets upset at being away from me, we'll know while I'm close by. And it will, um, give me time with Mr. Tall, Dark and Mysterious…"

"Good idea. Ken and Ethan can pick him up. Eight o'clock do?" Donna was very quiet now. She knew Beth's suggestion had little to do with practicality for Danny's first night away and nothing at all about a budding romance.

"Yes, that will be fine. Thank you. I'll pack his gear now."

"The boys will have a ball."

But beneath the words, the undercurrent of sorrow tugged at her soul. *I'll miss you.*

Beth swallowed the lump in her throat. She had no time for sentiment, no right to get so attached. If anyone went nosing around, and found out Donna had helped her escape—

She's safe. She doesn't know the truth.

As they'd prearranged, Donna asked no questions, said nothing extraordinary in case anyone was listening to the conversation. She yakked for a few minutes about her family and Danny and the school fete coming up, told a dirty joke and ended the call.

Old Harry Silver's words almost five years ago when she and Danny had arrived in the Bay area would always keep her safe from prying questions.

This is my granddaughter Beth, and her boy, Danny. They moved up here from Dunedin to escape the cold—and Danny's father. He's a bit of a psycho, so they ran from him. Hit her, you know. If anyone ever asks about her or the boy, let us know, will you?

Her entrée into Renegade River life was assured with that part-lie. Beth met Harry Silver through old Dan Cassell. Dan had been her beloved friend in England—her one-time land-lord and surrogate grandfather...the beloved old ex-spy who'd lost his life through his association with her. Harry and Dan fought their own unique war during World War Two. They were Special Operations Executive Pilots who'd smuggled goods, services and information to members of the French Resistance. They'd trusted each other with their lives more than once—and that utter faith had saved her life when she'd come to New Zealand.

With one look in her eyes, wise, seen-it-all Harry had seen all she'd wanted to hide, just as Dan had—and he'd created a "granddaughter" and great-grandson, complete with his name, and birth certificates to prove they were New Zealand natives.

Within hours, Harry had become the only family she had, the loving grandfather she'd known with old Dan. Harry had been the security she'd lost too soon, the one flimsy barrier between her and the blasting tide of Danny's father. She'd had Harry for two wonderful years, someone she could talk to, hold on to, leave Danny with while she set up her studio. Then, sudden and shocking as Dan's death, he'd had one gasp of chest pain and was gone, the last man she could completely trust.

If Donna thought her arrangements were to escape Danny's father, it was truth, but only Grandpa Harry had known the whole truth. Old Dan Cassell in England had sent him full details, in case she ever needed to flee.

Answering Dan's "boarders wanted" ad in rural England ten years ago—it seemed a lifetime—had been a gift from God. She'd never have escaped Falcone last time but for Dan's elaborate arrangements for her safety.

Lying to Donna was for her protection. If Falcone or his men came here, Donna knew nothing about Beth, past or present, beyond the number of the user account with the phone company.

McCall was watching her through the window. She felt him touching her with his gaze, even from this distance.

She looked for a moment, and turned aside, trembling. All he'd done was push a stray lock of windblown hair from his eyes, yet she felt seared. It didn't matter how long she kept up the pretense that she didn't see him, didn't care, she felt it still…his deep-forest river gaze roaming her face and body.

She shivered again…but not in fear or loathing. God help her for the pure feminine reaction to him, for even wanting to drown in his summer-hot, twilit temptation.

Risking it all to be with McCall made no sense—none—but the woman deep inside her cried out. *Stupid. You never forgot him, and he's using it against you now.*

Fool. For the second time she was drawn to him, wanting his touch, his kiss—his body. And heaven help her, she wanted to trust him, even though she knew he would only betray her as he'd betrayed his country ten years ago.

Pretending to wash her hands at the small washstand, she took the minute she had before McCall checked on her again, to make one more preparation for her flight from New Zealand.

Chapter 7

It was done; finally, after years of doing the silent drill, she was ready to disappear again. With one phone call and one security code, all that Dan had set up for her years ago, that Harry had added to and refined, had swung into action.

The gear would be waiting for her at the prearranged places. The taped conversation proving Falcone's involvement in ordering the murder of U.S. Senator Bernard Colsten, an avid campaigner for a worldwide system allowing the tracing of arms sales, was where Falcone would never get it. Even if she died, copies of the tapes would go to the directors of the CIA and FBI, with the original landing straight on the president's office by way of MI5.

Everything was done except packing the few things she'd need. *And outrunning McCall,* her rebellious mind whispered.

"Mummy! Come and see me!"

The one plea she could never resist. She moved to the door, looking out to where Danny held the football in both hands like a trophy, his dark, intense little face alight with joy. "I catched it, Mummy! Brendan showed me how to catch it!"

McCall stood beside Danny, arms folded, those steaming-hot eyes on her as always. She dragged in a breath and walked out to where Danny and McCall waited for her.

"Watch me, Mummy! Watch me!"

She felt the loving smile melting the habitual reserve on her face. Her beautiful, precious boy. "I'm watching, sweetie."

McCall turned his gaze on her for a long, nerve-racking moment; then he moved back with an easy grin for shy, insecure, easily terrorized Danny. "Here, pal!"

Danny tossed the ball to him, and he tossed it back overarm, gridiron style. Danny and Ethan both jumped high to catch it. Danny managed to grab the ball, then it slipped from his fingers as he toppled back to the lush, verdant grass, soft and spongy with the constant rain. Ethan ran after the ball and grabbed it.

Beth clapped and whistled, knowing the intense pride was glowing on her face. She knew it was foolish, exposing herself like Achilles' heel, to give so much away; but her love for Danny was as overwhelming as it was unconditional, and she couldn't hide it. "Go, Danny! That's wonderful, sweetie!"

An extremely wet, muddy Danny rolled over on the grass, laughing. "I'm not s'posed to *fall,* Mummy. I did it wrong. And Ethan got the ball."

"Danny, old pal, what did I tell you? It's the catch that's vital here—that's what you need to learn. Falling is okay. You've got possession for your team, even if you're tackled, and someone could score the touchdown. That's what counts. Yeah, running with the ball is best, but you'll get that later."

"Don't the other people take the ball off you?" Danny got to his feet, his dark eyes round and awed.

His father's eyes.

McCall laughed down at Danny. "Nah, pal—that's in Australian Rules football or Rugby Union. I know your country's world champions at Union when the Aussies aren't, but I've only ever watched that on TV, so gridiron—American football—is what you're getting. And it's learning to catch that you need, right? That's the same in any code of football except soccer."

Danny bit his lip and frowned. "But none of the kids at school know how to play 'merican football, just our football."

McCall ruffled the boy's hair. "Then you and Ethan have something special you can teach all the kids at school, haven't you? You've got a talent they don't have."

Danny's eyes lit, her sweet, shy baby who never felt as if he had the advantage with any of the boys. He and Ethan breathed a "Wow!" at the same time, and high-fived each other with big, cheeky grins on their faces.

But he won't have the chance to do that before I have to take him away from here, thanks to you.

No matter how nice he was to Danny, how damn-fool *safe* she felt while McCall watched her house, she couldn't trust it.

If she gave in to it, she could be dead tomorrow. And Danny's upbringing would be with a man who'd teach him to hold an assault rifle instead of catch a football. Her sweet boy would learn to order a hit on anyone who upset or bested him in business. He'd treat women as possessions rather than respecting them as equals.

So many reasons to keep up the lie of being Beth Silver, and all of them boiled down to two chilling words. *Danny's father.*

If only she knew who McCall represented and why he'd come, then she'd know what to do....

As things were, she had no choice but to put her plan into action. She dragged in a quick breath, and plastered a bright smile on her face. "Hey, sweetie, Mr. and Mrs. Richards have invited you to go camping with them this weekend, and I think you're a big enough boy to go. What do you think?"

Ethan and Danny yelled, "Oh, yeah!" together, ran and crashed into each other, performing wild war whoops of joy.

Seeing Danny's starry-eyed face, the *I'm-in-Disneyland* smile that showed his missing front teeth, gave her a bittersweet sadness. Danny wouldn't know until it was too late that this would be his first and last camping trip with Ethan. He might hate her for it later...*damn* McCall for being right...but he'd be alive and free. She couldn't make herself care about anything else.

She made herself speak briskly. "You're staying over tonight as well, because they're leaving very early in the morning."

"Can I go now?" he asked eagerly, his eyes shining.

"After dinner, sweetie. I have to pack your things, and I'd like to have one last dinner with you before you go."

Still laughing from watching Danny's intense happiness, McCall looked up at that moment, straight into her eyes. Seeing more than she wanted him to. She silently cursed her choice of words. His warmth cooled and gelled to something dark and intense in a heartbeat. Oh, he had the picture. He knew her agenda.

She just wished she knew his in return. The unknown quantity with the power of life or death over them both—with his arm around Danny's shoulders.

Keep him happy.

The decision made in that moment. "Would you like to stay for dinner, Mr. McCall?"

Wipeout. His face blanked. So she'd shocked him?

She smiled. "To thank you." Her gaze fell on Danny, flushed with happiness and achievement, then back up to McCall.

Slowly, he nodded. "I'd like that. What time—Beth?"

"Now." She paused, weighing her options, but she'd never been one to let a challenge lie. "Ex-Lieutenant McCall."

Rapier thrust met solar-plexus hit.

With a little, knowing grin, Ken Richards murmured, "We'll be back after dinner, Beth. And thanks for letting Danny come with us—Ethan's obviously thrilled," he added, laughing down at his still-capering son.

Beth smiled. "Thank you for inviting him. Go have a shower, Danny," she said when the Richards family had gone. "Maybe we can play a game of Scrabble with Mr. McCall before you go."

Danny gave a little whoop when McCall smiled and nodded,

and ran for the house; but McCall's smile faded as he looked back at her. "Thank you, Beth."

Tired of games, she just turned to the house, but he swung her back with the tiniest touch on her arm, an overreaction she couldn't stop. "What?" Despite her resolve to hide everything from him, she almost snapped the word. Three days of this stiletto-edged dance was three too many.

It appeared McCall was tired, too. His gaze was flat, harsh in a strange, despairing way. "Who are you, Elizabeth Silver? Are you who you say you are?"

She didn't even hesitate. "Are you, ex-Lieutenant Mc-Call?" The name itself, the title, was almost an accusation.

"Please." The word was quiet, but the emotion no less real, the need no weaker. "Please trust me. I have to know."

"Why?" She kept her gaze limpid, her secrets hiding beneath. "If you've led these people to us, what will happen to you? Could your whole world—the only one you have—fall apart if I don't tell you my life story? Could you die—could your son lose his life or freedom?"

"Do you realize what you just gave away?" he asked softly.

She lifted an eyebrow to distract him, in case he noted her thudding pulse. "So this Falcone person you're after is the only dangerous, obsessed man in the world? The only one who'd kill to get his family back?"

His hand fell from her arm. "I want to trust you with my secrets, Beth, but they're not mine alone, and lives other than mine are involved. People could die if the information gets to the wrong people. Just one wrong word and I could be responsible for the deaths of innocent people. Good people who are just trying to make a difference in the world."

Oh, how she could relate to that. His words rasped against her heart. She struggled to keep her conscience intact. "Remind me—your trust is important to me, because…?" She watched him, challenging him as he'd done to her. "What you're saying is, essentially, that your nonexplanation should be enough. So you want to trust me? How nice of you. What a hero—your hidden reason for me to tell a total stranger all about my life is to save others, people I don't know, or even if they exist.'' She folded her arms, in the same stance as the one facing her. ''You give me no proof, no evidence, just *trust me*. Yes, that makes sense. I'll hand our lives into your keeping, based on those few words.''

His eyes darkened with wariness. He didn't speak.

She gave a slow, challenging smile. ''Feel like swapping confidences, ex-Lieutenant McCall?''

McCall shoved balled fists into his pockets, his gaze dark, brooding. On edge as much as she, hiding the wildness, pushing it back inside him. ''If you go first.''

She made a considering face. ''Tempting, but…no.'' She turned for the house. ''Dinner will be ready in half an hour. I hope you like fresh fish.''

''I love fish.'' His voice turned deep and soft, with rumpled sensuality. ''You know, they say confession is cleansing for the soul, Elizabeth Silver.''

She turned back one last time, looked right into his eyes. ''I have no soul. All I have is Danny.''

I have no soul.

He shuddered even now, two hours later. Playing Scrabble with Danny and Beth in the beautiful old-fashioned dining room, with a gentle fire in the grate behind him, her words hit him with freeze-blasting force. The look in her eyes as she said them. The memory froze him to the marrow. Incomparable in their loveliness, yet empty. Dead. No life, no heart, no fire.

Soulless.

Was that why he couldn't break through to her? What had she sold inside herself to get away from Falcone that night?

Falcone's men were in New Zealand now. Beth's confession had to be soon, if it was going to come in time to save her.

Early this morning Anson sent him back stats on the photos he'd taken of Danny for the CIA and MI6 to compare with the few younger photos they'd found of Robert Falcone. If Danny wasn't Falcone's son, he could almost be his twin. DNA results on the hairs he'd taken from the studio floor would take longer. The lab would need to sort out whose hairs they were, but if Beth or Danny's were there, they'd soon know if they were related to Eduardo de Souza. Because of the manner of de Souza's death in a suspicious car crash, the CIA, and therefore the Nighthawks, had all the DNA samples they needed for comparison tests.

Damn it, none of this would work anyway. Anson was getting twitchy, wanting to take Beth into protective custody, but McCall *knew* she'd have the information they wanted in hiding somewhere, and no matter how long they held her she wouldn't give it up as long as they kept her against her will. She had to give it of her own accord, because she trusted someone.

Trusted him.

If he told Beth who he was, and who he represented—that he was a Nighthawk sent here to save her—maybe she'd hand over the evidence she had on Falcone, and he could get her and Danny the hell out of New Zealand before Falcone's hit men got here. Falcone wanted his son—and even thinking about the punishment the man would exact on his runaway wife made McCall shudder. Falcone's inside connection to the Nighthawks, whose identity they still hadn't cracked—damn it, was it Angel, Solomon or someone they didn't yet suspect?—would get Beth and Danny's whereabouts and pass the information on so that Falcone would get to them before McCall could get them safely out.

Yet Anson's orders were set in stone. *Don't tell her anything until she confides in you. Get a positive ID first.*

Never risk the Nighthawks' security. Never compromise. Never give in. Anson's damn watchwords had for years been McCall's own private obsession. To break the rules risked instant, dishonorable dismissal. He'd get away with risking it to gain Delia Falcone's signed affidavit.

But this wasn't just the job to him, or even international security. He wasn't fooling himself here. This was personal...personal right to his bones. He wanted this woman to be Delia. *His* Delia. No matter what the consequences were. But though his heart and body screamed that this was the woman he'd craved for years, he had to face facts. Delia and her cousin Ana were so alike they could pass for each other, and the signs of nerves the first day he'd come into her studio could have come from his own imagination. Yeah, maybe he'd wanted her to be Delia so much he'd made up the signs in his mind.

There was no way to know who she was, except through Beth's confirmation. Delia and Ana de Souza were "double" cousins, daughters of identical twin sisters who'd married twin brothers. According to experts, the girls' DNA might match almost perfectly, like identical twins—assuming they had anything to compare them to. All they could prove was a connection to the de Souza family at best, to Eduardo de Souza, but it wouldn't be able to state whether Beth was daughter or niece or distant cousin, or Danny a grandson or great-nephew. Fingerprints were unavailable. If either girl had ever been printed, they'd disappeared. The dead body in the ravine was charred beyond accurate dental graphics.

Not that they had any to compare. The only dentist who'd taken X rays of Delia's or Ana's teeth had disappeared with the files the day of the accident. He'd left Brazil and vanished into the mist, to another life.

"Brendan, what's a ravine?"

Without thinking, he answered Danny. "A deep, sharp cliff where people get rid of evidence, or hide secrets."

A stifled gasp made him look up, but by the time his gaze cleared, Beth had herself under control. It was only Danny's curious, "What's the matter, Mummy?" that told him the sound hadn't been in his imagination.

With obvious difficulty, Beth looked up from the Scrabble board on the lovely, dark wood dining table, and smiled at her son. "N-nothing. Do you want a hot chocolate before Mr. Richards comes for you, sweetie? Um, Mr. McCall? W-would you like one?"

Without a word, he nodded.

Her fingers shook as she moved to push back her chair.

On the unwilling alert, McCall gazed at the board...and it was only then he realized what Beth had seen. What he'd done to her, by the grace of fate or his overburdened conscience.

Hiding = eleven points.

Evidence = fifteen points with a double-letter score.

Death = nine points.

Tree = eight points with a double-word score.

Ravine = eighteen points with two double-letter scores.

For years he'd lied, played parts, fought and killed in darkness and silence, vanishing without a word. It hadn't bothered him once in fifteen years, either with the SEALs or the Nighthawks. His objective had always been higher than what he'd had to do, the target worthy of death or taking down. Those he'd lied to needed his anonymity as much as his protection.

Not this time. The steel inside him had been branded with a smelting furnace, his conscience burned with a searing iron. He couldn't lie to Beth; the secrets his long-buried conscience strained to tell her had finally come out in the last five words he'd put down.

McCall looked up at her, his dread acute. *I didn't mean it. I didn't want to terrify you. I don't want to hide the truth from you. Tell me what happened that night. Tell me your story, and I'll tell you mine. Let me help you. I can save you.*

He all but held out his arms to her. *Please come to me, Beth. Please trust me!*

There wasn't even a flicker of response. She barely glanced at him before she walked into the kitchen without looking back.

Chapter 8

As soon as the door swung shut Beth leaned against the cool, tiled wall of the kitchen, shaking.

It was one thing to suspect he knew, even to hear the names, but it was another to see cold hard evidence. He knew it all, even things the press had never printed. The only thing he didn't know was which of the de Souza girls she really was.

She had to get out of New Zealand tonight. Taking Danny's security away for now was only less appalling than the thought of the destruction of his gentle heart, loving trust and timid, stuttering shyness at his father's ruthless hand.

She would find a location in a place where she could buy safety from extradition laws, and get Danny back into a stable life. She'd dump everything, change their lives completely. She'd heard people could buy fake birth and death certificates through hackers on the Net. Maybe if she bribed someone to create graves, she could kill off both their identities forever, and start over—

"Here. Let me."

She gave a stifled cry as hot milk splashed over her wrist; she held back the gasp as McCall took the pan from her hands.

"Don't handle hot liquids while you're working out how to give me the slip." He stirred the chocolate into the milk, and shoved a mug toward her. "Drink that. It'll calm your nerves."

He knew.

With those simple words he'd robbed her of all breath, all thought. On autopilot she did as he bade her, but she couldn't taste the rich sweetness on her tongue. She felt hollowed out, empty, brainless, unable to continue her plans for escape.

"Ken and Donna Richards are here. I promised I'd take Danny his drink before he went." He poured the milk into Danny's mug with a steady hand. "Come and see Danny off, then we'll talk."

Graceless, nerveless, all she could do was put down her mug and follow him. How to tell Donna she had to collect Danny again tonight…that Danny couldn't go camping after all….

Her heart ached. Poor little Danny—such a simple thing to want, and she had to rob him of the chance. She knew he'd resent her for years for what she had to do, but at least he'd still be alive, with his innocence intact. She could live with his anger at denying him a normal life. She'd find his forgiveness one day for what she had to do to him, hiding in the shadows, watching through locked and bolted windows while others laughed and loved and lived, free of the constant, haunting shades of terror.

A life lived in fear is a life half lived.

Her eyes squeezed shut. *I'm so sorry, my baby. This is all I have to give you….*

As soon as she entered the living room, Donna's gaze sharpened for a moment; then, as if she'd seen Beth's inner stress, her face softened into a grin. "Looking forward to your get-out-of-jail-free card, Beth? Three nights alone for the first time in almost seven years…"

She forced out a laugh, and ruffled Danny's hair. "It hasn't been a sacrifice."

Danny was bouncing from foot to foot, even as he gave her a fierce, if brief, hug. "Can I go now, Mummy?"

She kissed the top of his head. "Go, sweetie. Enjoy your-

self.'' She smiled, watching as he bolted out the door with
Ethan and without his bag. With an understanding grin, Ken
tossed it over his shoulder.

With sudden inspiration Beth took a step back, and made a
sign to Donna—thumb to ear, finger to mouth. *I'll call you.*

Donna showed no sign of seeing it, but Beth knew she had
caught her signal when she turned to distract McCall. ''It's
been nice to meet you, Brendan. See you around—with Beth,
maybe? So where are you from, Brendan? Are you American
or Canadian? You have any family back home?'' She fired
question after question with a hint of archness in her tone.
Playing the nosy girlfriend to perfection. A deflection with the
skill of a professional—and McCall kept his face away from
Beth as he answered.

She dragged in a silent sigh. A moment's relief was all she
could ask for right now. The reckoning was in front of her
face, and she didn't have a clue how to fight it.

As soon as she shut the door behind the Richards family,
she turned and walked straight into the kitchen and stood with
legs splayed, holding the bench as if it were her last friend.

He came in and stood beside her, refusing to sit at the stool,
but towered over even her tall frame. Watching her. ''You
need to know what's going down before you make any decisions.'' His eyes lingered on her, assessing her. ''I got word
two hours ago. Falcone's on the move. He's left his island.
His men have already reached Auckland, and showing your
photos—you know the ones I mean—asking if anyone knows
you. It's only a matter of hours, maybe a day, before they
know where you are.''

The quiet words hit her with sledgehammer force. She
reeled, holding the bench to stop herself from falling over.
''W-who?'' she whispered in flickering defiance.

His voice was bleak, his wild, rugged face inscrutable. ''I'm
risking my career telling you this.''

Her defenses, and the life of her son, depended on her lie.
''Who?'' she asked, stronger this time. ''Sorry, I must still be
a bit weak from when I scalded my wrist.''

McCall's jaw tightened; he loomed over her like an avenging Fury, even as he checked her wrist, saw the red patch. Without a word, he grabbed a clean towel and wet it, then wrapped it gently around her burn, soothing it. "Danny's father is on his way to claim his son, and to kill you. Is that easier to cope with?"

Hearing what she already knew, but put so bluntly, made her knees give way. "N-no…"

McCall held her up with strong arms, his face stern and darkly beautiful in its concern. "I'm here. I'm here."

"And that's supposed to help?" She gripped the bench with fingers gone white from the unrelenting pressure.

"I want you to think so. I am here to help." Though his strength easily tripled hers, his words were gentle, tender as the arms that held her. "It's over, Beth," he murmured, giving her the name she preferred, giving her the dignity of being who she chose to be. "Please, trust me. I want to help you."

A dark, gypsy whisper, with an insidious sweetness almost compelling her to obey. She dragged in a harsh breath, releasing it only when she felt her diaphragm protest that it couldn't give any more leeway. *Danny's life depends on this. You can't trust him just because you want to!*

She kept her gaze fixed on the volcanic pattern of the bench top, drawing patterns on its surface with an absent finger. "You won't tell me who you represent, or give me proof. Do I hand my life over to you on the basis of a few words?"

After a long moment, he nodded. "You're right. But even if I weren't under orders, I've been trained to keep my career close to the vest for a long time." He expelled the air, and as he stalked past her, the scent of warm, sweet chocolate came to her. Luscious danger…the chained jaguar unable to reach its prey by conventional means, and she held her breath again, sensing that McCall was finally going to share something of himself, and his life. "My boss ordered me to tell you nothing until I have a confirmation of your ID, and the evidence we need to get the government of Minca bel Sol to overwrite their extradition laws and hand Falcone over. But my boss doesn't have a little boy whose life is on the line." He almost threw the words at her, his voice grating and stark. "I think the time has come for the truth—from both of us.'' He tipped her face up and looked in her eyes, his own hiding too many secrets and too much at stake to tell them all. "I'm sure from the way you never contacted me after our last date that your father told you about my dishonorable discharge from the SEALs. He would also have told you why it happened, at least as far as he knew. What he said wasn't the real truth, though we'll never know if he knew that or not.'' He rubbed his jaw, as if the late-night shadow on it bothered him. "I don't want to turn you against your father. I wouldn't tell you this if I had another way to convince you. I can't give you the details surrounding the terms of my discharge—it's highly classified—but it was always a fake. It's my cover, an intricate story with full legal backup to get me into where I need to go for my job.''

"And what job is that?'' she asked, losing the feeling in her hands as she gripped on. Everything hinged on his answer now.

Dragging in another harsh breath, he swung around to face her, his eyes the color of a storm-tossed ocean, and burning hot. "I could be court-martialed for what I'm about to tell you. I belong to a top-secret group of mostly ex-military fighter-pilots, a CSAR-combat search-and-rescue-team. Most of us were recruited from the elite squads, the most dangerous—Green Berets, SAS, SEALs, ParaRescue Jumpers, etcetera. Our job description includes gathering information and rescuing people in places governments can't or won't acknowledge they have vested interests in. We infiltrate drug and gun-running rings, fight in unacknowledged war zones, rescue hostages from deadly places—and we find people who don't want to be found.'' A little, grim smile. "We also find people in deadly danger who refuse to take help, or even admit they're in peril. People who put their own kids at risk because they're too proud and stubborn—or too scared—to reach out and trust us.''

She absorbed the information with a strange sense of calm. Much as part of her didn't want to believe him, it all made sense. She'd known all along that McCall was a hero junkie. It made complete sense that he'd be a spy who rescued people.

If he's telling the truth, why didn't my father know? As an ambassador to the United States, he'd have had clearance to find out.

The logical conclusion to that question was too painful to explore. So she lifted her chin, choosing defiance. "Would either of us be in peril—would this Falcone person know where we are if you hadn't come?"

She felt his shrug, the mental withdrawal, his own trust, and his unspoken hope withering under the quiet question. "We only got your name because Falcone's men were searching in the South Pacific region. He's been searching for you both for a long time. He never believed in your death, or his son's." His gaze sharpened. "You know the deal. We know you're either Delia or Ana de Souza. From there you hold the cards. We want the evidence to send Falcone to the electric chair. He'd be indicted in Texas. For that evidence, we guarantee your safety."

"I don't have any evidence. My name is Beth Silver." She kept her gaze on his face—no hardship, since looking at him was an addiction, as all-consuming as Ecstasy—as she had to deflect him. "You're not the first person who's confused me with Delia or Ana de Souza," she sighed. "Obviously this Falcone man has. Danny's real father did, too. He fooled me into believing he loved me." *Forgive me, Ana, for borrowing your story. Until he confirms who he is with reasonable proof, I must make McCall believe that Danny's father isn't Falcone!* "It wasn't until Danny was on the way that I saw his obsession with her had transferred to me. The violence and anger that I wasn't the woman he really wanted left me with no choice but to run. I've been running from him for years." She finally released her fingers from the bench, and the ache came, rapier-sharp, through her hands, but she welcomed it right now. Physical pain she could handle. "If this Falcone person takes us, believing us to be his wife and son, so help me, Brendan McCall, I will kill you."

His eyes bored holes into her soul, but not her story. "Are you telling me you're not Robert Falcone's wife?"

Dear God, Falcone's wife. She wanted to throw up. "I'm nobody's wife," she answered him with a queer sense of gladness that she could be honest in this, at least. "I never have been."

He frowned. His hunter's instinct had obviously heard the truth in her words. "You didn't marry Danny's father?"

She shook her head. "No, but it won't stop him trying to kill me if he finds me—and it won't stop Falcone taking my son, if he believes Danny to be his child." Again, her gaze locked on his. Moving closer to him, body against will. "You say your group is above the government, in league with the CIA and MI6?"

He nodded, his face wary.

"So are you responsible to them, or free agents? You promise protection in exchange for evidence, but do we have an expiration date? Do I get effective protection, or a so-called safe house that he could infiltrate in hours? Would your group betray my trust and my son's safety to achieve your higher purpose? Are our lives an acceptable risk to your boss? Would my son and I become collateral damage to him in a greater war?" she demanded fiercely, in total contrast to her tremor-shaken body.

The finger still touching the soft skin below her chin fell. Her knees shook; illogically, she felt as if her last support had vanished beneath her feet. "Damn it, woman, you know where to hit, don't you?" He wheeled away, dashing a thick lock of hair from his face with careless grace. "I won't lie to you. I can't guarantee he won't, Beth. I know my boss. He'd blow the world apart to save one of his operatives, to stop a war or bring down scum like Falcone, but though he'd expect me to give my life to save you during the mission, individuals like you and Danny are blips on the screen in the longer-term picture. He'd arrange for your safety, sure, but unless he had reason to believe you were in danger again, he'd forget about you when the next disaster came along."

A fire-streak of agony flashed through her brain, leaving her weak. "So why should I confirm or deny anything? Why should I try to bargain with you?"

He threw her an intense look over his shoulder. "Because I'm not my boss. I give you my word, Beth, here and now— if you trust me with your lives, I'd lay down my life before I'd let anyone touch you or Danny. I'd refuse direct orders, turn my back on my career, take another treason charge, stand in silence through a court-martial, even commit murder to keep you both safe. I'd walk through burning hell to save you."

The power of those raw words sent tremors through her entire body; but a flicker of doubt, of fear, made her ask, "If I'm Delia, you mean? What if I'm not her?"

His gaze narrowed for a moment; then he came back to her, putting his hand under her face again, caressing gently. Giving to her because he wanted to, not because he was trying to force her secrets from her. "I just gave my word to Beth," he growled, his dark, stormy face beautiful in its masculine intensity. "Don't you get it? It might be my job, and the right thing, to find out if you could rid the world of that filthy bastard Falcone with that tape, but I don't give a damn who you are. It's *you*…you and Danny I'd lay down my life for, whether you're Beth and Danny Silver or Delia and Robbie Falcone."

Aching, she whispered, "Prove it."

"There's only one way to prove it—and that's with my life." He released her chin and paced the room, seeming to take the night with him; then he stalked over to her and took her cheek in his hand, caressing her with tender reassurance. Close, too close. Never close enough. "I told you I'd walk through hell burning for you, and I would," he growled against her mouth, his breath mingling with hers. "Come with me, Beth, and I'll prove it any way I have to. If it comes to that, I swear to God that I would die to save you and Danny."

Chapter 9

I would die to save you.

Slow and unwilling, her eyes lifted to his face. Her eyes burned with all that was said, or had been left unsaid between them. After years of expecting darkness and torrential rain, she'd been led into the sunshine, and she blinked, dazzled by the power of it. Could she—*dare* she believe him?

In return his dusky forest gaze was unerringly gentle. "I can help you. I can save you and Danny. Trust me, Beth."

She drew in choppy breaths. Like a fool, she was praying for another miracle to show her the way, when all the magic she needed stood right here looking at her, touching her.

He didn't move, just kept his gaze locked on hers. Using his dark-eyed gypsy magic on her, willing her to believe. "Use your gut. Use your heart. You know the truth. You know me."

Et tu, Brute. And Judas betrayed his Lord with a kiss. "When it comes to my son's safety, I don't trust anyone." She pushed her hair behind her ear with a shaking hand.

Instead of the anger she expected, his face gentled with empathy. "I know, baby. How do you get your innocence back once it's gone? How can you look in anyone's face—

even people you've cared about—and *know* what they're saying is the truth?''

Speechless, she stared at him.

The small half smile was filled with understanding, yet
hard-edged in irony. Combined with his dark fall of hair and
a body made to bring a lover to unequaled satisfaction, it was
a lethal combination to a starved woman. ''Sometimes you
have to risk it on a throw. If you don't, you condemn yourself
to a life alone. Danny will grow up, Beth, and then what do
you have?''

So many answers she could give him to that. *A grown-up
son who can live, work, marry and have kids untainted by his
father's filth. A son who will see his twenty-first birthday without holding a gun or killing anyone who annoys his papa.*

For once, the answers felt like a hollow rehearsal; she
couldn't utter them. *A life lived in fear is a life half lived.* She
wanted far more than that for Danny…and for the first time
in years, she wanted more than that for herself, too.

A finger touched her face, lifting her gaze to his face. ''You
can't carry it alone forever. Give me the burden. Talk to me,
Beth—tell me who you really are.''

A king hit to the gut. She took the blow without movement
or signal, forcing her eyes to remain calm as she physically
restrained the tremors, stopped the tortured scream escaping
her throat. She lost more control with every second that
passed, giving her life and secrets into McCall's dark keeping.

But while she was unable to see the way forward, she had
to cling to the dangerous illusion that she had some control
over her world, by clutching at the only escape route she had.
''M-my name is Beth Silver. You—you don't know what
you're talking about. You don't know Danny's father. Please
go.'' *Even I can hear the tremors in my voice,* she thought in
disgust. *I give more away every second.*

So it appeared. His gaze was too knowing as he rasped,
''So you can run again?''

His hooded gaze remained locked on her, keeping her
pinned and still like a butterfly in a specimen case. Her only
movement was in her heart, beating like a wild thing, intent

on escape. *Keep your secrets. Keep control!* "Who is your group?" she demanded, still shaking. "W-what is their name? To trust you with my son's life, I have to know who they are. Who sent you here? Does the government know you're here? Will the local police back up your story?"

"No to the last. Almost nobody has heard of us, but the prime minister of Australia or New Zealand will confirm my story, and I'll take you to Parliament House to prove it if I have to. Come with me," he whispered, so tender, so under-standing. Not judging her for the things she'd had to do to stay alive and free. "I just risked my career—all the stability I've worked my whole adult life to achieve—to tell you the truth. You know what we want from you, and why. We know you took the tape as insurance against him. I was in Amalza trying to infiltrate his fortress. We'd only just discovered the tape was in existence. In return for your trust, and the tape, I will keep you safe—and I'll take Falcone down. You'll be free of him forever." He moved closer, filling her shivering spirit with heat and fire and the unerring force of his inner strength. "Lean on me. I swear, you will not be left alone. I'll be with you every moment until you have the safety and free-dom to choose your own life."

She couldn't make her throat work to answer. A dark web spun around her, terror and death and the fear of trusting any-one, enmeshed with tiny whispers of tenderness and hope and faith.

Was McCall the real deal, or a master spinner of lies?

She wanted, oh, how she *needed* to be able to trust him, but where Danny's life was concerned, could she take the risk? She looked down and away, shamed and foolish, made stupid by her own hidden hunger. "I can't afford to believe you, McCall. Just go."

"Is that really what you want, Beth?" His lush, graveled words, like knife-edged dark satin, unlocked a floodgate of desire inside her body she hadn't known until McCall strode back into her life, making her feel like a woman again with a single, searing look. "It's your call. I can go, and leave you alone. I can sleep on the sofa, be here to protect you. Or I can come to your bed and give you what your body's telling me you need so badly you can't think anymore.''

The heat his words evoked left her nerveless, breathless and *wanting.* "I—I don't know you.'' A flimsy defense even to her own ears, but like flotsam after a shipwreck, it was all she had left to cling to.

"Need like this doesn't follow convention. It just happens, and when it comes, it explodes. It's happened to you and me. I could control it, if it were only me—but it's not. You want this as much as I do.'' He turned her body so she faced him, and tipped up her face. She trembled at the touch and his hot, hot eyes, so much that her knees almost gave way. "You need the release from unbearable stress and fear of change—the emotional and physical freedom I can give you, even if it's only for a night. You can't be alone anymore. You're aching for me. You need me inside you as bad as I need to be there.''

Helpless for the first time in years, mesmerized by his eyes and his words, she couldn't speak, couldn't think. Her trembling hands reached up and brushed the fall of midnight hair from his dark, rebel face. Maybe she would never know this man, but oh, she *needed* him tonight. "Isn't it against all your spy rules?'' The words came out raw, filled with the *craving* that burst to life inside her. The greed for all he was offering.

He turned his face and kissed her palm. Then, slowly, he ran his tongue over her heated skin, and her body's need exploded. She swayed toward him, and he smiled against her palm. "I'm breaking so many rules with you, I've tossed the book,'' he growled seductively. "That rule book was all that kept me from crossing the line a thousand times since I became a man. But I can't remember what the rules are anymore. All I know is I need you like hell.''

A strong man does not need to blame a woman for his failures or his needs and weaknesses, encantador. Papa's voice came to her, a shadow of the past, from one of his heart-to-heart talks with her. She almost smiled, remembering how he'd call her *encantador,* a little fairy who enchanted him. *He does not need to hit her, or hide behind her when things go wrong. Trust a man who shoulders his own faults. Lean on him when you need strength, for he will need you, too.*

Until now she had never met a man who had fulfilled Papa's standards. Until McCall, who didn't blame her for his need for her, or even for breaking his rules, which could land him out of his spy group on his bad-boy ass. He took it on himself. *He* had lost control over *her,* and he wasn't ashamed to admit it.

His arms held her up when she fell into him. She leaned into his chest, her head on his shoulder. She breathed in his skin, his need, his heat, his fire and innate strength, knowing he wouldn't let her fall tonight.

"Say it, Beth." Jagged and hot with hunger, his voice rasped into the sensitive skin behind her ear. "If you say nothing else, tell me you need me like hell, too—at least tonight."

But she couldn't make the words come, and she was too far gone to care why. Her hands tangled in his hair and pulled his mouth down to meet hers.

Was there a word to describe what McCall made her feel? God help her, his touch made her drown in *need* until she had to taste him, inhale him, shed his clothes and hers, and be with him, skin to skin. Whatever this was, she felt dreaming and awake at once, in despair and in bliss, wanting to die and more alive than she'd ever been. And craving, *craving…*

You need me inside you as bad as I need to be there.

"Yes, yes," she whispered as he grabbed her by the waist and hoisted her onto the kitchen bench. He nipped at her throat with his teeth; his hands left her waist to fill his palms with her breasts. His thumbs found achingly hard nipples, and rubbed them with exquisite tenderness. And oh, the weakness of anguished desire filled her, body and soul, *aching,* pounding for release…

"Wrap your legs around me," he uttered hoarsely. "Do it, Beth. Show me you're as hot for me as I am for you."

She gasped at his blunt words—nothing pretty or tender or sophisticated for McCall—but they flicked a switch in her femininity she'd never known existed. More aroused than she'd ever been, she hooked her feet over his butt, her thighs around his hips, dragging him to her...skin to skin, hardness to her soft, hot dampness, if only these *clothes* weren't on...

She moved against him, moaning. Filling fingers and palms with that dark, muscled skin. Impatient, she tore at his shirt, pulling it away until she could see him, feel him. Gorgeous, so unutterably male, burning-*hot* and dangerous, so brilliantly *alive* and blatantly masculine, he terrified her, drew her irresistibly.

Come to hell, baby...

He ground against her, making a low animal sound of satisfaction when her body replied in kind. He flipped her T-shirt to the floor. "Beautiful," he mumbled between scorching kisses and a touch burning her alive and making her throat ache with the need to drag him to bed, take his body, right here and now. "Let go, Beth...yes, baby, that's it, let go..."

She couldn't outrun this desire, so she threw it on the fire he'd made between them, shuddering in the dark power of his words and touch, her mind and body screaming out a primitive chant, *more, more, more.* She barely knew what she did as she ripped, tore, dragged and drank him in.

McCall was no polite lover—he was a barbarian who would take her and give it all back again with that hard, savage *want.* Feeling raw and untamed, burning alive and aching, she wanted to let go—to be a bad girl for once. She wanted to be wild, to be the one to take him, to throw him on the floor, straddle him and ride him. To stake her claim on him, and oh, McCall would let her own him, chain him body and soul tonight—

What am I doing? Danny's father is coming closer by the hour...

"No!" She jerked back, shocked by her own wanton desire, by what he made her *feel*—by what he could make her forget. "I don't—I can't do this. Please go now!"

Expecting an argument, he stunned her again by moving away, but he didn't go far. He stood one pace back, folding his arms over his tight-muscled chest, still panting and flushed and hard. Half-naked, with his jeans unzipped—had *she* done that?—he watched her through that wild fall of dark, mussed hair, making no effort to hide his aroused state.

But why should he? He knows it's no different for me.

But McCall didn't look down at her half-undressed body, and she felt illogically threatened by his control, even by the respect for her she sensed in his self-command. He knew he didn't have to say a word. He could make her want to get it on with him, have wild, untamed sex right here on the bench, because the scratching of this heated itch they had for each other couldn't be called *making love*—with a single touch. But he gave her the choice. This man, who could have it all from her without a word, was waiting, giving her the dignity to choose her way and time. If she wanted him she'd have to come to him, walk straight into his dark, scorching-hot fire...

And oh, she felt so *cold* without his touch.

He turned to the bench, took the half-drunk mugs of now-cold chocolate and emptied them down the sink. He bent to the floor, tossed over her T-shirt and pulled on the tattered remains of his shirt, pulled his sweater on, zipped up his jeans.

She only just held in the cry of protest.

Only when they were both dressed did he turn to her, his eyes intense in raw truth. "I won't be far. I'll be watching."

Unable to control it, she shuddered.

"I loved your curls. I loved touching them." Slowly he reached out and touched her hair. A possessive gesture by a man who thought he was in control.

Control.

The illusive vision of budding trust vanished like a mist over the Bay below. She dropped from the bench—even just sitting on it seemed shockingly intimate to her now. She tried to make her face and eyes flat, though her lips and body still throbbed molten-hot from his touch. "This is my natural hair, McCall. You have the wrong woman."

"Tell me the truth, Delia," he whispered, and it sounded to her like a bomb ticking—and the explosion was the truth. And though he might get a promotion or commendation from it, the real consequences would only come to her and to Danny.

Yes, the term *collateral damage* seemed all too real now. And she might have to face the words in Danny's dying eyes....

"Delia again. A pretty name," she remarked, calm and cold. "You seem to be fixated on it—or on the woman who owns it. But she's *dead,* McCall. You say you want the truth, then look at it yourself. Delia de Souza died in a car crash years ago. You're chasing a ghost." Hating herself for the shadowy world of half lies she had to tell to survive, she told him as much truth as she could. "I've had to deal with too much obsession in my life because I look like her. I'm already trying to save my son from a man who's violent and unbalanced when it comes to us—do I deserve another one?" She sighed and shrugged, palms up, telling him the truth. "I've never met this Falcone person in my life. Accept it—I am not the supermodel who married that man, and gave birth to his child." Tired of the intricate, stiletto-sharp dance over a ravine as dangerous as the one that had caused Ana's death, she said wearily, "And if that was all you ever wanted from me, don't bother coming back. I'm tired of being a Delia substitute."

The heat and need she'd felt moments before snapped off like a broken light switch. He was all business now, cold and ruthless and dark as sin. "We got the original birth records for your year. The only Elizabeth Anne Silver in New Zealand is fifty-four. She lives five hundred miles away in Christchurch. And no Daniel Silver was born in New Zealand seven years ago, or either year around it." He threw the words in her face like a curveball.

She gave him a quick, bland smile. "I guess my mum and dad forgot to register my birth, and I sure as hell wasn't going to register Danny legally, with his father after us. The facts you have don't make me your girlfriend."

"Maybe not, but it does make you and Danny both illegal immigrants." He folded his arms across his chest. "You aren't on the naturalized list, either."

She shrugged. "So arrest me, and take me to your leader. I feel it's only fair to warn you, you won't find a thing to prove your theories as to my identity, and you won't see any of this so-called evidence I'm supposed to have, no matter how long or hard you search for it.''

He sighed as if he had the weight of the world already on his shoulders, and she'd just added to it. ''You know I've given you enough classified information to destroy me tonight, and we both know that you know where to use it.'' His voice was quiet and yet terribly harsh, as if she'd been the one to betray him.

She shrugged. ''Our definitions of destruction are a little different. Your 'destruction' is your career. Mine is the life of an innocent child, and sacrificing my life or freedom to a violent and obsessed man...whether the man is Danny's father or this Falcone person seems immaterial to me right now.''

''You're right.'' He withdrew inside himself; the blazing heat inside him vanished, and she shivered with sudden cold, and a tired kind of loneliness. ''But I'll be damned if I'll lie down for you to walk on me. You either trust me by now or you don't.''

Trust? With her baby's life and freedom on the line? With the possibility of her ending up dead? *Trust?*

The fury filling her must have shown on her face. He nodded. ''I guess that's it, then.'' His deep-forest gaze roamed her, face and body, and she shivered again, hot and needy. God forgive her for giving him the right to look at her with such intimacy—and God help her for the purely feminine reaction to everything about him, for wanting to drown in his dark, hot temptation.

Drawn to a man who would only betray her.

Judas with his silver. It seemed appropriate, since she'd been standing in a field of blood the past five years.

''I'll be watching,'' was all he said. Then he left.

Chapter 10

"**M**cCall! McCall!"

The scream froze him in his tracks, barely out the door. "What the—?" He turned back as the door autolocked behind him.

Damn! He bolted around the side and vaulted straight through the security-screened dining-room window, boots first, ripping the guts from the steel mesh and setting off the alarm system. "Beth!" he yelled, landing upright in a half tangle of ripped netting and mangled metal.

She skidded into the dining room from the hallway, her eyes wild. He heard her wounded cry through the shrieking alarm. "Somebody was here. He grabbed me, put a knife to my throat, but I slammed my elbow into his solar plexus and he dropped the knife and ran when I screamed your name," she panted, her face white and terrified. "I think he escaped through the manhole. I heard sounds coming from the laundry."

He had to recon the house, search for evidence; but he found himself holding her a nanosecond later. "You okay, Beth?" he asked gruffly, feeling the thumping of her heart against his chest as he smoothed her hair with the soothing touch reserved for the gentling of wild animals. For a man who had long ago accepted that he'd always be a loner, holding this woman in his arms felt so damn *right*...

She nodded against his chest. "You did this to me. You came here and my quiet, safe life blew up in my face."

One of life's grimmer ironies—he'd come to save her, but he'd merely landed her in greater danger. "I'll make it right again," he murmured against her ear. "I'm going to make life better for you and Danny. I swear it."

The slight shaking against his body worried him, until he realized it was soft laughter, dry and edged with the hysteria of released fear. "You know, McCall, you should try to get that God complex of yours under control. You *can't* fix my life, or anyone else's. You're only human."

He looked at her with wry humor. "Believe me, I *know* I'm not God...sometimes I wonder if I rank as human." The moment shattered with his words; he could feel her withdrawal. "I'll check the house. If someone got in here, they have to have been an expert."

One quick recon of the house confirmed it. And with her security system and his on top, this had to be the work of a pro. Hell, yeah. Through the roof and into the manhole—and back out again the same way—and all without setting off the intricate system he'd put in place for Beth's protection.

How? He'd covered the whole perimeter, every contingency planned for. How the hell did they disable no less than three sets of four-way systems with him in the house?

Suspicion confirmed. This had to be the work of an expert sneak thief—or a Nighthawk who had intimate knowledge of the system he'd set up.

Why would an expert who'd done such elaborate work to take Beth run at the first sign of trouble? Why not take her?

Danny. They were after Danny.

He didn't waste time with expletives. "Arm yourself. Lock this window, and everything else. Do it while I'm still in the perimeter. And stay away from the windows." He vaulted back through the window and bolted for his high-tech, full-throttle motorbike. He punched in a number on his cell as he ran. ''Break-in at subject's house—attempted abduction. Professional job—suspect rogue is in the perimeter. Target's son safe at another location. Will locate suspect and follow to be sure he's not after the boy. I'm moving the entire team in ASAP—two to subject's house, two to where the boy is.''

''Roger that, Flipper,'' Ghost replied tersely. ''We'll leave Australia tonight, as soon as we get clearance and call in the full team and equipment. We'll be in the vicinity by 0800.''

McCall disconnected, locked his semiautomatic and shoved on night goggles as he ran, checking the roof. Oh, yeah. One busted tile. Clumsy—too clumsy for an expert—yet he'd disabled two high-tech security systems without alert, and got away while he was right here. This was a pro who'd needed to escape in a tearing hurry, who had risked it all so that he wouldn't be seen. Which was fair enough—but something inside the story rankled. Was this some kind of crazy setup that made sense only to the perpetrator? Did he bolt because his primary target was Danny, not Beth—*or was it because the specialized Glock he'd have to kill McCall with would confirm his identity as a Nighthawk?*

A fading set of taillights on the southern road toward the mainland car ferry gave him the probable target. Checking the opposite direction in case of red herrings, he saw only dark emptiness. Flashing a high-beam flashlight he kept in his jacket at all times, he saw nothing hiding in the shrubs lining the road, no glint of light on metal, chrome or even plastic. So he had no choice but to go for the obvious.

He threw himself onto the Ducati and revved it up.

''Give me a helmet! You're taking me to my son.''

McCall started. Beth was already on behind him, snatching the helmet from his hands. ''We can't risk it. Go inside!''

''Don't waste time. He must be after Danny. I'm not waiting here for more of his men to get me—and you can't bring my son back to me on your own. Even you can't pull off miracles. You need help.'' She pulled on the helmet and moved against him, into riding position. ''I don't care who you work for anymore—you can get me to Danny, and that's all I want.''

McCall tamped down his impatience. He understood her need, but he'd blow this case wide open if only he could see the face of the person in that car. ''They went in the opposite direction of the Richards' house. Danny's safe for now, Beth—''

''What kind of spy are you, McCall?'' she yelled, crushing his ribs in her tight grip. ''You think he disabled a security system and broke in alone, in silence? If they were smart, they took two cars, one for distraction while the other takes Danny!''

''Yeah, they probably did, and if they're smart, they'll follow us there. *Think,* Beth! If someone *is* waiting in a secondary car, we could lead him straight to Danny, and they could outnumber us ten to one. Danny's safer without us there.''

''What if they followed Donna and Ken earlier, right to the house?'' she cried fiercely.

Damn, she was smart. ''I'll cover it. I'll move my people in to secure the Richards' house, and they'll call the local cops to help. Trust me, I'll make sure he's safe.''

''Fine,'' she growled, the wounded mother lioness wanting to protect her cub. ''But you can't guarantee he's not already in that car. I'm coming with you. Just go!'' she snapped, wrapping her arms around him, molding her legs to his butt and thighs. Snuggling against him as she'd done in the kitchen, when she'd had her eager hands on his half-naked body—

Stuff it in a sock, McCall. Danny could be in that car!

He took off after the disappearing car, knowing he had to go this way first. But if Danny wasn't in it, he somehow had to get back to the Richards' house or send backup, stat. As he revved the engine harder, he yelled, ''Can you grab the left handlebar? I need to ensure backup is following orders.''

Her breasts flattened against his back as she stretched, making small cries of frustration until she gripped it. ''I can't hold it for long,'' she cried.

He hit the button on the two-way in his jacket pocket, pulled out the attached earpiece and shoved it in his ear to receive.

"Nighthawks in Project Falcon, this is Commander One calling for immediate assistance. Wildman and Braveheart to 34 Post Road ASAP with all protective measures, including police. Target's son is to be protected at all costs. Child's name Danny. If approach necessary, tell him Brendan sent you. Panther and Heidi, head to subject's house to secure and collect evidence. Subject is with me, tailing suspect heading south on the road to car ferry."

Within seconds all operatives responded in the affirmative, and the directional device proved that each operative was in his or her proper place. None of the four of them could be the rogue, then…they couldn't have gone so far in five minutes.

He couldn't vouch for Beth's house remaining unmolested; but right now, Danny was all that counted—and finding the bastard who could terrorize an innocent woman but didn't dare face him.

But he wasn't so focused that he couldn't still feel Beth's arms holding him, her body curving into his back, butt and thighs like a lover's urgent caress—the starving-woman-on-fire caress she'd given him minutes before—and it shoveled testosterone on adrenaline like raw fuel tossed on an exploding fire.

He took the handlebar again and kicked up the accelerator to one-forty, letting it scream over the winding back road. Loving the speed, and the feel of Beth holding him so close, he could hardly breathe.

He leaned far out, angling his knees to compensate for bends like a motorcycle racer, but without padding, his jeans tore and his knees ripped and bled before the third bend. Didn't matter; he had Beth safe, and they'd catch up to this jerk. Close, closer—while the car before them screeched and swerved in the darkness and the night wind roared in his ears and froze his face.

McCall's heart thundered and his eyes burned, but for once it wasn't the thrill of the chase, or fulfilling objectives given by headquarters. This time he was totally involved, and he'd make roadkill of himself before he'd stop now. Good people were dying because of this filth, and Beth and Danny Silver deserved to have a happy life—hell, they deserved *a* life, a life free of the man who only wanted revenge, and an heir for his illegal empire.

They roared through the back roads toward the township. "Ferry's a few miles ahead," Beth yelled in his ear.

The only straight stretch of road came ahead. He blasted the guts out of the engine, came up behind the car and screeched around it until they rode alongside the back door of the sedan.

"Use this," he yelled, passing the flashlight to her.

The car careened toward them, and he swerved. Beth screamed, losing balance; the flashlight flew out of her hand and smashed on the road. He had to fall back. He'd take the risk with his life, but never with Beth's. Unlike him, she was worth something.

He tailgated the car, awaiting a chance.

A minute later, the twinkling lights of the car ferry terminal came into view, at the end of the gently descending road. The ferry was waiting on the north side of the water.

He had to try again. Revving the bike until the engine whined in protest, he flew south, ready to pass the turbo sedan.

"We'll have five seconds to do this," he shouted. "Check the car out as fast as you can." With that he roared around, revving the Ducati so that they'd pass the car before the driver could smash into them again.

Though they were doing one-forty, it felt as if they were inching up beside the car. Combined with the weaving he had to do to avoid the bashing attack of the big hard sedan, it felt surreal, as if he'd gone into another world, a movie set in slow-mo. But finally they drew level with the car. "Look fast!"

"I can't see him!" Beth screamed.

There was only one "him" she was interested in, and may Anson shoot him later for it, but McCall didn't even bother to look at the driver. "One occupant only, and Danny won't be in the trunk. Falcone wouldn't stand for such treatment of his son."

He felt Beth's body sag against his in relief. "I want to go to him," she screamed. "Please. I need to know my baby's safe."

A week ago, his answer would be a clear-cut *no way*. A week ago, he'd been a Nighthawk through and through, first and last, one hundred percent focused on IDing the perp in the car.

Now he felt torn. This renegade had taken Nighthawk lives and stolen their memories. He or she was aiding Falcone in his quest for domination of the illegal-arms world, but all McCall could see in his vision was a thin, sweet little face, with a smile like the sun and hands that trembled when he was scared...

There are operatives there in place, ready to protect Danny—

Wildman and Braveheart were the best operatives he knew, but they were big and dark and intense. Danny didn't know them, and he was so easily intimidated, because he was a little boy, only six, and he didn't have a dad to show him the way to be a man.

"Let's go!" As the car almost smashed into them again, McCall turned the bike and roared toward the Richards' house with only the briefest glance at the driver—a tall, blond— female?

Angel? He couldn't confirm ID. But he had a description for Anson, and right now, he had two living subjects for protection.

Racing through the night on an amazing machine he wouldn't have dreamed of touching as a kid, with the woman his dreams were made of, the career that had been everything to him a few months ago didn't amount to a hill of beans. Nothing seemed to mean anything compared to the woman clinging to him now, and the little kid they raced to find.

Chapter 11

They made it back to the Richards' house in a time that would make an Indy 500 record.

Not a moment too soon. Beth cried out as they turned into Post Road and saw the lights blazing at 34, the flashing lights outside of police cars. "What's happened to my baby?"

The headlights of one police car lit the night beyond the house, to the trees and scrub on the loamy ground of the vacant land next to the house, giving an eerie glow to the scene.

"Danny! *Danny!*" Beth cried.

He pulled the Ducati up in a swirl of wet grass outside the house. Beth was off the bike before he'd booted the kickstand into place, helmet tossed into the grass and running for the door. McCall was only a heartbeat behind her.

"I'm Danny Silver's mother," Beth said through gritted teeth when one police officer tried to bar the way inside the house. "Let me by. I want to see my son. Now." Her tone would have frozen fire.

"Let her in, Officer." McCall flipped his ID, showing his government clearance. Beth pushed past the cop into the house.

"Danny! Oh, baby, thank God!" she cried a moment later, racing down the hall. McCall let out the breath he hadn't known he was holding. Danny was all right....

A quick glance inside the living room told the story. A white-faced, pajama-clad Danny sat on Donna Richards' lap on a wing chair beside the fire, obviously traumatized. He was trying to shrink back from the towering presence of the cops, Wildman and Braveheart, his face filled with terror. Ken Richards held a gently snoring Ethan in his arms. Wildman and Braveheart wore gentle, reassuring smiles on their faces, but at six-two and six-five, and solid walls of muscle, they were seriously scary to a little kid, especially with their taut, protective stances, legs splayed and arms folded.

"M-Mummy...?" Danny looked around, bewildered, his eyes, hollow with tiredness, also held a sleepy fear, as if he was unsure he was sleeping or awake.

"Danny!" Beth cried, running to him, falling to her knees beside the rocking chair. "Oh, baby, I've been so worried about you! All these strangers with guns must have made you so scared..."

She reached out to him; but Danny, his eyes wild, his thin body shaking, turned his face into Donna's shoulder.

Beth turned to McCall, her face pleading for help.

Donna, looking distressed, said softly, "Danny, it's your mummy. Don't you want to go to her?"

But Danny shook even more. His hand pointed backward, right behind Beth, where the big, strange men all stood around the room like avenging furies. They might not be showing it, but they were all packing weapons, and sensitive Danny felt the haunting aura of unseen danger that the Nighthawks always brought with them.

The miracle was, Danny didn't feel any danger with him, the most dangerous Nighthawk on record...

McCall squatted beside Beth. "He's in shock," he whispered. "Don't push him now. He's been scared badly, and you weren't here when it happened to him. Donna's his security right now. He needs calm and quiet, and a lot of reassurance."

Beth nodded, shaking as much as Danny, her lovely face ghostlike, her pupils dilated. "I don't think I can do that. Help me, Brendan," she whispered back.

That was all the green light he needed. With a quick motion that sent all the cops and Nighthawks half a dozen steps back toward the hall, he concentrated on the shaking boy before him. "Hey, Danny-boy." Speaking in gentle reassurance, making no move to touch him. "It's Brendan, pal. How're you doing?"

No move. Danny didn't speak.

"What's going on here, huh? Is all this fuss for you? Why are all these big, rough, tough guys hangin' out with a little guy? They hear about your skills in two codes of football?"

After a long moment, the tiniest chuckle came, sounding more like a hiccup.

"I'm feeling threatened here, tough guy. I thought I was your special football friend. Did you find new guys to play with?"

"N-no…" A pair of dark brown eyes peeped around, half-terrified still, but with a tiny twinkle, too.

McCall grinned and wiped his forehead in overdone relief. "Well, that's good to know. Does that mean we're on for some more games soon, if your mom lets me?"

With a frozen beginning of a smile hovering at the corners of his mouth, Danny nodded. "Her name is Mummy. You say it funny."

"Yeah, I do. Maybe because I haven't had a mom—um, a mummy, to practice on, for a really long time." He smiled at Danny with a tenderness he'd never known or felt in his stark life. "I wish I had a mom—mummy like yours. Mothers are very special people, you know. And I think yours really needs a hug right now."

Danny blinked at him, obviously not yet ready to leave the security of Donna's lap. "You don't have a mummy?" He sounded shocked, and more than willing to think of something aside from the recent terror he'd endured.

Solemnly, McCall shook his head. "My mom took my sister Meg and left me with my dad when I was eight, and my dad died when I was fourteen. That's how I know how lucky you are to have a mummy like yours. To have a family that loves you so much.''

Danny's gaze switched to Beth, who was making a valiant effort to stem her tears, swiping at them with her sweater sleeve. ''Mummy?''

Beth smiled at him. ''I'm here, sweetheart. I'm right here with you. You're safe now.''

Danny frowned and bit his lip. ''Brendan's mummy ran away and left him all alone when he was just a little kid.''

''I would never leave you, Danny.'' She reached out, tentative and slow, and touched his face in a gentle caress.

Danny rubbed his face against Beth's hand, in a gesture of total security. ''I know, Mummy. But Brendan's all alone. He's real nice, and he plays good games with me,'' he added in sweet earnest as he hopped off Donna's lap at last and snuggled into his mother's arms, his head on her breast.

Beth blinked, slow and unsteady. A gentle flush mounted her cheek. ''Yes, Danny.'' She snuggled his head beneath her chin. She looked up and met McCall's gaze. ''He is nice.''

Nice. A damn stupid understatement in most things, yet when Beth agreed with Danny's assessment of him, more of that thick, black ice around his heart sloughed off. For the life of him, he couldn't make his throat work. He stayed frozen on his haunches. The man trained to go in with both guns blazing, the man named The Untouchable and The Ice Man, couldn't move or say a word as he watched the two people he'd been assigned to protect calling him *nice,* completely stunned, utterly speechless.

Danny smiled up at his mother, sweet and trusting. ''You like him, don't you, Mummy? So do I. So can we 'dopt him?''

Now he couldn't breathe. With every word he spoke, little Danny Silver rocked McCall's entire world.

Choking sounds came from behind him, sounds of amused disbelief from men he'd worked with for years. They only knew the dark, silent ''Ice Man'' who was always on call, always ready to fight, and rarely joined in any camaraderie on the job.

Which he had been; the job was him, defined him. Until this assignment he'd wrapped himself in isolation like a cloak, accepting that he'd always be alone. Flipper, Commander of Team One, was a complete career man who didn't need anyone.

Out of the mouths of babes. Shy, stammering Danny Silver had seen straight through the walls he'd used as a shield to hide his loneliness since he was eight, watching his mommy walk out on him without a backward glance. Danny had seen beneath the withdrawn darkness of Team Commander McCall to the unhealed heart of little Brendan, needing love, aching not to be alone anymore.

After all these years walking through the wind-blasted darkness of his isolated world, he thought he'd given up hope on finding love, or a normal life. Danny had shown him that the wound had only festered with time, not healed. Mom had abandoned him, taken Meg and never returned. Delia left him the same night he'd proposed to her and she'd never called or come to him.

Love was a delusion, a myth only idiots believed would last. So he left the women he'd bedded before he could remember their names. Why hang around for the heartache?

After a silence in which Beth seemed as shell-shocked as he did, she answered her son. "You can't adopt grown-ups, Danny." She kissed his spiky shock of dark hair. "Brendan's a man, sweetie, and he's older than me. I can't adopt him."

"But—but that's not fair!"

"I know, sweetie." She kissed his forehead. "The world isn't always fair, and good people sometimes don't have people to love them." Her gaze met McCall's, and clung.

With a tiny smile, Donna Richards made a motion with her hand. The room emptied in silence; the door closed behind them.

"But everybody needs a family." After a frowning moment, Danny launched out of Beth's arms and into McCall's lap, snuggling in as if he belonged there. "Do you live all alone, Brendan? Have you been all alone since your dad died?"

McCall swallowed something the size of a brick inside his throat as he held Danny close. It didn't occur to him to lie to the boy. It would be as if he lied to the voice of his own heart. "Yeah." *Except when I was with Delia. When Delia loved me, I never felt alone.*

He felt Beth's gaze on him with the words he'd left unspoken, and felt her doubt, her fear and wonder touching his skin, like a living current arcing between them. Strange that with so little trust between them, the connection was so strong he could read her every emotion right now, and she could read his. They were both scared, so damn scared to reach out and trust....

Yeah, they were opposite ends of the social spectrum, the dark-souled, hard-ass McCall and Princess Beth, but in essentials, they were two of a kind.

"Are you lonely sometimes?" Danny snuggled into him, sliding toward the wonderland that is the right of every child at sleepy-time. "D'you ever want somebody to just *hug* you?"

McCall closed his eyes. Before today, he couldn't remember the last time anyone touched him without violence, or just straight-up raw sex, a slaking of long-denied male need with a woman whose name he'd never be able to remember by the next morning. "Sometimes."

"Mummy's lonely lots of times." Danny had almost gone right over into dreamland now. "Sometimes she cries when she thinks I'm sleepin'. I think she wants a big guy to help her and hug her, y'know. Like I hug Bark." Danny sighed and snuggled in more. "I think she needs all the kissy-kissy stuff grown-up girls like."

McCall, seeing Danny had fallen into sleep with those final words, glanced at Beth. "Shall I shatter his illusions, and tell him big guys like it, too?"

Beth shook her head. "Let him be innocent for as long as he can," she whispered back, looking at her son with melting tenderness. "But one day he'll need to know." She looked up and smiled, and the sweetness in her eyes socked him in the gut. "He'll need to know it's all right to want a girl to kiss and hug him."

The brick in his throat became a boulder. Just as he'd been ready to give up, had Beth seen past the cloak of dark mystery and violence to glimpse the man inside? "So it's all right for me to want you?" he asked in almost a whisper, not wanting to wake Danny. Wanting her so bad he ached and burned— the sweet torture he couldn't seem to live without.

Her gaze fluttered to his mouth, and her gentle hunger touched his lips like butterfly wings. She leaned toward him. "Yes," she breathed. "Yes, it's all right..."

And she kissed him, there in the warm half-dark of the firelit room, sitting on their knees and a sleeping child between them. A chaste, barely there kiss; yet as their kiss earlier tonight slammed into him body and soul, this one tiptoed inside his heart. All he could see, feel, smell, taste was *Beth*—Beth was all around him, surrounding him, inside him.

The kiss went on, slow and gentle and so infinitely tender. A kiss that shimmered with promises...promises to give him all he'd lost—all he'd never had.

Promises. Yeah, sure. Delia had promised him forever ten years ago, and left him with nothing...

From between them, a sleepy little hand reached out. As if guided by God, that little hand landed right over McCall's heart, speaking silent words foreign to McCall's experience. *Trust us...*

As if she felt his gut-tearing emotion, Beth's mouth grew softer on his, enmeshing him with a gossamer web of tangled emotions. Hope and fear, need and wanting, and the promise of sweet, sweet love.

Damned addictive, gut-clenching, soul-destroying love, that turned a strong, independent and functioning man into a mess of need and hope and fear and jealousy.

He wanted her like hell, and that was all. He'd do his duty by her, but he'd walk away this time. Love only led to trust, a belief that he had someone to care for him, and then he was alone again, alone in the darkness, aching for promises unful- filled. Love could be damned, too. He lived alone, and he'd die alone. But he'd make a difference in the world. That was all he had, and it was enough.

But *damn* it, he couldn't make himself desecrate this moment with quick, hard passion.

You're a fool, McCall. You've been a fool for this woman before, and you're making yourself one over her again.

Goodbye, Brendan…

It took all she had inside not to let the tears fall as she kissed him and he kissed her, but Beth managed it. For the first time in ten years she had seen inside the soul of the man…and the woman, locked away too long, cried out in answer. Needing to touch, to take and give in return. To claim McCall as her man, now and forever, in the most elemental way a man and woman can. To give him the love he hadn't known in his life.

But she had to leave him—and if he followed, she had to make him think the worst…even if he had to hate her, so be it. The truth could make him become those two words she'd outrun the past ten years.

Collateral damage.

Tonight, Brendan had proven himself as the man he'd claimed to be. She and Danny were safe, against all odds, and it was thanks to McCall's mysterious group of spies.

And Falcone would have McCall mowed down for it. He'd know the name of the man in his way, and have it wiped, deleted like a virus in a computer. Falcone had had Dan Cassell, an eighty-five-year-old man, shot execution style through the head for helping her. If she let McCall into her life, let Danny love him, she could only imagine what Falcone would do to him.

Years ago her fame, her father and a team of bodyguards had protected her from becoming a victim to Falcone's desires—or any man's. Then Ana's innocent curiosity led to a meeting, diamonds and yachts and a wedding ring within a month. And Falcone, who had married Ana under the name Delia de Souza, obsessively believed he had the right to claim the real Delia, body and soul.

Or kill her for taking his son away from him.

It was only now that she realized the foolishness of making

her dream come true. Yes, she was normal, invisible, anonymous—and she had no protection apart from that anonymity, and the measures Dan and Harry had set up for her. She had little to no chance of getting away.

She wasn't invisible enough. She had to disappear completely this time—all traces of her existence had to vanish.

But she couldn't make herself break the kiss. Oh, how she needed him close, needed that taut, hot body beside her, making her feel *alive* after a decade of cold, dark shadows.

It was the baby sigh, the little hand fluttering from McCall's heart to hers, that brought her back to reality. *I have to leave. I have to betray him, for his own sake, and Danny's.*

With exquisite slowness she pulled back, watching his face.

He looked as moved as she felt. In the warm firelight, he looked sculpted, a thing of intense masculine beauty crafted by flame. His eyes were black with emotion. "Beth..." The name was a guttural whisper, as if he wasn't capable of speech.

Shaken, she reached out with trembling fingers and brushed his hair back from his face. "I know," she whispered back.

As if her tender touch undid him, he closed his eyes. His face followed the movement, and he kissed her palm.

The smiling lips warming her skin melted what little ice was left around her heart.

It was at that moment that she realized the truth. Whether she believed his story or not was immaterial. She loved Brendan McCall, in all the sweet flush of first love with which she'd loved him ten years ago. Maybe she'd never stopped. She'd probably never know. Papa's words had destroyed her trust, and put her heart in permafrost, waiting for Brendan to come back to bring them, and her, to life. She'd become a shadow-being the day she'd learned of McCall's treason, frozen inside, a dead thing encased in a living body, existing for Danny alone—until he came back to her.

Only McCall could save her from this invisible cage, trapping the woman within. Only he could awaken her from the deep-frozen emotional sleep she'd put herself into.

But she had to leave him behind. Too many people had

already been destroyed by Delia de Souza. Delia had to remain dead. Forever.

So she smiled when she desperately needed to cry, made her eyes twinkling when they stung and burned. "It's time for this boy to go to bed—and I smell hot chocolate waiting for us."

"It's probably cold by now." McCall smiled back at her, warm and strong and all man, his barriers of remoteness smashed to pieces at her feet, and she melted all over again. "We seem to have bad timing with hot chocolate tonight."

Bad timing. It seemed to be the chant of their relationship, both times they'd been together. She longed to ask, *Did my father lie about you?*—but McCall's sense of duty was strong. Within hours his spy group would have his confirmation of her identity, her decisions out of her hands, taken over by the CIA, MI6 or any other governmental or international organizations after the tapes on Falcone. She'd be in protective custody within hours, separated from Danny while they asked day after day of questions.

And the moment they got what they wanted, they'd turn their precious resources to more important witnesses on other cases, and she and Danny would be left to the mercy of Falcone's hired hit men. And what he'd do to McCall—

"I'll put him to bed. Which way is the bedroom?" McCall looked down at her son, cradled in those big, strong arms. Oh, how she wanted to nestle there, too, to find safe harbor finally after years of dark storms.

Again she fought the pain, willed it away with a smile. One hint of her pain and he'd know, know she was going to run. "Down the hall, first on the left," she whispered.

One lithe movement and he was on his feet, so smooth Danny's breathing barely changed rhythm. With the grace and silence of a jungle cat, he left the room. She averted her gaze—it seemed held there, dark magic holding her will—and she, with far less grace, uncurled her legs and forced leaden feet to the kitchen.

She had more codes to give to Donna.

Escape tonight seemed impossible now, with the police, McCall and his friends watching, but she had no choice.

She couldn't even give Danny a day to run and play with his friend, a day's innocent camping fun, one more day for Danny to stay in sweet childhood. Oh, for just one day, one day to cement all her plans.

Don't lie to yourself. You want one more day with McCall. One more touch, another kiss…

Disgusted with herself, she forced her thoughts onto escape.

Chapter 12

She was going to run.

He didn't know how he knew. Instinct. Razor-honed gut guess. Maybe no other guy would pick it up—Anson sure as hell would laugh at him for it—but he *knew* her. Her face and voice were calm, but her words...the tripping of her cultured tongue—the almost rhythmic hand movements as the ums and ahs came—

Morse. It was like Morse code, the way she spoke to Donna Richards in the quiet warmth of the kitchen, and the strange responses on Donna's part, so utterly everyday.

Too commonplace. Like a code long devised.

Was he going nuts, or did the other Nighthawks, sitting in silence at the kitchen table with their prosaic hot chocolates, pick up on the code?

He looked at Wildman, then Braveheart. Saw the half-confused recognition of men who didn't know what was happening, but their radars were out and screaming.

He didn't know why she was going any more than they did. He didn't know how she'd manage it with Danny here. He just knew she was planning on leaving. Without telling him a thing.

His gut churning—how, *how* could she kiss him like—like she *cared,* and calmly plan to run out on him?

Hating this whole charade he turned away, pretending to look out into the quiet darkness of country night, and reached into his pocket. The pager was a part of him after eighty-odd missions with the Nighthawks; he knew how to use it without looking.

Ghost. Subject planning escape. Check all charter plane companies for hire by anyone, man or woman, and block it.

Moments later, the silent vibration of the pager told him Ghost had received and understood.

It was more than he knew Beth would. She'd probably never forgive him for the betrayal. But *damn* it, he was doing this for her—for Danny. She couldn't get out of the country alone, not with the forces Falcone had marshaled against her. Alliance with the Nighthawks was her only hope of survival and freedom.

He had to get her alone, to talk to her. And no kisses this time…no sweet, drugging kisses that made the operative in him submerge like the *Titanic,* becoming all needing man, believing in her while she made plans that didn't include him.

With a motion, he left the kitchen to the backyard, Wildman and Braveheart nanoseconds behind. "What happened tonight?"

Wildman shrugged. "Cops took jurisdiction, sir, but it seems they ignored our orders and woke the family, demanding to see the boy, concerned for his safety. They scared the hell out of the poor little kid."

McCall nodded grimly. "The subject is planning escape. Ghost will be checking all hired escape routes. Buses and trains are too slow, but I want you to check out any fast routes to a sea escape, or to airports. I can't see her using commercial airlines, but she might have fake passports for them. Check all incoming and outgoing calls and Internet bookings—call in the telephone company for data during the past twenty-four hours."

Wildman frowned. "What about the kid? She wouldn't leave without her kid, and he's here."

"Danny," he snapped, knowing naming the boy betrayed his feelings about his subjects, but unable to stop himself. "She's got something going down with the Richards woman. Rendezvous, pick-up point, something. Panther will watch the house and follow them wherever they go. They won't know him, and he's our best at invisible tailing. Heidi can back him up in a second car at a prearranged point." He turned back to the house. "We've been out here long enough. Procedure clear?"

"Hoo-yah, sir," Wildman answered, and McCall could hear the grin in his voice. Yeah, he'd given away that he was in way over his head this time—but the cheek in Wildman's tone told him that he wasn't going to rat. McCall believed Wildman had his own, unspoken reasons for keeping quiet. A tall, blond, very sexy and full-of-attitude reason—one Wildman had made every excuse to not work with for the past year.

Another career man in over his head...because Wildman's personal reason may have held a knife against Beth's throat less than two hours ago, and driven into the night after trying to kill them both. And while the thought of the fiercely efficient and seemingly loyal Angel's being the rogue Nighthawk got to them all, it seemed to torture Wildman.

"Roger all procedures, sir." Braveheart's tone was quieter, with respect for more than McCall's commander rank. Braveheart carried on a constant, if quiet, rebellion against the Nighthawk anonymity policy, annoying Anson whenever his fanaticism got in the way of operatives' personal lives. His answer now was his way of saying that his superior's relationship with Beth and Danny Silver was nobody's business but his own.

"Good. Leave unobtrusively within five minutes and start obtaining objectives, including a tracking device on the Richards' car. Report back to me with any progress, and keep the exclusive channel open. You may need to close in within minutes."

"Roger that, sir." This time the men spoke as one. They

dipped their heads in acknowledgment of the orders, and went inside to thank Donna Richards for her hospitality.

And through the pretty bay window filled with potted flowers, a pair of eyes slammed him with unspoken accusation. She was determined to do this on her own. Stubborn woman. Why wouldn't she accept the help he offered her—

Falcone.

He closed his eyes. God damn him for a blind, infatuated fool! He might have forgotten, but she never had, not for a moment. That kiss in the living room had been her way of saying goodbye. Because of their passionate encounter in the kitchen tonight. She might have wanted it, but she knew she had no right.

He'd done a lot of low things in his life, but tonight he had almost made love to a woman on her kitchen bench…and no matter what she'd said earlier, he couldn't believe she wasn't a *married* woman. He'd known she felt alone and terrified and vulnerable, needing comfort, and he'd used that to slake his own need.

He'd hit a new low in a life marked by foul takes, lower drops. Tonight he'd downgraded from badass to pond scum. He was a Nighthawk, sent here to protect Beth and Danny. No matter what his feelings were, he was not supposed to seduce her, either in word or in deed. He was here to find out if she had evidence on Falcone, and save her life. And from now on, he'd keep his hands off her lovely body. It didn't exist for his pleasure.

But Falcone, the conscienceless slime, believed it did—for his pleasure alone. And his pleasure was, if his sources in the world of organized crime had it right, to kill Beth himself, for making him appear a fool in the eyes of his associates. And though he wanted his son, he didn't care enough about Danny's feelings to leave Beth alive. Danny meant nothing to Falcone personally. The boy was merely the heir.

McCall swore one thing at that moment—he'd set her free from Falcone, no matter what it took. He was a trained killer; he knew ways to take out filth without leaving a trace. And whether she chose to come to him once she was free, to give and receive the full promise of pleasure they'd known tonight, would be up to her. He'd be waiting.

Liar. He'd claim her, brand her with a searing iron the second Falcone was out of the picture. McCall's woman. He knew he could make her want it as bad as he did.

Walking into the kitchen, he placed a tiny device by the door before entering. He nodded to Beth, as remote as he'd always been on point, as detached as he wished to God he felt. "Thanks for everything, Donna. We'd better go back and check out the damage to Beth's house, and secure it so she can sleep."

Beth gave a little gasp. "Thank you, Brendan," she said, giving him the personal name she only used in front of others. "I'd forgotten about the break-in."

He didn't waste words. "Let's go." He smiled and nodded at Donna, and, while shaking her hand, placed a listening device under the kitchen-bench top.

He placed another tiny device by the front door near the Richards' bedroom. They couldn't leave without the Nighthawks knowing. Before they left, he checked that the tracking device was in place. He revved up the Ducati and pressed the button that lit up the small screen beside the speedometer. A tiny red dot, not yet a blip, showed that the guys had done their job.

Whatever plan Beth had had with Donna Richards was over for tonight. Wherever they went, the Nighthawks would be there.

And McCall would be beside Beth—or right behind her.

Beth half expected to come home and find the house ransacked, since she'd jumped through the window right after McCall, leaving the whole thing open, but the house was still, silent, peaceful in the slumbering darkness. Every piece of damage repaired, apart from the broken roof tile. Two people stood in the shadows of the living room—people who nodded at McCall and melted into the darkness outside when he waved his hand.

Beth wandered through the house, dazed. Why hadn't there

been another attack? Were the kidnappers the only people Falcone had sent? Surely not. And surely they hadn't just allowed McCall's friends to come in and take over, securing the house and—

She went hot and cold all over. *What if they were watching?* Waiting—seeing if she took a man into her bed? Reporting on her life as they'd done in England right before they shot Dan?

She'd been attacked tonight, straight after she'd almost made unbridled love with McCall on the kitchen bench. What if the attack had been a warning from Falcone? If she gave Falcone's perfect prize away, McCall would pay the price.

Her mind working furiously, she turned to McCall, who was checking out the repair job his people had done on the mangled screen. "It's safe enough for tonight. I'll order another screen to come tomorrow. In the meantime, just keep the window locked."

"I will. Once you've gone." She put her hands on her hips, glaring at him. "I want you to leave. Now."

He folded his arms over his chest, his eyes cool and amused. "So you can run? I'm not going anywhere."

"This is my house." She spoke through gritted teeth. "So get out or I'm calling the police."

An eyebrow lifted in that untamed face; he leaned against the wall with a cool, dare-you-to-do-it smile. "And that's supposed to scare me? Baby, I've dealt with the dogs since I was eight…and one word from me and they'd be out the door. You saw it tonight. You couldn't even get to Danny until I told them to let you in."

The breath dragged into her lungs as though it carried a noxious smell. Eyes closed, jaw clenched, she decided to pick up his gauntlet and throw it back, in spades. "Those people were from your organization, weren't they? This whole kidnapping was set up to make me trust you when you brought me safely to Danny!"

Apart from the other eyebrow lifting, he made no move. "Nice excuse, baby, but it's not cutting the ice."

She had to restrain the urge to scream, yell, throw things at him. *Please God, if you care for this man like I do, make him go!* "You aren't staying the night here. Don't you get it?" she cried, wringing her hands in real anguish—the terror she couldn't show him. "In Danny's father's eyes, I belong to him. If he's here and sees you stay with me, he—he'll punish me for the rest of my life," she finished, knowing the words *he'll kill you* wouldn't cut the ice either, not with a man like McCall. "He'd take it out on Danny, and make me watch, just to prove he owns us both."

Though he didn't touch her, the cool arrogance fell from him like a cloak he'd shed. "He won't get to Danny—he'll never get that close. We've dealt with Falcone before, Beth, and we can do it again. I meant what I said earlier. You might be way out of my league, but for what I'm worth, I'm with you, come hell or flood or Falcone's hit men. I might only have my strength and my dreams, but if it's enough to save you and your son, you've got it…for as long as you need me."

Fight it, fight it… She clenched her fists even as her body swayed toward him. Oh, how she ached to take what he so freely offered; but she was fighting, not for her choices or Danny's freedom alone—she was fighting for McCall's very life. The life he'd all but laid at her feet just now. And though she'd give herself up to take that offer, she wouldn't risk his life. She had to trample right over that selfless, beautiful offer if she was going to keep him alive. She'd rather he hated her for the rest of his life than be forced to cry over his grave.

"Sweet offer, really it is—but not enough." The words grated harsh and flat, like a magpie's cawing call. "You can leave now. I gave you your reward for taking me to Danny. I hope you didn't imagine you'd ever get more than a few kisses from me."

Hating the harsh implications of her words, her gaze flew to his and saw that she'd obtained her objective. His face might have been carved in granite, it was so cold. His eyes glittered, cold and unfathomable. He'd withdrawn so deeply inside himself she wouldn't even know how to follow him.

"Nice one, Beth. You just hit a new low in manners. Your

parents would be proud of you—I can hear the applause from heaven. Rule one—don't waste yourself on the hired help or lowlifes that crawled their way out of the gutter, like me.'' As if her words hadn't affected him at all, he took his time strolling to the window. ''Lock it after me. If you feel like slumming again at any time, I'll be on the roof, fixing the broken tiles. Got to keep the princess safe.''

Her eyes squeezed shut in agony. She pressed her lips hard to stop her rebellious heart from recanting the words.

She couldn't stop him from following her when she made her move, but she'd done what she could to save him from the certain death that knowing her seemed to bring with it. This way, Falcone might think he was just an operative, and race to beat him rather than taking him out. A minuscule chance, but it was all she had.

Even if she went to her grave aching for what she'd lost tonight, he had a chance of staying safe and alive…and she couldn't allow herself to want any more than that.

Chapter 13

She left in the dead of night—0345.

He'd known she would—he'd prepared for it, even knew the Richards family were on the move with Danny, and their direction—yet McCall felt sucker-punched by the betrayal. What was it about him that made the people he connected with on a personal level, the rare ones he cared for, run in the opposite direction?

Don't think about it.

He watched from between the heavy old trees by the quiet bay, away from town with its bustle and noise of the daily tourist traffic. She struggled with a stuffed-to-the-gills backpack, a suitcase and Danny's puppy. Nice of her to bring the dog as a security blanket against the changes about to rock Danny's world. She walked from her lovely home without a single glance back, giving up everything she had to save her child.

Well, she would—she loved him.

Do the job. No mercy this time. No softness. And no faith. She's a case like any other. A killer's woman we need for the evidence she's got. And the ten million in traceable dollars.

They'd traced the money back through the Brothers of Retribution, a group dedicated to continuing war in the Balkans who'd used Falcone's guns to kill off thousands of their greatest political foes, and from there to an English ammunitions factory, and a massive theft seven years back.

So from now on, that was all she was—a case, and her kid to save. And what was left of the ten million bucks, probably stashed in the backpack.

Through his night goggles he watched her move like wind in the trees, graceful even in flight, burdened with the backpack, the suitcase and the puppy. Running from him.

Damn her. For years he'd sold his soul, bargaining with unknown forces just to see her face one more time.

Well, now he'd seen her. Time to get on with the job.

He moved like a shadow in the deep night. The rest of the team had backed off, waiting at every available exit point. Panther was currently heading south, following the Richards' car. Everything was in place: cars in every direction, two planes and a chopper on its way from Auckland. Every charter-plane company provided records to show they hadn't hired a plane or pilot in the past two days to anyone who wasn't a bona fide tourist.

Beth headed straight for the Bay, her thigh-high rubber boots sloshing through the smelly slush of low tide, toward—

At the sight awaiting him he swore. Hard. Cursing that he'd given her fifty feet leeway, and wouldn't make it before she—

She put the puppy on the floor of the high-powered jet boat, tossed the backpack over then climbed in. She shushed the puppy's excited yipping in gentle, frantic quiet. Then she took off, making the craft almost fly over the small, tipping waves of the Bay, heading for the open sea. She'd either had intensive lessons for years, or had used speedboats from her cradle.

He fired up the Jet Ski awaiting him—turbo powered, of course—and all but flew, himself, to keep up with her. Within moments the noise of his engine, and the high-powered light he'd rigged on the front, told her she wasn't alone. She revved the guts out of the engine, sending it skimming over the waves as they grew stronger outside the Bay. He had no choice but to push it, until the hard whine of the engine told him it had reached its limits, could even blow at any minute.

Her frequent glances back told him she felt some concern for his safety, but every time she'd assured herself that he was still alive, she opened the throttle further. He jerked his back hard in his effort to keep up. He had to lash himself to the handlebars with rope to stay on—an awkward, one-handed knot that would never hold at this pace, but made him feel a little safer, and as in flying, confidence was everything in the chase.

But she only sped up more, curving across the waves to avoid rips and reefs, always angling the boat just at pre-keeling-over level. She drove the boat like a damn pro racer.

Where, when did she get the prowess? Who had taught her?

Maybe the reason she's surprising you so often is that she's not Delia. Nobody knows all that much about Ana de Souza...

"No," he growled. "It's Delia. Delia's alive."

Jerk. Lovesick fool. Just as butt-stupid as all the starstruck fans in her modeling days, certain they were soul mates based on their feelings when they looked at her airbrushed image.

But that was what he'd always been, the past ten years. A dumb-ass jerk in blind infatuation with a dream.

She was edging away, and the Jet Ski was on full throttle. He had no choice. "Ghost!" he yelled into the small machine strapped to the handlebars, with a magnifying speaker. "Subject's on the move, heading southeast on the open sea. Her jet boat's outgunning me. Estimate she's heading for the airstrip inland from Waitanamako Bay. Check for hire cars, taxis, anything that will get them there, and tail it."

"Roger that," was Anson's instant response. "Don't let her out of sight, Flipper."

"No choice in that, sir," he snapped, losing control for the first time in over five years. "Subject has a Super Sport with 240 horsepower, fuel injection and a V6 engine. I can't gun to that in a damn Jet Ski!"

"Why the hell didn't we know she was a pro with a speed-boat?"

"Maybe because she's not who we think she is!"

"With the primary target's son? Yeah, right. Get out of your gonads and think like an operative. You're too involved."

He swore beneath his breath, knowing Beth wouldn't forgive him for this. "Ghost—"

"Did you think I didn't know about your past with her? I've given you leeway considering you had a greater chance of getting her on board than any of the rest of us, but this is beyond your control, Flipper. We're almost in the area now. There's a chopper waiting for us on landing. ETA ten to twelve minutes."

"No!" he yelled. "You get a bird above her and searchlights and she'll panic. This is a dangerous stretch of coast with wild seas. She's no use to us dead!"

"We'll be discreet. What's your position in ten minutes?"

"I don't know my position now! I'm just trying to hold on and keep up!" He shot a quick glance around. "Between eight and ten miles south of the Cape Brett lighthouse, hugging the coast. She's about a quarter mile ahead, and gaining."

"Roger that. If anything changes, report stat."

"Roger and out, sir."

Beth's boat surged farther ahead. Hugging the coastline—too much. He'd studied the topography—any second now, she'd hit—

"Beth!" he yelled, but it was useless: she'd hit the enormous part-hidden rock beneath the ocean, and flip—but with a smooth swerve, a swing back in the boat averted danger, with barely any decrease in speed.

So she'd even rehearsed riding over this tidal eddy before.

The chase continued, both crafts lifting off the water in frantic speed, their faces slapped by seawater and predawn rain stinging their skin, dousing clothes. Lashed to the handlebars, he felt as if he'd hog-tied a bronco with cotton thread. The Jet Ski leaped from the water. He jerked and flew with it, revving the throttle on constant max with a big crazy grin on his face.

Maybe he was a jerk to feel so exhilarated by the chase, by the danger...but he couldn't change his nature. He was a boy of the sea, an adrenaline junkie who'd first cheated death at eight, falling off his dad's fishing vessel in a storm. He'd pulled on fins and a suit at eleven, became a navy diver at nineteen, dived straight off a chopper into turbulent ocean at twenty-four to save a fellow SEAL. He'd never turned down a challenge, never thought about death, and never felt fear— not for himself.

And despite being scared to all crap for Beth now, his most dominant emotion was a *well, what do you know* admiration for her ballsy attitude to life, even when she was probably more scared than he was. When it came to Beth, still waters ran deeper than any of them knew.

Then, in the most treacherous stretch of the current-run shore, she swerved right, toward land. "What the…? There're rocks like knives in that bay! Beth, stop!"

But she evaded every rock with smooth, practiced ease and pulled the boat up to the sandy shore without a problem. Maybe the sun, just rising above the clear horizon, helped her.

He wasn't so lucky. By emulating her moves he got around the biggest rocks, but came to grief on a tiny protrusion. The Jet Ski flipped over the rock's knife edge into the deep, cold ocean.

He came up sputtering, half-numb from the cold, with a gash on his upper right arm where the rocks tore through his skin and muscle and a blow to the back of his head that left him reeling.

He'd never make it to land before she took off. Being the best combat swimmer on his SEAL team wouldn't help without a wet suit and fins in a near-freezing ocean against the tide, with half his strength gone from the deep, jagged cut tearing his muscle almost in two.

He tore off his heavy boots, pulled off his socks to make a fast double-compression bandage, using one hand and his teeth to tie it; then he struck out toward land in an awkward butterfly motion, using only his left arm. He struck out for land, swimming hard and fast, ignoring the pain and lightheadedness, as training dictated.

Where was the chopper? And why hadn't he used surveillance equipment on her so he'd be a step ahead in the game?

Because you're just as big a dumb-ass jerk over her now as you were ten years ago.

And now, just like then, he was paying the price for his naive half hope that this beautiful enigma would turn to him. Trust him in the most primal, elemental way a woman can, with her heart, and her secrets. Giving up that deep, untouched ocean of secrets beneath the tidal cobalt of her eyes.

The whirring of props, the spinning of water flying out from behind moving floats, told him how stupid he'd been to hope for anything from her. Trust and Delia de Souza were a dichotomy.

Alpha 849Y8 Delta…red, white, blue seaplane…

But as he floundered, lightheaded with blood loss from the weak, left-handed compression bandage, he heard the whirring sound come closer, right up to him, leaving him thrashing in the sudden waves the seaplane created. The passenger door flung open and she leaned over, her eyes blazing. "Get in."

With the last of his strength he swam to the seaplane and used the float to push himself up. "Thanks."

She pushed a huge beach towel at him. "I wouldn't leave a bleeding dog in that freezing water to die. Shut the door. I don't have much time before your reinforcements arrive, do I?"

He pushed dripping hair out of his face with the towel before he looked at her. "No."

She nodded, and with a ruthless efficiency he was coming to expect from her, she swerved the seaplane around the final rocks, headed for the open sea and reached the required level of knots before she took off. "Thermal blanket beneath your seat. Warm up. I have enough on my conscience without adding your death to the list. Did you notify your boss about the seaplane?"

"I flipped before I could."

Her mouth twisted. "Uh-huh. So when do I expect the cavalry to arrive, courtesy of a chopper?"

Man, she was quick. "Any minute. I expected it by now."

"Right." She pulled on the throttle. "There's a medical kit in the armrest compartment between us. You need a better compression bandage than that or you'll bleed all over the plane, and this one isn't mine.''

He kept rubbing himself down. "The dog's awfully quiet." In fact, he was asleep, belted awkwardly into a passenger seat.

"I gave him a light sedative," she replied curtly. "It probably started taking effect about fifteen minutes ago."

"Nice of you to take him. Danny will need the comfort when he finds out he's not only not going camping, but leaving home for good." He flicked a glance at her. Her mouth tightened; her face, already pale by the early morning light, grew even whiter, but she didn't answer. She probably didn't know what to say. He moved on, knowing he'd have to pry answers from her. "So, where did you get the plane? When did you learn to fly and drive that boat?"

Her mouth curled again; she gave a cynical laugh, daring him. "How long have you lived in Australia? How many names have you used in the past few years?"

Shutdown, and showdown. "Beth—"

She glanced at him, eyebrows raised. "Oh, so you do remember my name now. That's nice. With the amount of times you called me by your girlfriend's name, I was beginning to wonder if one of us would end up with an identity crisis."

"Maybe both of us has one now," he said quietly.

She laughed again, but this time it was softer, sweeter. "Maybe. And maybe we're fooling ourselves, not each other. Wanting things we can't have will only drive us both crazy."

He got out the medical kit, no longer up to a war of words. "You could have left me in the water. I couldn't have stopped you from getting away."

She shrugged. "You wouldn't have left me in the water, if only because your boss wants me alive and whole, either to own me or get me to hand over whatever it is he thinks I have. If you'd been out to kill me, I'd have left you there to die."

The probable truth of that felt like a sharp knife slitting his skin. He put antibiotic cream over his wound before binding it. He wouldn't take anything for the pain until the Nighthawks were in sight—anything might put him to sleep in this condition, and if he awoke too groggy to fight her, she might dump him somewhere. When he finished with the wound, he finally answered her. "I'm starting to believe you would."

A flash of pain crossed her face for a moment, the shadows chasing each other across her skin. Tiredness, angst, fear, uncertainty. And he wished he could take his words back. "I'm sorry," he said, loud enough to be heard over the noise of the engine. "I won't hurt you, Beth."

"You bet you won't. Like I told you, McCall, you won't get the chance to be close enough." Without conscious effort, she turned the plane toward the southwest.

Exhausted, wound throbbing and frustrated by her constant deflection of anything he said—perhaps because it reminded him too forcefully of himself since he'd become a Nighthawk, or maybe years before—he snapped, "You're too cynical."

Another shrug. "Cynicism is a safe bolt-hole when you're too scared to take risks. Naiveté—or trust—can get you killed when you have a man like Danny's father on your trail."

He had to shatter the cynical defenses she used somehow, or he'd keep bashing his head against the fortress of her secrets. "Say his name, Beth. We both know what it is."

"Have you got a tape recorder or sound device in a safety-seal bag somewhere to catch it for posterity, or your boss?" she retorted without skipping a beat.

He pulled off his coat, jacket and shirt, awkward and one-handed. "Can I ask where we're going, at least?"

She flashed a look at him. Her gaze caressed his half-naked body before she turned her head, and shook it in negation. "I don't know what kind of surveillance equipment you have on you."

"I could have a tracking device on me. I could already have notified my people of our whereabouts," he pointed out, almost kicking himself for not wanting to do just that. "My boss is already hot on our trail."

Her mouth twisted. "I realize that. But I still haven't figured out which side you're all on." She flung up a hand as he opened his mouth. "I know—you're a knight on a white Jet Ski, and your team is out to save me and my son from ourselves, right? Sorry if I don't quite put faith in that yet, McCall." His name was tossed at him like a casual insult.

Brendan, he wanted to yell. *My name's Brendan. You know my name…you called me Brendan when you smiled at me, held my hand, kissed me and touched my body all those years ago. You called me Brendan last night when you touched and kissed me. I'm on the side of the good guys, a Nighthawk sent to save your beautiful neck, and your son's, from that slime bag Falcone!*

What was the point? She wouldn't believe him. And Anson's instructions were set in stone. A silent sentinel he was, and had to remain so, even in his own mind, until the tape proving Falcone's guilt was in Nighthawk hands and she was in safe custody. Anything else put them both, and Danny, in danger.

He didn't have the strength right now to keep pushing. He had to conserve himself. If he fell asleep she could—

"You're bleeding through the bandage."

With an effort he turned his head, but it felt too heavy to go the whole way. "Can't—awkward, one-handed…"

Through the fog in his mind, he heard her make a savage sound. "Right." She put the seaplane in autopilot and turned to him. With deft motions, she unwound the lopsided crossover bandage. "You're dizzy, aren't you? You've gone pale."

His head fell back against the seat. He hated falling asleep at any time—it indicated a lack of control he refused to show, a deep, dark loneliness he couldn't stand—but he knew that this time his body was going to force the issue. "Hit—my head on a rock." Let her do what the heck she wanted with that information.

She inspected the head wound, then the wound on his arm, and made that harsh sound again. "No wonder you're losing blood—you need at least seven stitches in that. I've got ten minutes before I need to change course, so I'll do what I can."

He frowned and blinked, trying to make sense of her words. "You can—do that?" *He* could—it was part of his medic's and combat/rescue training—but a model?

An odd laugh, almost derisive—or self-mocking—burst

from her lips. "Yes, I can, McCall. I did an advanced first-aid course more than once. A woman and child without legal ID—or on the run from someone who has resources to check computer databases—learn how to fend for themselves."

Yeah, he supposed they did. He gave up the battle with his eyes and closed them. "And you—"

"I wouldn't dump you in an isolated spot and escape while you're injured and have a possible concussion, McCall." She sounded wounded by the implication he'd been about to make. "I do have more morals than that...and I know how much I owe you."

Her gentle touch on his wound, cleaning the salt from it, preceded the quick jab of a needle. "Local anesthetic. I'll give you antibiotics when I'm done."

He was sliding into sleep, his mind as numb as his arm was fast becoming. "Where...?"

"Your curiosity will be the last thing to leave you, McCall." Her voice now sounded gentle with laughter. "I didn't steal them. There are places you can get these things, no questions asked."

Yes...he knew most of them. He'd—he'd have to... Anson...yeah...the pull and tug of the curved suture needle going in and out of his skin was strangely rhythmic, soothing. He felt himself sliding into the first deep sleep he'd had in over a week, trusting that she'd take care of him. Trusting that she'd still be there when he opened his eyes. "Beth...?" he mumbled.

She couldn't have heard him over the engine, yet she answered. Maybe she'd been watching his mouth? "What?"

He sighed. "Thank you."

Though he'd never know how later, he felt more than heard her answer. "You're welcome—damn you, McCall, for making me want to care." A light hand touched his bandage. "You probably have a light concussion. I'll wake you every half-hour."

He nodded. "Thanks," he mumbled again.

"You're welcome."

The last thing he felt was a flutter, as of butterfly wings, across his mouth, so light and fleeting, it felt like part of a dream already forming in his spinning mind.

But he knew, *knew*. She really had kissed him, kissed him of her own free will. Not a kiss of passion, nor of exasperation, or even of response—it had been a *comfort* kiss. As though she knew of all his years alone and aching for what he thought he'd never have—and she wanted, by some crazy miracle, to take all that away from him. A kiss better.

Well, what do you know…

And the darkness he fell into this time wasn't so lonely, as out of control, as it had always been before.

Chapter 14

He only slept for an hour before he jerked awake. Instinct, training, he didn't know; but he never ignored the imperative warning call. He awoke to full awareness of his surroundings, what he was doing, and why. The throbbing head pain had receded to a dull ache, even though she'd shaken him awake twice to ask what day it was. He didn't have a concussion then; at least not one strong enough to keep him down.

Well, she hadn't ditched him. A moment's check of the sun's position told him how long he'd slept before he checked his watch, and their current direction. They were heading for Auckland, or somewhere nearby.

A soft pulling feeling at his ear made him start. Beth had put a headset on him while he slept, cutting off noise—how had she done that without arousing his fight instinct?—and now she turned on the sound to speak to him. "So Prince Charming awakes too soon. You don't get enough sleep, McCall."

"Habit." He rolled his shoulders, stretched his neck to clear his head. "I can't ever remember sleeping a full night through."

"Ever?" She sounded incredulous.

He shrugged. "Not that I can remember." He'd always slept like a cat, with one eye open. When he was little, looking out that his dad didn't fall on him in a stupor, or belt him unawares; and later, hoping Mom would come back for him. Hopes and fears so tightly interwoven he no longer knew how to separate the two, and trusted neither. "Just weird, I guess."

"I suppose so. By the way, McCall, would you consider switching sides for a million dollars? Would you help me get away from your people then?"

The question startled him—shook him to his core. Was it confirmation of who she was…confirmation he was no longer sure he wanted to have? And why did she choose *now* to say it? Because she wanted that damn distance put back between them? Did she regret a single kiss so much that she had to *remind* him that he was the operative, she his subject? "How does a single mother get that kind of money? How could someone who lives as modestly as you appear to be able to offer me that kind of bribe?"

With the last word, she flinched. "For my son." Her voice was flat. "For Danny." She turned to him, her eyes filled with unshed tears, blazing, *pleading* in the soft, unfocused light of sunrise. "Don't make Danny go back to his father. He'd eat my baby alive."

Hate slammed into his soul. Dear God, gentle, stammering Danny being left to Falcone's tender mercies. That beautiful, shy little kid would morph into a damn hit man before he turned ten. No wonder she was going out on a cracked and shaking limb here. Any mother would. Well, maybe not his mom, but Beth loved her son. "You don't care for yourself?" he asked, low. "You know what he'll do to you if he gets you."

An equally low sound, like a ripping shudder, tore from her throat. As she turned back to the cockpit, her shaking hands held on to the controls like a lifeline as she dragged in breath after shaking breath. Her face, so pure and lovely, had the faint, creamy-grass hue of a woman about to throw up.

She didn't have to answer him after that. Those few seconds had been more than eloquent enough.

He hated to push her now, but he had little choice. He had to know where she was coming from—and where she was going. "Is it his money you're offering, or yours?" Silence greeted the question, and he heard his voice, rough and demanding. "Come on, Beth, you have to trust someone!"

But she'd reestablished control, and confidences, or even pleading, were at an end. Her words were measured. "The only two people I ever trusted with my life—or Danny's—are dead."

More words that echoed inside his own soul. A page in his own life history. Hell, they had so much more in common than he'd dreamed…such a sickening, gut-churning shame it was all negative. "How?" She shook her head, and felt a sudden rage, totally out of proportion to the level of *need to know* in the question. "Tell me, Beth!" he all but yelled, feeling foolish even as he yelled.

She turned back, her eyes blazing. "A chopper's following us—sent by you—and you're upset because I don't give you irrelevant information about a dead man who was in my life? Oh, poor McCall. Shall I just lay myself and Danny down on the ground to play dead for you and your boss while I'm at it?"

He tried to thud a fist against his thigh, but the arm fell back, useless. Damn it, how could he tell her the whole truth? It put his whole career, everything he'd worked for the past ten years, on the line. It compromised the mission, put him and the whole Nighthawk team at risk.

And her telling you could kill her—and Danny. And she loves that kid more than she'll ever love any man.

"By the way, I haven't seen your friends yet," she remarked casually. "Does that mean they're damn good at their job, or that you, the perfect watchman, fell asleep before you could notify them of our direction?"

Yeah, she's putting distance between us all right—and it's deliberate. The only thing he didn't know was why— why now?

He didn't ask any more questions. What was the point? The stakes were too high for them both, and their cross-examinations were fruitless, like a pair of roller coasters on a one-railed collision course, slamming against each other in painful carnage but still going nowhere. But he took careful note of the direction, the local landmarks.

Moments later, pretending to look out the window, he took his pager out of its waterproof cover. Pressing the silent option and keeping it well beneath her line of sight, he used his left hand to press the buttons. *Injured, request backup, stat. With subject in seaplane, WSW. Alpha 849Y8 Delta. Expect airstrip outside Auckland to collect son. She will leave me behind. Repeat, subject plans escape.*

His gut clenched before he pressed *send.*

Moments later, he got a silent reply. *Roger. Five miles back and following. Start tracking device.*

He felt sick with betrayal—she hadn't broken her word to him, and though he'd made no promises, they both knew, understood, the unspoken accord that she hoped for. But still, he pressed the GPS-tracking button on his pager. Even though he knew all he was doing was his dead level best to protect Beth and Danny, he still felt like a traitor of the worst kind.

And with a sinking feeling in the pit of his gut, he knew Beth would never forgive him for what he'd just done.

The Nighthawks' chopper reached the small airstrip northwest of Auckland before they did; and though Beth half expected it to be there, the betrayal burned right to her gut. "Congratulations, McCall. Your people won the race." She put no inflection in her tone. "World peace wins over individual rights, and my son and I become collateral damage in your righteous war. I hope you can live with what you've done—and what it will do to Danny."

He unlocked his seat belt. "Where is Danny? I thought Donna would be here by now. Isn't that what you worked out with your um-and-ah, hand-signing Morse-code communications last night?"

"Damn you, McCall," she whispered, shaking. "You don't

know what you've done. It's all about you. You and your save-the-world friends don't care if my son and I live or die.''

He turned on her, the wind-blasted darkness of his soul hitting her from those incredible eyes of his. ''Clever, self-reliant Beth, always so sure you're right. Maybe it's you who don't know what you're doing. You think you've outwitted Falcone all these years? You think his only obsession was with you, the perfect Delia? Well, think again, baby—seems like he's a one-obsession-at-a-time kind of guy. The reason you've been left alone all this time was that he had another woman on his mind. He spent five years chasing Verity West, the singer. It seems he was willing to let you keep Danny if he could have her; he talked of having an heir with her. But when Falcone got too close, Miss West recognized that she needed help. She might have been cold, but she wasn't stupid. She didn't try to get away from him on her own. She trusted us to help her—and we got her out of danger. Falcone's only turned back to tracing you and Danny because she married another guy and disappeared from public life altogether.''

She felt herself start to shake, in rage, in regret for the contempt she'd engendered in McCall by her deliberate cruelty earlier, but she had to keep him alienated to keep him alive. ''And you think his wanting another woman would *bother* me? The only part of his chasing the poor woman that upsets me is the empathy I feel for her. I'm glad she got away. I just wish he'd turn his obsession onto a woman that wants it. You idiot. You *fool*. What makes you think you know *anything* about me?''

He blanked out. Literally. She watched the barriers come up in his eyes so fast she all but felt herself slam into them. ''Nothing. Nothing at all.'' He opened the passenger door and vaulted out in a smooth movement. Ready for action, despite his injury and little to no sleep the past four days. ''You'd better get that evidence on Falcone ready, because you just told me who you are—and this time I did tape it. And my boss will have a search warrant on him, and a female operative ready to search you. Get your bags out, baby. You just blew it. Big-time.''

Beth watched him greet his boss with a nod, and hand over the recording machine, wanting to scream, cry, tear out her hair. Oh, she'd blown it all right. By her callous rejection she'd made McCall, the most fiercely loyal of men, an implacable enemy. She'd sent him back to his first allegiance by throwing his every offer of implicit protection and utter caring back in his face.

But I did it for you, Brendan. I did it for you!

It was too late now. Maybe it had always been. A love as fatal as it was fated, and as impossible to start as it was to end. A love as unforgettable as the eruption of a volcano, and as unforgiving—unrelenting and destructive as seasons out of time. Had she killed it, or was it always going to happen this way?

A dark sedan came down the runway, lights off and traveling with quiet speed. The car pulled up beside the seaplane, and Donna's worried face appeared at the darkened window.

"It's all right, Donna. Thank you so much for your help." With a tired sigh, Beth hitched the backpack on her shoulder, lifted the suitcase in her hand, and managed to get to the ground. She put them down carefully before climbing back in to grab Danny's still sleeping puppy from his seat.

"What's happening, Beth?" Donna whispered, her frantic gaze taking in a barefoot, mussed McCall talking to the group of people in anonymous fatigues and hard boots.

She shrugged. "I think I'm about to be arrested."

Donna gasped and laid a hand on her arm. "May I ask…?"

Beth spoke loud enough for them all to hear. "My guess is for being an illegal immigrant—charges that they'll offer to drop as soon as I give them what they want. That's how people like this do business. No honesty or honor." She leaned down to the shorter woman and kissed her. "You've been a good friend, Donna—the best. If I get through this—"

"You will," Donna all but growled, her soft blue eyes shooting fierce sparks in McCall's direction, "or there will be hell to pay. Absolute and extreme public hell for all concerned."

Beth bit her lip. It had been so long since someone had

cared with such utter unquestioning faith. "Thank you," she whispered again. "Go, Donna. You know nothing about me from this moment—it's safer." She turned to the car to take a sleepy Danny out.

McCall had beaten her to it, was lifting Danny up in those strong arms…and though she knew he was only helping, her fury, barely contained until now, boiled over. "Don't touch my son."

The freezing scorn in her voice got to him. He wheeled around to face her, his eyes blistering, meeting her ice with the heat of disbelieving contempt. "Do you think I'd hurt him?"

"When it comes to you, I *don't* think. I don't want to know." She moved fast, and snatched Danny from his arms. "Don't touch my things," she added as he started slinging Danny's backpack onto his shoulder. "I don't need your help."

He froze in place, his face a mask of barely contained fury to match her own. "What the hell *do* you need, Beth?"

She met his gaze, stinging from the contempt she knew she'd earned. Hating herself at this moment only marginally more than she hated him for forcing her to words and acts so far beneath her. "Nothing from you. I don't need or want anything from you."

A tall, rugged blond man who looked to be in his early forties was waiting right outside, with four others standing like silent sentinels behind him—and one woman. A woman whose appearance had been subtly altered to look like hers. She was even wearing similar clothing, the unusual sweater bought from the same store. She wouldn't pass for her close up, but she could lead anyone following them on a wild-goose chase.

What did that mean—were they going to replace her for Falcone to follow…or was she going to conveniently disappear?

The intensely handsome blond man spoke, in a slow, sexy Southern drawl that washed over her turbulent emotions like dark molasses. "Hello, Ms. Silver. My name is—"

"It's not your real name, so don't bother." She kept walking toward the plane she had ready. "You're McCall's boss. Excuse me, please, unless you have a warrant for my arrest."

The man produced a piece of paper without a word, holding it before her eyes, since her hands were full.

She felt the blood drain from her face. "So I suffer arrest for being an illegal immigrant or go with you. And of course you put us in protective custody, separating us until I give you whatever it is you want." *And where Danny's father will get at him with his crooked cops and his millions of dollars.* "I have no choice, then—but don't rejoice, because you won't get a damn thing from me." Shaking with terrified fury, she refused to look McCall's way, but stared defiantly at his boss. "God help you if anything you do this night ends up hurting my boy."

"We're here to help you." McCall's voice came from behind her, low and fierce. "You have to—"

"I don't have the least interest in anything you say." She kept her gaze trained on the blond man. "I suppose there's no use in saying this, but I don't want McCall near my son. I'm sure you have a *whatever-it-takes* credo, but I have to pick up the pieces of my son's broken heart after you all go—if we're still alive. And my little boy's started hoping that he could have a daddy."

Behind her, she felt McCall flinch at her words; but no satisfaction filled her, just an emptiness of heart. Maybe he'd had no choice but to tell his superiors, but he'd destroyed her one chance at anonymity. With this gun-toting circus of people around her, she had no chance of getting Danny out of New Zealand unnoticed. Somebody would see them—someone who needed money—and Danny's father would know in which direction they'd gone before long. His kind of money precluded silence, or honor, or loyalty. Or trust.

Maybe she was warped, no longer a normal woman, but at least she and Danny were alive.

"Flipper, take the other plane—the one Ms. Silver has. Take Heidi and go to the South Island. From there, separate and find your ways to the arranged checkpoint by noon tomorrow."

Obviously the blond man's word was law in this spy group. McCall and the slender woman made up to look like her moved without argument to the plane.

"You'll need these." Beth held out a set of keys. "I'll have to unlock the system for you before you can start the engine."

"Go ahead," McCall said curtly without turning around. He leaned against the plane with a hand, his back turned to her, as stiff and cold as the morning slowly coming to life.

The blond man took a still-sleeping Danny from her arms, and walked over to the DC-10 primed and ready behind him.

She unlocked the system of her plane with a complicated setting of five keys—the right one in the right groove the first time, or the computerized system would fail. Then she turned away. "You can fly normally now. There's no trick to taking off or landing, but there is a system to disable any unofficial tracking from the ground or the air. Just use the button beneath autopilot. If you fly at a high enough altitude you shouldn't be seen at all. Please leave it safely in a hangar somewhere. And bring me back my keys. I hope your group can arrange to have it flown to wherever I'll be living for the time being?"

"Of course." McCall turned to her then; his eyes burned into hers as he spoke. "I'd have died to save you, Beth, do you know that? Shows what a stupid jerk I am. I'd have done anything to keep you and Danny safe. But you're running again—running from imaginary fears as much as the real thing. You'll ruin your son's life, cheat him of a real life so that you can stay a coward, safe inside those damn fears of yours, never trusting anyone." He added, so low no one else could hear, "Are you willing to spend the rest of your life alone, refusing to really *live* just so you won't have to reach out and accept that someone cares about you, or that you might care about them?"

He had no idea of the chord he'd just struck in her inmost heart and soul. She wanted to cry out, *I don't want to live my life alone. I don't want to fight Danny's father on my own, but he'll kill you if he had a clue of how much I love you...*

"Do you?" she said softly, hating that she had to push every button he had to stop him from staying so close. "Do you *live,* or hide behind your save-the-world philosophies? Do you rescue people because they need it, or because *you* need to justify your existence? To prove to Mommy that she was wrong to leave you all those years ago—that you're something better than your father was?''

He flinched as if she'd struck him, but didn't answer her. He stood tense and silent watching her, arms folded, big and dark and hot, all man, stalking the cliffs inside her soul. She drew a small, ladylike breath. *Control, control!* ''Goodbye, McCall. Danny and I will see you at this checkpoint tomorrow, I gather.''

By what miracle had her voice come out sounding so unmoved?

She walked back to the larger DC-10 waiting for her without looking back.

Chapter 15

So she was back in Australia.

Strong instinct told her Danny's father knew nothing about their arrival here—a deep-seated sense of safety, a kernel of peace, settled inside her soul and wouldn't be shaken by her old friends, fear and distrust. Whoever these people were, whatever they wanted from her, they were not in Falcone's pay.

Five years ago she hadn't been outside Kingsford-Smith International Airport. She'd only seen parts of Sydney from the air. A change of clothes and hair, a wig for Danny and, using the fake passports ready for them, they'd flown straight to Wellington in New Zealand. Escape, completely according to plan.

And she and Danny vanished from the world. Anonymity for five lovely years, with no sign of Falcone—until McCall found them.

"Sandwich, Ms. Silver?"

Beth started and turned to the blond American, who'd only introduced himself as Mike. Yeah, right, and his last name was Brady, too, he was so innocent and wholesome.

And Beth's your real name? an inner voice jeered.

It is now. She refused to identify with McCall's people. Arguing over ethics was a waste of time, sitting with a bunch of flak-jacketed, heavily armed people after evidence.

She shuddered. They'd changed tactics, that was all. They hadn't found what they were after by intimidating and arresting her, so they were trying some overdue kindness. The protective stance that had gotten McCall almost everywhere with her…

Not again. Control!

"Thank you." She took two plain meat sandwiches, unwrapped one and gave it to Danny, then ate hers in silence, looking out over the fading horizon of the sunset.

"Where are we, Mummy?" Danny mumbled, half-asleep still.

She patted her son's tousled dark mop of hair. "Don't talk with your mouth full, sweetie. We're in Australia. You'll have to ask that man there if you want to know where." She gave McCall's boss an ironic glance, which he returned with a bland, unconcerned smile. He obviously didn't give a hang what she thought or felt.

Unlike McCall, who'd be here any minute. He'd radioed his estimated ETA to his boss a short while ago.

Wherever they were, it wasn't heavily populated. A vast, flat land of red earth, pea-green scrub and stunted, twisted trees standing beside their taller, proud, ghostly cousins—the famed Australian eucalyptus trees, perhaps—and this deserted airstrip with the scrub-and-rock carpet beside the red-earth landing strip. Ready for as soon as they drove off, or flew away, to cover all traces of their presence.

Fight it as she would, she felt a horrifying sense of kinship to these people—a creeping sense of belonging. No names, no permanent identity, change at a moment's notice. Leave no traces behind. Even her house in Renegade River would be empty by now—the faceless removalists who'd never seen her or spoken to her would have her stuff in storage.

And, even though she knew she had no choice, no say in this crazy life she led to keep Danny and herself free from

Falcone's putrid corruption, her stomach churned and her heart slammed against her ribs. She'd judged these people for living the same life as hers. She had no idea what they'd given up to lead this life, or why they did it. She'd just hated them, despised them without the benefit of a fair hearing.

And she'd judged McCall most of all.

A small, blinking light appeared above the fading horizon, like the first star of evening, like the reassuring wink of an old, loved friend. He was coming.

"It's your choice from here on in, Ms. Silver."

The quiet voice made her start. The rugged, handsome American was beside her. He looked as if he saw everything going through her mind, and understood her dilemma. She gave him the same dignity, refusing to prevaricate. "Give me the options."

He smiled a little, refusing to charm her. "Only in whose car you ride, Ms. Silver. The rest is nonnegotiable. You're going to one of our training facilities, west of the outback town of Bourke. No one can even scout the place from thirty thousand feet without our complete knowledge. You'll be safe there."

"I never understood the premise in books and movies that an isolated place, like a shack in the mountains, can be safe."

Her bland remark made his smile grow; yet still he gave her nothing, and she sensed that was the Nighthawks' regular way of life. He seemed invincible yet somehow elusive, insubstantial as a tired phantom walking beside her in the night. "This house has trip wire every five yards for the first mile in, a tracking system so intense that we can trace mice after crops in the next property. Everything's hooked up to our satellite system. Nothing for ten miles moves or breathes without our knowledge, and the system's unbreakable. There's a runway, and four planes in the back hangar ready to go should we need them."

She nodded, and, her heart thudding again, watched in silence as the small plane landed before them.

"Your choice," he said quietly.

"Does—has he—" She clamped a hand over her mouth,

aghast that she'd even started to ask. What power was there inside this strange man that inspired confidence against her will?

McCall's boss gave her a single glance, and answered her unasked question in blunt honesty, words with rough edges, telling the unvarnished truth. "He's never compromised a case for a woman—not until now. So make your choice, Ms Silver. But remember, even men who walk in the shadows, who don't have names, are human. They feel pain and bleed like any other man. They have hearts just like yours."

She bit her lip; but by the time she'd turned to face him there was only gentle half darkness, as if he'd melted into the dusk. Another one of the disappearing people.

Just like her.

Then McCall's plane was landing, and every other man vanished from her thoughts. With her heart knocking a soft tattoo against her ribs, she watched as he brought the Cessna in with a grace rare even in experienced pilots. He vaulted out within moments, landing catlike straight from the cockpit.

He didn't even look at her. He crossed to where his co-workers were rolling out the carpet of earth and scrub, and helped them cover the runway. He didn't so much as turn in her direction. He smiled down at Danny as her little boy jumped around him like a puppy, but he didn't speak to him.

I don't want him anywhere near my son.

He was obeying her, yet she felt snubbed. He'd turned his back on her just as she had to him, and it hurt. A lot more than she'd allowed anything to get to her since—

You are a young woman, niña, *but you are still a girl. You dream and wish like any other. One day you will find the one man who wrings your heart's blood from you with hopes and dreams and needs and desire. Then you will understand why your father means more to me than life, and did from the day we met.*

And oh, she did understand—even why Mama had stopped breathing within a month of the car crash that took Papa's life ten years ago.

I'm sorry, Mama, I can't afford to let that happen!

But it had. That kind of love, that once-in-a-lifetime love had come to her a decade ago, and her heart had held on to it with all the tenacity in her being.

Denial was her only life preserver in a storm-tossed ocean. Loving McCall might not be an option she had, but whether it brought her to her knees or not, she *would* maintain control. For Danny's sake. McCall would take Danny's trusting baby heart and crush it beneath that cloaked heel as he strode away from them, back to his world of shadows and phantoms.

Until Falcone was gone from her life for good; until McCall spoke, until he stepped out of his protective darkness and gave her what she needed to know, she dared not risk her baby's heart—or her own—on a man who had only promised to save them from Falcone, not to stay forever. Danny had been hurt enough, lost enough, without losing the dream of a daddy as well.

"Nothing, sir," Heidi reported quietly to Anson, her lovely Asian features reflecting the frustration they all felt. The entire team had been at this remote outback site for more than twenty-four hours, and Beth had given them absolutely nothing to work with. No evidence, no admission of her name— even when Anson played the tape of her voice talking about Falcone—and nothing to show her ID as anything but Elizabeth Anne Silver. "I've been through her things four times and searched her twice," Heidi went on. "Not a sign of any identification that she's anyone but Elizabeth Silver, and no sign of the tape."

"The house?" Anson snapped at Panther.

The lean, sleek man, dark and elegant and dangerous, shrugged one shoulder. "Empty. I even took her garden apart, broke the few pots left. She had the place cleaned by experts."

"And what the hell are we?" Anson growled, pacing past each of them while they stood in silence like recalcitrant children. "This is one woman. *One* woman! How the hell can she outwit trained professionals?" His gaze flicked to the monitor, making sure Beth and Danny were still there.

Heidi spoke again. "Maybe because she's a trained professional? This woman either appeared from thin air, lived as an illegal alien all her life, or is a current or former pro to the game, with a life and identity we can't crack. Have you sent her prints to all relevant organizations to be sure?''

''Of course I have,'' Anson retorted. ''She's absolutely clean.''

''Are you sure, sir?'' Only Heidi would challenge Anson when he was this furious. Only Heidi kept this cool under the wilting flame of Anson's fire. ''Are you sure one of the intelligence organizations isn't taking countermeasures to protect her, even from us? If they don't want her to be in the public eye—''

''They'd have arranged an accident if she were in their league, and that delicate an issue,'' Anson snapped. ''You don't play with the big boys and disappear on your own terms—you should know that, Heidi.''

''But it seems to me that she's done just that, sir.'' Heidi's chin turned just a shade more square, a touch more stubborn. ''She's evaded Falcone's boys—and us—for years, sir. She's been in the game, in my humble opinion. We just need to know whose chessboard she was—or is—playing on.''

''With the utmost respect, sir, I agree,'' Nightshift, Team Commander Three, intervened. ''No single woman with a child could have made it this far, evading even detection, let alone capture, by so many professionals, without being a pro—or having expert help. She hasn't had that, as far as we can see.''

Anson gave a short, pithy return to Nightshift's opinion, but then, any other answer was unthinkable for the unbeatable, indestructible Ghost.

As team commander, McCall needed to be privy to the lives and backgrounds of every operative in his region, but he knew only the basics about Anson. Like McCall, Anson had dragged himself up from a neglected childhood on the streets, but he'd come from the swampy dirt and muck of New Orleans rather than the gang-ridden streets of L.A., to make it this far through guts, ability and decades of hard work. No man like Nick Anson would handle the news that a young woman alone—

and burdened by a small child, at that—had outwitted his best, handpicked team, yet again.

McCall watched Anson's internal battle against disbelief versus unassailable facts in silence, feeling raw and idiotic, and yes, relieved that it wasn't only him that had been so stupid or blind. Did all his operatives believe Beth was a current pro? He looked around at his fellow operatives, and saw them all nodding, with the complete lack of surprise that meant they'd already had the idea in their minds.

And if this had been any other case, with any other woman, he'd have been the first to toss the idea in the air. It explained the ease with which she flew planes and raced speedboats, got an identity and accent so damn flawless that it took the Nighthawks years to crack it. They'd known of the existence of Elizabeth Silver for three years, yet she hadn't even become a strong probable for Delia until a casual cross-referencing with the actual written records in Dunedin proved that no Elizabeth Anne Silver had been born there within twenty years of Beth's age. It also explained her stoic silence in the face of arrest and search, the perfection of her escape system, and her code with Donna Richards.

He flicked a glance at the monitor. Yeah, Beth was playing perfect mommy, reading a Dr. Seuss book to Danny. Yet despite the storybook loveliness of the picture they made, too many pegs were fitting right into their holes. If Beth was in the game, it was no wonder she'd twisted him in knots. She'd know how to get an operative on edge, even to knowing the way that would make him back off, if she had a dossier on him.

Turnabout was fair play. Time to go for the double bluff.

With all the coolness he was far from feeling, he doused the heat of the argument. "With all due respect, sir, we can thrash this out all night, or we can test the theory."

All heads snapped his way, their eyes filled with startled respect, and McCall realized how close he'd come to losing point on this operation because of his personal involvement. Anson's eyebrow lifted in the way it did when he didn't want to concede the right to someone else. "Well? Are you going to throw the bomb and leave it there, or defuse it for our delectation?''

McCall grinned, feeling sudden adrenaline kick in. Anson was willing to give him point still. ''It's obvious that Ghost has told most of you about my involvement with Delia, before her marriage. And this woman and I have the same kind of attraction, have done from the minute I walked into her studio.''

''And?'' Anson snapped a pencil between his fingers.

His heart started knocking out the hard tattoo of coming excitement, of knowing he was right. Yeah, this was going to work. It had to. ''She wants us to believe she's a single mom on the run from an obsessed lover, mistaken for Delia. So let's call her on it. She told me she never married Danny's father, which means, if she told me the truth, that she's free. So let's give her the one thing she won't be able to resist.''

''You're not Hercule Poirot, Flipper. We don't appreciate the dramatic pauses here,'' Nightshift interrupted irritably. ''If you have a point, I'd appreciate it if you'd let us in on it. It's been a long two days with little reward thus far.''

''It's obvious, Nightshift.'' Anson was grinning now, all but laughing with the boyish look he always got when he had the chance to outwit someone who'd got ahead of him. ''Give her the full Monty. We offer her a new name, a new country and identity, and a big strong daddy for her little boy. All fully documented and tied in a red ribbon, complete with a wedding ring.''

''Dated back seven years, for added safety when Falcone's men check her out,'' McCall added, grinning, too. ''Make me Danny's legal father, too. Give her the anonymity she craves, and see what she does. An active pro with anonymity as her top priority would take the offer and try to take me out within hours, by temporary disablement or death. An innocent woman genuinely attracted to me, seeing me as a man tortured with love for her and willing to let her disappear again, will be grateful for the help, touched by my pain…and maybe she'll trust me with the truth.''

''And you get lucky in the interim,'' Panther commented

languidly from behind him. "Damn lucky, with that body and face. She is one superb woman."

"Now that's what I call a perk of the job," Nightshift added, his irritability vanishing with the quiet joke.

"That will do," Anson interrupted, his tone clipped. "We have work to do, so let's get on with it. What do you need, Flipper?"

McCall turned to Braveheart, one of his two most trusted team members. "Get the details into Births, Deaths and Marriages stat. I'm a dual American-Australian citizen—make her one, too, and date it back seven years. Give her American background, living in Australia. Get her onto the U.S. records now—have her born there, preferably Texas or New Mexico, but came out here at least twenty years back, to account for her accent. It's mostly only Aussies and New Zealanders that can tell their accents apart, so Falcone's men will swallow that Danny and Beth are Australian."

Braveheart, U.S.-born and Australian raised, a man of action who loved tinkering with any kind of gadgetry, computer or otherwise, grinned and nodded. "You got it, sir. This is gonna be fun." He left the room within seconds.

McCall turned to Wildman next, a Texas boy and a fully trained ParaRescue Jumper, the other man on his most trusted list. "Form a team, Wildman. Whoever you want, it's your call, but at least twelve CSAR experts. Your job is to follow us discreetly when we run. You'll need to be ready for anything—rescue, arrest, whatever happens. Have all equipment ready to go at any time. Full military-rescue ability at all times."

"Hoo-yah, sir." Wildman saluted him and marched out.

Anson lifted that eyebrow again. "What's my job?"

"I need a doctor and nurse here, stat, preferably Irish and Songbird if you can recall them. I need a team ready to attack us—people the subject has never seen and never will see again."

Anson nodded. "Done." He picked up the phone.

"And me, sir?" Panther said in the dark, sinister growl of

his, cool and lethal, that led to his code name. "What do I do?"

McCall chuckled. "With your expert marksmanship? You work with Nightshift on his op. You get to face us if you have no other recourse. You're the official fall guy."

Nightshift lifted an eyebrow and spoke in his elegant, drawling British accent. "At this point in the proceedings, I almost dread asking, but what exactly is my task?"

McCall held in the exuberant laugh. Man, this was taking point in a way he'd never dreamed when he joined the Nighthawks under Anson's irascible and unquestioned leadership. He hadn't had the chance to get so inventive since he left he SEALs. "I saved the best for last…and it's a job right up your alley," he told his fellow team commander, a man he liked and respected, a former operative in MI5—a real-life James Bond. "I need you and Heidi to set up a murder for me."

Chapter 16

3 a.m. Time to go. Seven minutes and counting.

McCall nodded to Irish, Team Two commander and Nighthawks' doctor, called in from his honeymoon—but his wife, Songbird, not only understood, she was right beside him this moment. Heidi lay on the floor outside Beth's door in a flat sprawl, a broken blood capsule beneath her back, staining her clothes and skin and the carpet. She lifted an arm; Irish injected her with the serum. Her eyes closed in seconds. Her delicate frame stopped the rhythmic lift and fall of breath, and her skin took on a sick pallor as her body, responding to the chemicals injected into her, cooled faster than a normal death.

"Go," Irish whispered, and disappeared into the shadows of an open door. "I'll be here for her."

McCall opened Beth's door, stepped in silence over Heidi's body and closed the door. He'd need a moment of privacy with Beth before he sent her into either operative mode or total shock.

The sight in front of his eyes almost made him hesitate. Two single beds, one with a sweet-faced child cuddling the puppy against his face, and a teddy bear clutched in his other hand; the other bed held the woman of his dreams—a decade's worth of dreams. In the soft, unfocused light of the half moon outside, her sleeping face was perfection of face and form in shadow and marble, living and warm, cool and remote.

Six minutes forty seconds.

He crossed to the bed and touched her shoulder. ''Beth.'' It wasn't hard to inject the name with urgency—Heidi's life depended on exact execution of this op. ''Beth, wake up.''

She flipped her body toward him as by instinct, because it was obvious she still walked in the land between sleep and waking. ''Hmm…Brendan…my Brendan…''

He almost reeled at the tone, saturated with sensuality and something deeper, sweeter—wild and wanton and longing, as if in her eyes, his name was beautiful. If she'd spoken his name like that two days ago…hell, if she'd said his name at all—

Six minutes twenty seconds.

He tried to shake her, but his rebel hand drank in the sweet warmth of her half-bare shoulder, and he caressed her instead. He swallowed a groan as the heated silk of her skin shivered right into his needing body. ''Yes, it's me.'' The dark huskiness of his voice, hot and urgent with sexuality, disgusted him. *Be an operative!* ''Wake up, Beth,'' he growled.

''Mmm.'' An arm hooked around his neck. ''I was dreaming of you,'' she whispered in a half-dreaming voice. ''I dreamed of you touching me. You're always with me when I'm alone and afraid. You haunt me even when you're not there…you stalk my soul, you live and breathe inside me, and I can't forget you, can't leave you behind…never. You're with me, always with me. Touch me…''

The man heard the words, the operative understood what they meant for the mission—but their power and beauty speared the heart of the child with too many unhealed wounds, lost and alone and *needing.* The dark-hearted little boy who'd lost his mommy looked out that stark, lonely window into empty night, and saw her once more—not his mom, but the face that haunted him, the hand that could dry ancient tears, fight his fears for him, walk through life holding him. "Beth…" His voice cracked.

Five minutes fifty seconds.

Just one kiss…

You're a fool to believe in this, even for a moment. She'll only deny it when she's awake.

Five minutes forty seconds…

I don't care. Just once. I'd barter my soul for this.

His mouth moved over hers with all the joy of a captive finding release from dank chains. Beth's arms held him with such sweet ferocity…she responded to his kiss with sweet abandon, her mouth drinking him in, her hands twining in his hair. Her lovely body, her nakedness sheathed only in a swathe of satin, lifting to touch his; her hands pulling him down, down until he fell to the bed, drowning in his moment. If he paid with a century of torture, it was worth the pain, having sweet, lovely Beth in his arms, being in her arms where he belonged.

Four minutes thirty-five seconds.

If she stops breathing for longer than seven minutes, brain damage can set in. Heidi's life is in your hands!

The jolt brought the operative back to the fore, even as he touched Beth, caressed her, kissed her, and his body moved with hers in a rhythm that told him he could be inside her right this moment, finding release and long-overdue peace in her welcoming body. And the torture kicked up a notch. It was physical agony, but he tore his mouth from hers. "Beth…"

"No." She pulled at him to bring him back to her. "Tomorrow will be the same as today—it has to be, or you'll die. But they can't see me tonight, and I can have what I want…I can have you…"

He kissed a searing path from the base of her throat up to her mouth, and he growled in intense satisfaction when she gasped and writhed beneath him. Her words made no sense, but he didn't care right now. "Baby, you can have me whenever you want. That's a promise. But now—"

"Yes, now," she whispered into his mouth. "Now… always. I'll always want you. Always."

Four minutes ten seconds.

As the man drowned, the operative kept count—and delivered the TKO to his needs. "Tonight, baby. I promise," he muttered, hoping to God it would come true. Bartering his soul on that hope. "But now, we have to go. You and Danny are in danger."

The one word guaranteed to bring the mother forth from the sensual siren beneath him. Her eyes snapped open. "What?"

He spoke rapidly, submerging his aching desire beneath cold hard lies. "The safety of this place has been breached. One of the Nighthawks has compromised the operation. Someone's here, and they're after you, Beth—after Danny."

"How do you know?" Her voice was low, half-terrified as she jerked up in the bed, half lifting him off her with the force of her movement. She was with him already, but needed proof.

Three minutes forty-five seconds.

He vaulted over the bed and opened the door to reveal Heidi's sprawling body, the expert fake blood seeping from beneath her.

"Oh, dear God…no, not again. Not again…"

At the first sound of the cracked, teary voice, McCall glanced at Beth, and felt sucker-punched. She was as stark white as Heidi's chemically induced comatose body. She swayed as she sat, her face taking on a greenish hue. She clapped a hand over her mouth, but her body jerked forward, and she threw up over the bedcovers in horrifying silence.

So he'd been right about her. No pro in the game could be so shocked at death, or act this well, but justification had never come at so high a price. He couldn't even take the time to comfort her. *Three minutes ten seconds.* "Get your things, Beth. We have about ten minutes before they sweep the hall again. We have to be long gone by then. Two minutes to pack and run, Beth."

Did he sound urgent enough? For Heidi's sake— "Follow me out of here," he added in the imperative, authoritative tone that made people in war zones follow him in SAR ops. "I know the layout of the place. I helped plan the traps."

Beth nodded. "I'm sorry," she murmured, her voice scratchy and aching. "I've made a mess…"

"Just get up, sweetheart," he said quietly, aching to comfort her. "I'll get Danny and the pup, you get a few things together. Go light. We have about ninety seconds to get out."

"But the poor girl…she must have been hurt trying to—to help us…" Without warning she flew off the bed to Heidi, and felt frantically for a pulse. "We have to help her! We can't just leave her here like this!"

Confirmed: Beth was no spy. Even Mata Hari couldn't act this well—and she wouldn't have cared enough about Heidi to start an imperfect round of CPR on her, as Beth was now. "She's gone, Beth. She's lost too much blood. We have to go—now." *Two minutes fifty seconds.* He could almost feel Nightshift's fury, and Irish and Songbird's frantic need to take the six steps to Heidi's supine body and inject her with the adrenaline-based antidote. Damage can set in as quickly as seven minutes after injection if the subject isn't fit, or has heart/lung problems.

Heidi was a mountaineer and champion gymnast, and a former agent of the Australian Security Intelligence Organization, ASIO. Surely she could handle a few more minutes.

"We can't leave her!" It was as if she sensed his urgency for Heidi and relayed it back to him in a pulsing beat of guilt. *Two minutes forty seconds.*

If he didn't get her out of here, Heidi wouldn't die—Anson would see to that—but they'd have to reveal the ruse before Beth's eyes, and then they'd never get the tapes or her trust. He had to go through with the whole charade, or lose everything.

Do something! He felt every operative in the hallway screaming silently for him to act.

"It's her, or Danny," he uttered brutally. "A woman you barely know, or your son. Sixty seconds. Take your pick."

Beth gasped and vaulted to her feet as he'd done a minute

before, and ran to the backpack, leaving the suitcase behind. "This has all we need. Let's go."

With lethal efficiency, McCall bound electrical tape around the muzzle of Danny's pup. "We can't let him bark...and we can't let Danny cry out, either." He put a gentle hand across Danny's mouth before he lifted the child, startled out of sleep, into his arms. "It's Brendan, pal," he whispered in the boy's ear. "We're going on an adventure, me, your mom and Bark...but you have to be real quiet. Okay?"

Danny's eyes swiveled to Beth's; and though she looked startled and still somewhat green, she managed a smile and nod for her son. "You missed out on your fun with Ethan, sweetie, so we're making it up to you."

One minute thirty seconds.

Danny struggled against McCall's hand until he was free; then he smiled up at McCall with the instant, unquestioning love only a secure child can give. "Can we go camping? Can I see a kangaroo and a koala?"

"Sure, pal, as soon as we can manage it." He made himself smile at the boy. "We're going to my place first—but that's in the countryside, so there are wild kangaroos and sometimes koalas. We'll have to go hunting at night for a koala, okay?"

Beth's face was rosy with the flush of sweet shyness. Yeah, she was thinking about it, about being alone in his place, and her words a few minutes before—and his. *Tonight, I promise.* Long nights alone in his house, loving her body, her loving his—

Fifty-five seconds.

He cocked his head. "Close your eyes, pal," he whispered to Danny, and the ecstatic kid didn't even question the command. He stepped over Heidi's sprawled body. "Don't look, Beth. This way."

But he saw that Beth *did* look down at Heidi again, a quick, helpless glance, longing to help. She shuddered as she stepped over the body. Guilt speared through McCall as he led the way through the labyrinth of security measures. No matter how he justified it, some things couldn't *be* justified. Terrorizing an innocent woman to prove her innocence when she'd already been through the mill more than once, ranked right up there.

His life thus far may not have led to his being able to trust many people—not even the woman who'd just given him a precious piece of her trust—but the word *lowlife* resonated in his mind. A tired reproach for the man of phantoms, lies and shadows…but tonight, it seemed to take on a whole new meaning.

"Hurry," he whispered, continually looking left and right to keep up the pretense of urgency. "I'm on official watch tonight, but my relief will come any minute." They reached the side door that led to the hangar. "I've disabled the security system, but it has automatic reversion within ten minutes. We have to be on the plane within two minutes, Beth."

She nodded and increased her pace.

They made it halfway down the path to the hangar before Panther led the "attack" on them, swift and stealthy, a sneak attack worthy of his code name. With military precision, he hit the puppy with a—

Danny cried out, "Bark!"

McCall dropped to the ground, put Danny and the unconscious pup down, and got out his tranquilizer gun, checking that Beth, too, had dropped out of range. "Shh, pal, it's okay—it's just a sleeping shot. Bark will wake up in a few hours, good as new. These aren't bad guys…they don't want us to go is all. They'll try to put us to sleep and take us back to bed."

"How do you know what they are?" Beth whispered fiercely.

"These are specialist darts, used when our search teams need to immobilize witnesses without killing them." He gave her a savage grin. "I worked with our team doctor to create them. I was his star guinea pig."

She gasped, her lovely eyes running over him as if to check for damage. A warm shiver ran through him at the intimate look. *Had* anyone looked at him like that, with such caring?

Another shot came whizzing through the darkness. The operative responded by diving out of range, taking Beth down with him. "We have the advantage—they don't want to hurt us," he whispered in her ear. "Use your backpack as cover and run like hell, keeping low and your arms swinging. It's harder to hit a moving target, and chances are they'll hit the backpack. I'll keep Danny covered." When she nodded tensely he whispered, *"Run."*

The terrifying *whiz* of darts flying past chased them all the way into the hangar. McCall felt savage gratitude when some darts hit the backpacks. Beth was too smart—and given their track record and her obsessive self-reliance, she'd be looking for holes in the plan before long. Any reason to run...

He swore with a viciousness that wasn't feigned when the hangar door was locked. "I opened this!" With another curse, he muttered, "Quick, Beth, get my gun from my coat and shoot out the lock. Can you do it?" He dodged another dart that flew past his ear as he spoke. Oh, yeah, he'd have words with Panther when they met again. His sense of perfectionism had gone too far this time.

Beth didn't hesitate. Even dancing with the need to evade the darts, she grabbed the Glock, fixed the silencer and took out the lock with one clean shot. "Do you want the big doors done while you put Danny in, or do I cover you?"

"Cover, then shoot the doors and throw them out fast," he replied, treating her as an operative without thinking about it. "Can you jump up into the plane while it's moving?"

"I can try. Go!" she cried, turning to where Panther and two other operatives were still firing darts. They hit the door and wall beside her crouched form with tiny, sickening thuds. He had to physically squelch the fierce desire to cover her with his body. Trusting Panther to follow procedure as he'd always done, McCall tucked Danny into the back passenger seat of the Partenavia P68 Turbo, which could reach speeds of 322 kilometers an hour. Nothing else in this hangar would catch up fast. He threw himself into the cockpit. "Beth!" he yelled. She heard the plane fire up, grabbed a massive toolbox and pushed it against the door. She ran to the massive double doors and within moments, shot the locks one after the other, *blast, blast, blast.* No hesitation, no fear—not one miss.

Pilot, speedboat racer, a shot to qualify for the Olympics, and, even burdened with a small child, she'd eluded capture from both the bad guys and the best of the best for years.

Even now, she threw the doors open, shooting with a steady hand as she did so, not thrown back by the force of the shots, not fazed by the darts still coming at her thick and fast. She dodged them with the smoothness of a pro, sprinting for the plane like Cathy Freeman heading for gold. Using the handle of the open passenger door as ballast, she swung up and into the cockpit beside him with barely a hitch in her breathing.

Well, damn, if she isn't someone's operative now, Anson will do his best to recruit her as soon as she's free.

Just as he would have done, if it were anyone but the woman he'd step in front of a bullet for. And every protective urge screamed at him to stop that happening.

Every selfish urge. Face facts, McCall. Yeah, the kid who couldn't remember having anyone all his own to love him, finally had a shot at being loved…*my Brendan,* she'd said…and he wanted to grab at it with both fists and hang on like grim death. He wanted to keep Beth and Danny all to himself—

"Brendan!"

McCall looked at the closing doors and swore. Stupid jerk! Panther was losing it. Perfection in execution had its limits, and attacking them when they needed to get out fast was bordering on insane! With a muttered curse, he snapped, "Can you fly this?"

She ran her gaze over the console. "Doesn't look hard."

"Then get this out of the hangar and onto the runway any way you can. Don't run anyone down or shoot unless you have to."

He dived out of the cockpit and landed on Panther, more than ready to make this real.

The man in the ski mask and dark clothes wasn't Panther.

He'd sparred with Panther enough in training sessions to know. The taut, lean fury that was Panther wasn't fighting him now—this guy was a wall of muscle, and he wasn't mock fighting, he was trying to bloody kill him. Whoever he was, he was a street-fighting expert. Each punch and kick changed direction, into a different method, from karate to kickboxing to drunken boxing and starting over—all planned to get him off balance.

Too damn bad for him that he faced a former SEAL and street fighter himself. The rhythm was too familiar, and McCall blocked each blow and kick with the ease of coming home.

The moving plane created a deeper shadow over their wrestling bodies as Ski Mask pinned him down.

Three seconds. One, two—he used both feet to launch up, sending Ski Mask flying over his head and straight into the moving wheels from behind. The man grunted, collapsed for all of two seconds, then came back for more.

Rough as diamonds, smooth as silk. This guy was in the game somewhere, not just a hired mercenary. Not Falcone's man, then.

The Nighthawk rogue. No one else could get through the military precision of the security arrangements—

Except that I turned them off.

Ten minutes. That was all. Ten damn minutes. No way was it enough time to let an outsider in here, with a fifty-acre shield all around. The satellite was still in full force, tracking every movement—Wildman's team needed it to follow them. If this guy had come in from outside, he'd have been seen. Unless he'd been—no, how could he have been here the whole time?

He could have if he'd been seen as one of my team, absolute and unquestioned. And, damn it, I ordered Panther's team to back off from this point and shoot wild only. This guy's using my own plan against me.

Either he was one of the team, or he was someone he trained in breaking through a security system this complete. Someone who knew the way his mind worked, and waited for his chance. Sliding into McCall's plans, smooth as silk, to frustrate them.

Even as his mind worked through the possibilities, he kept fighting. It was second nature to him, the fight mode. He'd been in his first fistfight at five years old, with his goody-

goody cousin Stephen, who'd started the thing; yet he, Brendan, had not only been blamed, but forced to apologize by his mother. She'd stood grimly over him as he'd stuttered out the words to his smirking cousin, and his shocked, self-righteous aunt, who'd sworn, "My Stephen would never stoop to fighting!"

"Oh, Brendan would," Mom had replied grimly. "And he will apologize." Later, she'd had harsher words for him, when he wouldn't back down. *Show me you can be better than this in front of my family! Show Mommy that you're not a gutter rat like your father. Show me you have some manners, some conscience, Brendan!*

He'd done it—groveled for Mom's sake—but Stephen hadn't smirked later. It took him three years, but he'd made Stephen swallow that damn smirk—and that time, he didn't back down.

That had been the final straw as far as Mom was concerned. Tired of a husband who did little but drink and fight, she'd wanted better for herself…and her daughter. She'd wanted no traces of Jack McCall in her life—and that included his son.

A bitter life lesson he'd never forgotten. He'd never apologized since for self-defense, or even for attack. Never. The only apology he'd ever made since he was five had gotten him nowhere. *I'm sorry I was such a bad boy, Mommy. I'll be better. I won't fight again, I promise—not with Stephen or anyone. Please take me with you! Don't leave me with Dad…*

Even as he relived the humiliation, he fought his adversary with ruthless efficiency, and no emotion. Slam. Cut. Block. Kick. Fall, roll, launch onto feet firmly planted apart, ready for more. And, finally, the opening—and an open-palmed hand pushed upward, under Ski Mask's chin. And since they needed him alive to trace him backward to his source, or to identify him, and eliminate him from the Nighthawk team, it was a hit with surgical precision, aimed to disable not kill.

McCall heard Ski Mask's teeth crash together, saw his jaw displace—yeah, he wouldn't be talking to his boss for a while—then his eyes rolled back in his head, and he crumpled.

Using the Nighthawk standard-issue plastic cuffs, he put the guy's feet together—Panther could finish this job. He could take the mask off, identify this creep, even take the kudos, for all he cared. Into the two-way, he snapped, ''Panther, team attack, collect hostile witness inside hangar, stat!'' And then he bolted from the hangar to catch up to the plane, heading steadily toward the runway to the ugly melody of missed shots.

He had more important things on his mind right now than identifying this jerk. He had a bride to marry, a sweet and timid six-year-old son to reassure. Because if he could make her agree to his idea, that's what they'd be from this day forward: his wife, and his son. For the first time in his life he could become part of a real family, and it made his heart pound and sweat break out over his body, far worse than any danger he'd ever faced in the SEALs. What the hell did he know about making others happy? What if he blew it? What if he went on a mission and didn't come back? Would he leave them to grieve or worse, would they feel relieved that someone like him wasn't in their lives anymore, just like his mom had? And the real biggie, what if he asked her today and she laughed at his presumption? In his world of constant impossible situations, this was the biggest risk he'd ever taken, because it had the potential to be the biggest no-win of them all.

Chapter 17

For the first time since McCall walked into her studio last week—had it only been a week?—Beth felt at peace. McCall had brought her here to his own small property, the haven he'd shown no one before. He'd let her into his life.

She wasn't a fool. She knew the reason he'd brought her. She could almost hear the words he'd use: *If I let her into my life, she'll let me into hers. If I become the Brendan she loved, she might become Delia again, and give me her secrets.*

He knew her too well. He'd seen that she'd long since tired of carrying her burdens alone. He'd gone right into her soul to the lonely woman beneath, aching to share her secrets with someone—no, with *him*.

She couldn't fight the need anymore—the absolute *imperative* urge to give him…everything. Her body, her secrets—and her heart. It was coming. Now they were alone, and safe—for now—from Falcone's men, she could finally give back to him…

She sat on the porch swing of the sun-soaked veranda of McCall's rambling old farmhouse, watching Brendan play with an ecstatic Danny. They'd let the football drop almost an hour ago, after spending what seemed hours teaching her son how to improve his ball skills. He'd also shown Danny how to let go of his fear of being hurt and dive "into the ruck"— a term that mystified her, and made her terrified that Danny would break his neck.

But Danny was safe, and now on Brendan's shoulders, exploring the flora and fauna unique to Australia, in the free forty acres around the house. Surrounding that was a buffer zone— the security measures he'd put in place for them. And some of those measures were courtesy, she was sure, of the next-door neighbors he'd introduced when they'd arrived here just after sunrise—Mitch and Lissa McCluskey, and their four children, Matt, Luke, Jenny and new, adorable, curly-haired baby Natalie.

Beth knew the McCluskey parents for fellow spies within minutes, with all the unspoken-speak between the three of them. The kind of silent talk she'd had with Donna.

Had McCall felt as locked out watching her and Donna, as she had, watching him communicate with the McCluskeys? Even knowing that the communications or orders pertained to her safety, she'd resented it, hated being so shut out with him. Turnabout didn't feel like fair play. She wanted to know, to be a part of everything he was—to walk into McCall's world.

Then let him into yours. Trust him!

Crunch time. All her fears and her obsessive need to keep Danny safe from everything and everyone boiled down to this day, this hour, this moment. Putting her life, and that of her beloved child, in McCall's hands instead of clutching to her chest.

She had two choices now. To admit that she was human, and her support systems were now exhausted, and tell him her whole, crazy story…or run again. Walking through the underbelly of life, living a half life, existing in the shadow-world of terror.

Was there an option, really? And if there were, would she want to take it?

Danny made frantic hand gestures until she looked at her son. "Mummy, look, a kangaroo and her baby," he mouthed to her, his eyes alight as he pointed downward from McCall's shoulder.

Decision made, she smiled and got to her feet. Goodbye independence; she didn't want it anymore. She wanted her time in the sun with her son…and McCall. *Brendan.* It was Brendan she wanted to share her life with now. It was Brendan who'd brought her to life ten years ago with a smile; and if it had been McCall, her dark sentinel, who'd brought her back to life again within a day, after years of trusting no one, she had to accept the entire man, murky past and uncertain future.

Approaching with gentle steps, she saw the Grey kangaroo, a baby in her pouch, standing with a nervous tension about fifteen feet from Danny and McCall. "The baby's called a joey." She spoke in an undertone to not scare the wild creatures. She couldn't help smiling at the picture they made, the big Gypsy of a man, no longer so dark and remote with the tender smile on his face as he held her bouncing-with-excitement little boy on his shoulders, Danny's puppy frolicking at his booted heels.

Her men. Her family. She hoped.

Danny's eyes grew round. "Joey?" He peered down at McCall. "You weren't joking, Brendan? The baby kangaroos really got named after the guy on *Friends?*"

Beth choked on laughter as McCall's twinkling eyes met hers. "Well, sort of, pal," he replied, his voice rich with shared amusement, and the smile resonated inside her soul. "They—"

"Liked *Friends* so much they named baby kangaroos after them," Beth put in, smiling. "The mothers and fathers have names, but the poor babies didn't. It wasn't fair to them."

Danny's eyes turned round with awe. "Wow. The guy on *Friends*—did he come out to do a show about it or anything?"

At that McCall put Danny down, chuckling outright, and the startled mother kangaroo turned on her thick tail and bounded away, Bark hot on their trail. "I don't know, pal." Again, his gaze sought Beth's, shimmering like dappled sunlight coming through the forest. She caught her breath at the sheer beauty of his expression.

Caught in a net she didn't want to escape from. The latent heat came to life, radiating like raw power from within as his gaze locked with hers for that one moment.

She bit a corner of her lip, and smiled. Personal. Intimate. Welcoming. A look he didn't have to read—it was all there for him to see, the need, the yearning.

"Hey, Danny-boy, I think you'd better grab Bark before he falls into the McCluskeys' waterhole. I can see Jenny, Matt and Luke there, too—looks like they're trying to catch tadpoles, if you feel like playing for a while."

"Oh! Tadpoles!" Danny's eyes were enormous now as he lifted his face to Beth's. "Can I, Mummy? Can I?"

Her heart squeezed tight, then faltered to rhythm again. Poor baby. It was time for him to believe in fairy tales and his right to play. "Of course, sweetie."

"Woooooohoooo!" Danny bolted over the low wooden fence to the neighboring farm. "Hey, guys, can I catch tadpoles, too?"

The three very grubby McCluskey kids turned with friendly smiles. Jenny handed him a net, and Luke put a jar beside him.

"He'll be cold," Beth said softly, watching as Danny got his track pants wet wading into the waterhole.

"He can warm up later. Boys don't notice the cold—or mud." McCall's voice was warm with affectionate laughter as he watched Danny wipe mud on his face like warrior's paint, the way Matt and Luke had. "He'll come back home coated in muck, happy and hungry, and will whine his way through a shower—that is, if he comes home at all. Knowing Mitch and Lissa, they'll keep him until at least tonight if you'll let Danny stay."

He didn't look at her as he spoke. No inflection resonated in that deep, smoky voice. Yet in its smallest corners she heard the lingering…the expected rejection of anything he suggested. He expected her to disrespect anything he said, to argue with anything he wanted. Why, *why* did she only seem to hurt the people she would give her life to protect from pain?

"I think that would do Danny the world of good, especially since he didn't get to camp with Ethan for long."

"I'll call Lissa and let her know we'll pick Danny up later, then." He didn't look at her; he nodded, watching the kids play. Keeping a distance from her greater than the few feet that separated them. As if they hadn't shared laughter minutes before, or he hadn't even seen the look on her face moments ago, or as though he couldn't bring himself to trust it. Couldn't trust *her*.

A deep breath for courage, then she said softly, "Why are we here? I can sense your tension, the secret you're keeping. What is it you're not telling me?"

He hunched into his long coat, then said it. "You want to be safe. Right? You want to be safe from Danny's father for good."

Not knowing what to say to that, she nodded.

He turned toward the sun, which was slowly falling behind the western hills. He lifted his face, as if needing the warmth, or maybe he didn't want to look at her. "I can arrange it." When she didn't speak, surprise rendering her silent, he went on. "They're not just idle words, Beth. It's all arranged."

"What is?" she whispered, aching to touch him, to take the frozen night inside of him and bring him to the sun he sought so desperately.

"Say the word, and your former life is wiped, yours and Danny's both. I can give you both new birth dates, whole new lives. All you have to do is agree. I can fix it so that you've been my wife for the past seven years, with a birth certificate and Australian citizenship, and Danny, my legal son. In the eyes of the law, he'll be my flesh and blood child." He still didn't turn to her, even when she gasped. "I have all the legal paperwork; the data's ready to go into the register. Lissa and Mitch are waiting to enter the marriage in an old church register, and sign any documents as our witnesses. Another operative is at a Sydney hospital, ready to enter Danny's name as having been born there, three months before his real birth. As far as the world would be concerned, Suzanne Elizabeth McCall is my wife, and Joshua Daniel McCall, our son." He shoved his bunched fists inside his coat pockets. "All you have to do is agree."

Oh, sweet heaven, and she'd mistrusted this man? Her eyes stung and burned. "You can do all that? You'd do that for me?" She couldn't seem to talk above a whisper.

A single jerk of his averted head. "But it won't hold up in court if anyone can verify your ID with fingerprints or DNA as another man's wife, and there's a full investigation. It's legal so long as you're a single woman, as you said you are."

She gulped so hard it felt as if she'd dislodged a tendon there. "I told you the truth. I never married Danny's father."

Watching the kids as if his life depended on it, he muttered, "Then our marriage will be legal. If you want it. Your call."

Implications and ramifications walloped around in her head like warriors in savage battle, but her heart grasped only two things: she and Danny could be safe permanently, and McCall was willing to mortgage his own life and future to make hers safe.

The terrified mother, the woman on the run too long, spoke first. "Do it."

Without a word he turned and strode up to the house. For once, she was left chasing him. And suddenly, she knew she'd give everything she owned to be able to take back those terrible words of the other night. *You can leave now. You got your reward…*

She found him sitting over a laptop computer. The strange buzzing sounds of connection to the Internet filled the room. "It will only take ten minutes, so be sure you want this. It isn't so easily reversible."

"A lot of things are hard to erase, no matter how much you want them gone," she agreed softly, her gaze drinking him in, taking his pain inside her heart. "But this is one thing in my life I won't regret…Brendan."

Nothing. He just kept watching the screen, and punched in numbers. "Panther. Team Commander One. Go ahead with the operation." He disconnected, and dialed another number. "Lissa? Hi, it's Brendan. Can you tell Mitch the op is a go? You've signed the register already, haven't you? Yes—thanks.

Oh, by the way, Danny's at the waterhole with your kids. Do you think you can—yes, we discussed it.'' He listened for a moment, then gave his rich, strong chuckle. ''Is that so? I think tomorrow's fine, but you'd better check with Beth. Hang on, I'll put her on.'' He handed her the phone. ''Lissa wants to know if they can keep Danny overnight. She says his presence is stopping Jenny from smothering Natalie to death with love.'' His eyes twinkled. ''It appears he has a fan already.''

Despite her aching heart, she smiled as she took the phone. ''Hi, Lissa. How are you?''

''Pretend to laugh, all right?'' Lissa McCluskey said quickly. ''I have something to say and I don't want Brendan to know.''

Intrigued, Beth laughed, and waited for more.

''Beth, I like you,'' Lissa said forthrightly. ''I see a kindred spirit in you. And because I do, I want to stop you from making all the stupid mistakes with Brendan that I made with Mitch.''

''Oh, really?'' Beth replied, chuckling through a throat that hurt. ''What happened then?''

''If we're kindred spirits, so are Mitch and Brendan,'' Lissa went on. ''Mitch was dumped on a church doorstep soon after he was born, rejected by his birth parents. And because of that, he never felt he was good enough for me. So when I started taking things out on Mitch—things that happened with my first husband that Mitch didn't deserve—he took it as proof that I could never want him as a man, or ever truly love him. He was sure I was too good for him.''

''I see.''

''Do you?'' Lissa's voice was gentle, yet penetrating. ''At least Mitch never really knew what he was missing. But Brendan…did you know he rarely sleeps more than fifteen minutes at a time, and it isn't just because of his SEAL training?''

''Yes,'' Beth replied quietly, as something small, cold and ominous snaked up her spine.

''You know we work with him—I saw it in your eyes this morning. Until we had the baby and semi-retired, offering the farm you're on as a training facility, Brendan was our Team

Commander. Mitch especially has worked with him, but we only got to know him well after he bought out the other half of our farm. We became friends, and he doesn't have many because he won't let them in.'' Lissa sighed. ''The reason he won't sleep is because he talks when he goes into a deep sleep. He asks his mother to take him with her, that he's sorry, he won't be a bad boy if only she won't leave him there with his dad. He also dreams of his father beating him up—he begs his dad to stop hurting him. We only heard him when we transported him home after a mission went bust last year—he was knifed almost in two. So he trained himself not to sleep. As Team Commander, he's on call 24-7, and that suits him fine. He doesn't have to dream of her then, doesn't have to relive his mother walking out on him, and whatever it was she said to damage him so badly.''

A slow, shaking hand came up to cover her mouth; she forgot to hide her emotions. ''Dear God…''

''Yeah, exactly.'' Lissa sighed. ''Don't destroy him, Beth. He's already been abandoned one time too many.''

''Thank you, Lissa,'' she whispered. ''We'll pick up Danny in the morning. I'll call later to say good night, all right?''

''Sure, if I can pry Jenny away from him long enough. She seems to think she's found the love of her life.'' The cheerful mother-next-door came back. ''Anything he can't or won't eat?''

The conversation turned prosaic after that…as ordinary as Beth's shaking voice would allow. When she hung up, she stood lost in thought until McCall broke into her thoughts with a voice as cool and remote as New Zealand's snowcapped peaks. ''It's all done. Here's your marriage certificate. I have a ring, too.'' He handed her a small box. ''Get another one if you don't like it. And we'd better train Danny to call me Daddy. It's for his safety. People on the hunt may be less likely to look twice at a secure-looking family to find the boy…or you.'' He spoke with a clinical, detached air, as if he had no emotional input in either the certificate or the ring, or in what Danny called him.

Having heard all Lissa McCluskey said—or left unsaid—

Beth now knew better. "Thank you, Brendan," she said quietly, as she opened the box with hands that trembled a little. "Oh," she gasped. "Brendan...it's—it's so lovely..."

And it was. The soft tulip pattern engraved on the simple rose-gold wedding ring gave it an aura of commitment and caring, sweetness and sharing that choked her up. "Where did you get it?"

He shrugged. "My McCall grandmother left it to my sister Meg in her will, but she'd gone with Mom. I hid it from Dad—he'd have only sold it for booze or gambled it. Figured I could start a family tradition or something. But if you don't like it—"

She couldn't stand it any more—she'd do anything to give warmth and light to that chilled, dark soul. With two quick steps she was crouched beside him, her hand on his. "Don't you ever say that again," she uttered with all the ferocity she felt. "This ring is beautiful and special, and I love it, Brendan McCall. Now I want you to do something for me."

He eyed her with all the wariness a man would give to a wild animal, or a vision he couldn't believe in. "What?"

She held out both hands, the box in her right, and her left bare. She kept her gaze locked on his, knowing that her eyes shimmered with tears unshed. "Marry me for real, Brendan McCall. Make me your wife. Be my man...in more than just name."

He looked at her fully then, his gaze hot and black as the smoke of hell burning. "Don't, Beth. If you're going to leave, walk out now. The marriage is still legal. You and Danny are still safe. And I won't stop you, or chase you. But don't make promises you have no intention of keeping. You haunt me too much now."

It was now or never. A tear fell down her cheek as she told him the unvarnished truth. "I deserved that, for saying what I did. I'm so sorry I hurt you. I didn't want to, but I had to save you," she whispered. "Danny's father killed a man before, just because he helped me get away. I couldn't bear it if I lost you, too."

Looking deep in his eyes, she saw the flinching, an infinitesimal recoil that showed how little he believed her. "I said don't. I don't need a pretty send-off in bed to thank me for your freedom." His words were gut-raw, as blunt as a knife sawing at his skin and as black as the smoke in his eyes. "And you didn't say anything that wasn't true. This marriage won't be real. We both know you can do a lot better for yourself than me."

Tears rushed to her eyes as she watched him force his attention back to the details on the laptop. "No, Brendan, it's not true. You saved my life, saved Danny—"

"That's what I do." His mouth tightened, but he kept typing. "What I *am* is a snot-nosed punk who thought with his fists for too long. That's why my mom walked out on me. She said I'd end up like my dad—a foul-mouthed, hard-ass drunk who beat the crap out of everyone he met. She only took my sister with her, and it didn't matter if he took it all out on me."

His unemotional recounting of Lissa's painful tale of his life seemed more harrowing to Beth. She felt torn apart, raw and bleeding from internal wounds—*his* wounds. She ached to comfort him, but it wouldn't help now—only truth and justice could neutralize the poison rotting his soul. Still crouched in front of him, she laid her hands on his thighs, gripping them hard. "Was she right? *Are* you just like him?" she asked fiercely.

His hands froze over the keyboard. "I just told you—"

"You told me your past. Tell me your present. *Are* you like him? *Are you?*"

"I'm a professional killer," he said harshly. "You tell me, am I like him, or even better? Or should that be, even worse?"

"You've never taken one life without government sanction, and even then, I bet you hated it. I *know* you did."

"Doesn't matter." His voice was gravelly. "I remember the name of every person I've been assigned to kill."

The stifled anguish in his voice pulsed into her like a living thing…and she knew this was another reason for his sleepless nights. "Doesn't that make you a person of conscience?" she asked quietly. "Those people are—were—real to you."

"Not Stephen. He was my cousin," he said slowly. "I hated

the little weasel. I beat him up twice. My mother called me a barbarian.''

"How old were you?" she demanded, hating a woman she'd never met with all her heart and soul, for the damage she'd done to an impressionable little boy.

''Five the first time." He threw it at her like it was something awful. "Eight the second time. Mom left that night.''

In other words, he'd driven her to leave—or so little Brendan had thought. "What did that boy do to you?"

He shrugged. "He pinched me the first time. He didn't touch me again after I hit him, though he smirked when Mom forced me to apologize. The second time he tried to play "show and tell" with my sister. Meg was a gentle kid who liked to draw and play with her dolls, and the little pervert lifted up her dress, even when Meg cried and said no. I got mad, like dear old Dad, and broke his collarbone. Mom couldn't stand the shame of it. She said leaving me with Dad was my punishment for acting like a wild animal. She wouldn't let me contaminate Meg with my bad ways.''

Beth's heart bled for the child inside the man she loved. How could any mother be so cruel? Had that woman ever taught him how to behave, or shown a little faith in him so that he could have some in himself? Or had she found a convenient scapegoat for her own shortcomings as a mother…an *eight-year-old* scapegoat? "Did you keep doing that?" she asked, somehow sensing that, as shocking as it was that any mother could leave a little boy with a man she knew would abuse him, that this wasn't the full crux of his self-hate. "Did you beat up everyone you met?"

He turned away, slamming the laptop closed. "For a while, yeah. Then, just before Dad died, I ran away. I joined a street gang in South Central L.A., and I did what it took to belong.''

As protected as she'd been, even she'd heard of the notorious activities of street gangs. She couldn't hold back the shudder. "Did you—''

"Steal cars? Steal liquor and drink myself stupid? Attack other kids who invaded our turf? Break into stores to get TV's and stereos to sell off for booze and drugs?'' he asked brutally. ''Well, that's what you have to do to belong, right?''

''No!'' she cried, shaking her head in vehement denial. ''No, I don't believe it. You wouldn't have gotten into the SEALs with that kind of record. And you wouldn't join the navy and hide your past, not with that on your conscience. I know you too well to believe it.''

McCall slanted her an odd, almost disbelieving look. ''You can't know that.''

''I *do* know! Don't tell me you did any of that, because I won't believe it! How long were you a part of the gang, and when did you get out?''

He shrugged, his mouth tight.

''How long before you left? *How long?*'' she almost yelled.

He shrugged again. ''A few months. My friend Casey came to see me. She was the only nice kid at school who'd ever liked me. She was a nurturer, I guess…one of those girls who'd pick up wild strays and nurse them. But when she came, it was my ''jumping in'' night, when all the kids would beat me up to see if I was tough enough to take it. I was— hell, Dad had probably broken just about every bone in my body already—but Casey wasn't.''

This was it. She felt it, knew it. ''What happened to her?''

''She got there just as it was about to start. She hugged me, and one of the girls—hell, some of them were worse than the boys—said hey, girlfriends get jumped, too. Casey was terrified. She begged me to get out, to leave with her then. She said I was better than this. But I was a guy, right? If Dad taught me anything, it was that I had to hang tough or lose respect. And where else would I go, home to Dad? I had to fight to keep my place, keep my respect. But I wasn't letting Casey get hurt. So I stood in front of her and told them they'd have to go through me to touch her.'' His fists clenched, and his face whitened, cold and hard.

''Tell me,'' she said quietly.

''You don't defy anyone in a gang. Twenty of them jumped me. I couldn't fight them all; most of the kids were bigger than me. I told Casey to run, but the girls made her watch

while the boys beat me unconscious, then they turned on her.''
He squinted, staring out the west-facing window to the deep,
peaceful indigo of the afternoon sky. He looked like a sculpted
piece of marble, cold and uncaring, but his hard, flinty voice
told her the truth. ''They left her in a gutter near Santee Alley.
Thank God someone found her in time to save her life, but
she was in the hospital for six weeks.''

''How long were *you* in the hospital?'' she asked softly.

''You don't get your hurts seen to in a gang, Beth. You
have to be tough and show them all you can take it. I couldn't
walk or eat for a couple of days. By the time I could, I was
out of there. When I found Casey, she wouldn't see me. Her
family guarded the room and threatened to call the cops on
me if I didn't get out and stay away. So I headed back to the
docks. Dad had been buried the week before. The house was
rented. All his stuff was gone. So I walked around the city for
a day or two. I woke up in an alley filled with the smell of
vomit, and worse. I looked at myself and felt sick. Just as my
mom predicted, I was turning into Dad. I was hungry and
hurting, lost and sick at heart. So I handed myself in to a
welfare office. When I got out of the hospital, I was put in
foster care south of Long Beach, away from my old life. I
took my foster parents' advice and went back to school. For
Casey's sake, I wanted to make something of myself. Show
her I could be somebody, even though the family moved away
as soon as she was out of the hospital. She was the only person
who'd ever shown faith in me.''

The late afternoon chatter of cockatoos and galahs taking
flight and kookaburras finding their nests was raucous, but
Beth barely noticed. She stayed crouched in front of him, so
lost in thought she barely felt the cramping protest of her legs.

What could she say? Horror filled her, but *for* him, for all
he'd had to suffer with no one to help him, to bind his wounds
or tell him they loved him no matter what.

But it was too late for trite phrases. He'd seen the problem
all along: there was a yawning gap between them, and not just
in birth. All her life she'd been adored and flattered, so much
so that she'd run free from the stifling atmosphere of being

constantly in such high demand. She'd been worn out in spirit because everyone wanted a piece of her.

Brendan probably would have given his left arm to have *one* person love or want him the way everyone had loved her. He'd probably give his life to have her pristine, clean background.

No wonder he'd never told her any of this before, when they were together. She now understood why he didn't feel good enough to lead a normal life. Even with all he'd done for the greater good in his years with the SEALs and the Nighthawks, all he saw in himself was a street fighter with a license to kill. Trained only to see the worst in himself and to try harder, reach higher, all he ever saw were his flaws. He had no idea what a wonderful, *magnificent* man he was…because when he looked in the mirror, all he could see was his father's reflection.

She knew how desperately he needed redemption, to forgive himself in a world that demanded perfection of him, but how could she help him find it? "W-why did you join the gang?"

His face twisted in self-mockery. "Because I'm a jerk, like my dad. I didn't care who my friends were. I found my level."

In agony, Beth closed her eyes. How could she make him see the man he was, the courageous, *honorable* man who'd risked his life for her when she hadn't deserved his help, had come from the boy he'd been? "You said you joined before your dad died. He died when you were fourteen?" He nodded. "So you were that young when you joined the gang?"

"Yeah," he growled, letting his hair fall over his face. Hiding the self-hate. Lost in the eternal night of self-recrimination, living and reliving his mother's words. "I was already a bad-ass punk by then. On the road to damnation."

"But you got off that road. You finished school, went to college, joined the SEALs, and now the Nighthawks. Can't you see it?" she cried when he shook his head. *"You were a child.* You didn't hurt Casey, you tried to save her! Do you think I don't have parts of my life I wish I could live over? You've spent the last twenty years proving who you really are. You're a man of courage and honor. Rising above your past—''

"Don't tell me you understand." McCall lifted a tired hand. "You can't. How do I atone for the things I've done?"

"Don't tell me I *don't* understand! I know what haunts you. It's with me, too, day and night."

His head snapped up, and Beth raised a shaking hand to her mouth as she realized what she'd said. But she couldn't take it back, and if she was honest with herself, she didn't want to. "I watched someone die." She let out a tiny sigh. "Someone who was too young and should have lived. I was also responsible for the death of a dear old man who helped me. Can I give them their lives back? I wish to God I could, but all I can do is thank them by keeping Danny and myself alive. I can't forget the things I've done, but will sacrificing my life make my past go away? Will it make me a better person to constantly hide beneath my mistakes, making it an excuse not to move on? All either of us can do is what we're already doing. Learn from the past, and do the best you can with your life from that point." Finally the cramps in her legs became stabbing bursts of pain, and she slowly rose to her feet. "So how is your life different from mine, except by accident of birth?"

Again he wouldn't face her, but only shrugged. "I'd bet yours were accidents you couldn't change, right?"

"No," Beth said quietly. "I have as much guilt to carry as you do. Maybe more."

He only shook his head, and Beth ached with tears unshed for the child led to believe that nobody could ever be worse than he was. Sad little Brendan, neglected and abandoned and abused, was still alive, tortured inside a man who wouldn't allow him to find absolution. A boy desperately needing to belong somewhere had done some stupid things, made some bad decisions. The boy had left that world of his own free will, made something better of himself, yet the man he'd become refused to see it.

After decades of self-hate, how could she show him the way to forgiveness when she barely knew the path herself?

She bit her lip, knowing that if her anguish couldn't make him soften, a simple reassurance wouldn't go anywhere near what he needed to know. Her hands started to shake, and she didn't know what to say, what to do. She'd given him all she had, and he still didn't believe. "I want to be with you, Brendan."

"Don't, Beth. Don't make the sacrifice because I did what I had to do for you." He reached for an untouched bottle of Scotch on the old-fashioned walnut cabinet beside the dining table he'd been working at. He now sounded only weary as he dropped his face into folded arms. "If you're going to run again, *damn* it, take Danny and *go* while you can. I hate booze, but I promise to get too stinking drunk to chase you!"

He was willing to give up his entire career to ensure her freedom—he'd said it all. He could be charged with treason—*again*—by letting her go...

She no longer needed to ask why he was dismissed from the SEALs. No matter what reason was given on paper, Brendan McCall was a decent and honorable man, upholding every code the SEALs lived and worked by.

Papa, you were wrong about Brendan...and your loving snobbery has caused him—and me—ten years of terror and pain.

A sharp-edged rock seemed to be lodged in her throat, and all the tears coursing down her face did nothing to ease the pain. She'd run out of words.

So don't use words.

A feathered kiss across the back of his neck was enough to get his attention. He lifted his face as slowly, gently, she trailed her fingers through his hair, bringing him up with her as she rose, turning him around to stand face to face. The next kiss was on his mouth, slow, deep, with all the love she felt for him. Her hands slid through his hair, bringing him closer, but he resisted her mouth and hands, holding back an intrinsic part of himself she craved to reach. It was as if he was waiting for some untold miracle...for words whose cadence she couldn't hear.

So she said the only words that came to mind, words touching the core of her own soul. "Can we get married properly when this is over? I'd love a real wedding in my local church, with my priest, standing before God and my friends. It might seem silly to you, but I'd like to be a bride walking down the aisle."

He drew back, his eyes searching hers, giving nothing. There weren't just shutters up inside him, there were brick walls. "Even when it's me you're walking to?"

The band around her heart tightened. "*Only* when it's you. Don't you get it?" she cried when he made no move, toward her or away. "I'm sorry I hurt you, but I was trying to save your life! If Danny's father sent the man who broke into my house and we'd so much as kissed while we were under surveillance, he'd have had you killed for touching me! I couldn't stand it, I couldn't *bear* standing at your grave when I—"

"No." The growl was quiet, but terribly harsh. He pulled away from her, tugging his sweater down over his aroused state. "Stop playing these stop-and-go games. I don't know what the hell you want from me."

Beth shook her head, but it wouldn't clear. He'd only accentuated his body, his ready state, by tugging down the sweater. Now a slow, delicious spin dominated her body, making her belly heat and starting a sweet pounding between her thighs. "I want you," she whispered, reaching out to lift the sweater he'd pulled down. *"Want you…"*

He froze for a moment before he growled a particularly crude obscenity, yanking his clothes back down. "I've done a lot of low things in my life, but I haven't stooped to getting lucky out of gratitude."

In the sweet whirling of her mind she heard the words, but couldn't process them. With a tiny sound of distress, she reached for his sweater, but he grasped her wrists, his eyes blistering-hot with need and denial. "No," she moaned. "No, please…"

"*Damn* it, Beth, will you *go?* I can't hold out much longer!" His hands still grasped her wrists, gentle but unbreakable. "We both know you'll regret this in an hour."

Without warning, she started shivering. "C-cold, Brendan…I'm so c-cold," she whispered. The words tumbled from her mouth. "Ten years of cold, without you. There's this big empty space inside me, this pit of black ice and it *hurts*. Hold me, Brendan…make me warm again, like you used to when the world made me feel so small and frightened…"

He froze. For long heartbeats, he didn't breathe. When he spoke it was guttural, a bare growl of disbelief. "Delia?"

Her fight was over. Secrecy had given way to the woman who only knew she needed this man so much, needed to help heal him so badly she couldn't think beyond him. With simple relief, she nodded. "Did you get your car back in one piece after that night?" she whispered, trying to smile.

A slow grin came to life, making his rugged, remote face warm and strong and beautiful. "Yeah, your Papa's right-hand man got word to me about a month later that it was at my apartment."

She blinked and frowned. "A month? After the scandal broke, and you'd left the States? He knew where to find you?"

He nodded, his smile slipping a little. "Yeah. I guess he did. I didn't think about that until now."

So it was true. Papa had known all along that Brendan was innocent, and he hadn't told her. *You will be happier in your own world, with a man who knows where you come from,* he'd said. *Is that not obvious from your lack of judgment with this man?*

She didn't want to think about it, not yet. One day she'd have to come to terms with what her father had done to her life, but this day, this moment, she could only think of one thing. "Hold me, Brendan. Touch me. The world's been wrong too many years, since Papa threw you out of my life, and only you can make it right for me again." She took a deep breath. "I need you—all of you. Everything that's made you the man you are."

She felt the trembling in his fingers before he let her wrists fall, and *at last* he gathered her close, his hard warmth filling the chilled places inside her. He rested his cheek on her hair like he used to a lifetime ago, when she was innocent, and believed love was all that mattered. "I knew," he rasped, "I knew this feeling in me couldn't be wrong. I saw you and *knew*.''

She nodded against his shoulder, her arms wrapped around his waist. The long-overdue sweetness of peace seeped into her heart and body with his touch, with the beauty of truth between them. "I hated lying to you, but after what Papa told me, and running from Robert Falcone—''

The frown was evident in his voice. "Falcone—''

The shudder worked its way through her. "Not now.'' She moved closer to him, burrowing in. "Please, Brendan, not now. It's been so long since I felt alive…you've haunted me for ten years like a ghost. You hovered around me, an un-healed wound that wouldn't go away. I was so *alone*.'' Her hands bunched up his sweater, and moved under it to find the heat of his flesh, caressing him in eagerness, in greed. She kissed his throat, a heated trail to his mouth. "I've missed touching you so much.'' Her voice was a throaty rasp, flinty with need. "Touch me, Brendan. You said I could have you. You promised…''

He lifted her face; his mouth met hers, hot and hard and *needing,* and she reveled in the hot-blooded glory of being with him again. "Be sure, Beth. Be very sure you want this,'' he rasped against her mouth, "because if you have me, you're mine, too. I'm a street fighter, baby, and I'll take on the whole damn world to keep you. No man will ever come between us again.''

Even as her blood sang hot in her veins in response to his raw words, she found herself looking at him in wonder. "You called me Beth.''

A small, lopsided smile. "You said Delia was dead. You want to be Beth.''

"Brendan, ah, Brendan…'' She gave a cry of joy, and launched herself into his arms.

Chapter 18

"Ah, Brendan, *meu querido, meu amado…*" A torrent of passionate words came bubbling from her in her native tongue, between fast, hot kisses all over his face. "We are going to make love—now—and you'll be mine," she uttered fiercely. "My man." She lifted her chin and faced him defiantly. "You think you're a jealous lover, McCall? Don't try to tell me the names of the women you've been with the past ten years. I'll scratch their eyes out."

He gave a low, husky chuckle, and nuzzled her neck. "I've got a tigress on my hands."

"Baby, you ain't seen nothin' yet," she said huskily. She unzipped her boots, and kicked them off; her socks followed; then, one by one, she loosened the buttons of her cotton-knit shirt. She shrugged it from her shoulders until it fell behind her, revealing her shimmering creamy bra.

"Beth." His voice came out strangled, harsh with hunger, watching her strip for him with eyes of a forest fire, burning alive. He reached for her. "Baby…"

She put a finger to her lips and shook her head, giving him the little mysterious smile of an aroused woman. "No, *meu amado.*'' She shimmied out of her button-up jeans and let them pool at her ankles, then kicked them away. A flick of her fingers, and her bra fell to the ground. Her panties followed, and she stood nude before him, proud of her golden, lithe model's body for the first time in a decade when she saw by his face what she did to him. ''Now. Put your hands on me. I want your hands on my body. I want you to do all those things you promised to do to me that night in my house.''

He made a strangled sound. ''I might find some things hard to do with my clothes on.''

She smiled again, and led his hands to her breasts. Her head fell back in abandon, in bliss, when he caressed her intimately. ''Yes,'' she murmured in a soft purr. ''When—when I can think again…ah, *Brendan*…''

He lifted his mouth from where he'd just gently suckled at her, with a smile. ''I love looking at you when you're aroused…it turns me on so bad I can't think,'' he growled, touching her breast's hardened peak with his tongue—and she writhed, crying out with the amazing unbearable *beauty*—

He nipped gently at her ribs, holding her up when her knees began giving way. ''Say my name again, Beth.'' A guttural command as he kept sipping softly at her, nipping with low, sexual growls between, saying all the things he wanted to do to her, with her, all the things he wanted her to do to him.

She gasped, soaring higher, burning brighter than she'd ever known before, even with him. ''Ah…ah, Brendan…yes, *yes*…''

''Take my clothes off, Beth. I want to be naked with you.''

She almost collapsed in a hot puddle at his feet. ''Yes, oh, yes,'' she muttered, and in joy, finally pulled that sweater from his body. Hunter had become prey, the tigress tangling with her mate, her master. ''Oh,'' she gasped, drinking in the sight of him.

''I've got a few scars from the job,'' he said, as if it was an admission of guilt. ''The big one is ugly.''

''Scars? I—don't—'' was all she could say. She couldn't see any imperfection; all she could see was Brendan, *her* Brendan, his glorious, dark, honed body half-naked and in anguish for her. Trembling hands reached out to touch the white-hot male beauty standing before her. "Oh…" She filled her hands, her senses, with him. Her mouth caressed the ridges and curves of his strong chest. Unbearable, shaking excitement grew in her as she caressed the hard ridges of his back, his waist, and kissed the flat planes of his belly, the pounding *want* so rich and beautiful it almost hurt—"Want," she whispered. She made a tiny sound of frustration when she reached his jeans and couldn't kiss more of him. "Want. Oh, want…" she muttered, her stupid tongue so filled with the ache inside her, she couldn't make any other words come.

Seconds later his jeans were gone, his underwear shed with them, and she groaned, looking at him, drinking in the rough-edged male beauty of him. "Want…oh, want…" She curved her hands around taut buttocks, kissed his legs, making guttural sounds of need and joy and discovery. Beautiful, glorious, perfect *male*…

She cried out in protest when he lifted her to her feet again. "No, Brendan…no…"

Then she wasn't on her feet, she was up in his arms, on the way to the bedroom. "Baby, it's now or I'm gonna lose it. Seeing you touch me like that—"

"No…want…" Unable to say more, she buried her heated face in his neck.

"I want, too," he growled. "I want to bury myself so deep in you I'll never find my way out."

She looked up at him, shocked and thrilled and intrigued by those crude, blunt, intensely sexual words. "P-please."

A slow smile curved his mouth, as one of his hands cradling her moved in soft, heated promise against her bottom, the inner curve of her thigh. "Oh, baby, I'm gonna please you all right. All the rest of the day, and all night."

She gasped, so turned on it was pain inside her, the sweet, lilting throb of her blood a hard, hot thudding driving her insane. "Brendan!" she cried, all but reeling with the explosions in her body. "Brendan, *now!*"

"Yes, now. We've waited too long." He laid her on the bed.

Arms feeling cold and empty within seconds, she opened her eyes and reached for him. His gaze was fixed on her, and she glowed at the hard hunger and raw male appreciation in his eyes, knowing that in his eyes she was beautiful, and more importantly, she was *Beth.* "Don't ever try to run from me again, baby—you won't make it a mile. You're mine now, and I keep what's mine."

She lifted her chin as her hands dragged him down. "The same goes for you, McCall. You're my man, and if you try to leave, or even look at another woman—"

He gave a low chuckle, lethal, sexual as he moved beside her, one leg trapping hers beneath him. "Yeah, you'll scratch my eyes out. So long as you try it in bed, do whatever you want to me."

"I'll remember that." Her gaze, even to her, felt as if it would send metal into molten blisters. "I'm no princess, McCall, I'm a woman who's—"

"Possessive, territorial and a tigress who purrs like a kitten when I do this…and this…" Hands and mouth worked their magic on her, and that low, helpless sound ripped from her throat as she writhed under his touch, and the hot, wet pulsing was unbearable. "Yes, *meu amado,* yes…please, love me now!"

With one smooth motion, he lay on her, his hands parting her thighs and his eyes hot and smiling at once. *"Meu amado,"* he said softly. *"Meu querida.* You know I speak seven languages, including Portuguese, and I know what you're calling me?"

She was beyond caring; her flushed face thrashed from side to side on the pillow, seeking coolness, seeking relief. She needed him so much she could barely breathe. "My love, my darling—you are, Brendan, you know you are. Please, now!"

She'd been prepared for pain, but when he filled her, after the first second of tearing her virginity, all she felt was a surge of exquisite gladness and relief. A torrent of Portuguese came from her lips, words of love, of need, of joy; when he stopped, gazing down at her, stunned, she grasped his hips. *"Não, não, meu amado, não pare, não agora, necessito-o…" No, no, my love, don't stop, not now, I need you.*

"Beth, what the hell—Danny can't be—"

"No," she cried, bucking beneath him in her anguish. "Be my Brendan now. Be the team commander later, I promise I'll tell you everything. Just love me now!"

But he held off, his eyes still glazed with shock. "Why?" It was as if he couldn't say any more.

She'd give him anything to make him love her body now, even the truth. "I couldn't live for me, not after what I'd done to her, and Danny lost his mother. And—and the thought of being this intimate with any man but you was obscene," she cried, twisting and writhing. "I couldn't make myself look at any man after you. I've felt dead inside for so long. Don't make me wait anymore. I want to *live*, and only you can bring me to life…"

He frowned and blinked. *"Obscene?"* he said slowly, looking completely stunned. "You waited for *me?*"

"Yes, I waited for you, and yes, *obscene!* When the people in my family love, it's for life, and no matter what they said about you or did to separate us, I love you, I always have and I always will!" Her hands moved over his body as she spoke, with all the urgency she felt, all the glorious anguished sweet hot *need.* "Please, Brendan, this feeling is pain, it's exquisite torture inside me. Can't you feel my pain? I need you now!"

Finally, oh, finally he moved in her, and she groaned with the release of exquisite pain into a pleasure so intense, so overwhelmingly beautiful she could barely stand it. She sought his mouth, letting him drown her cries with lips and tongue.

And when the gentleness stopped and he set the rhythm— oh, the rhythm, she couldn't breathe, couldn't think, could only *feel* and *be* and it grew, grew and shone like the sun, brighter and glowing, and her body took over everything, she wasn't in control and it didn't *matter,* for once nothing mattered but this moment and Brendan, *her* Brendan inside her, loving her—

Her cry was wild and unstoppable as the whitewater rush of sensation gripping her, taking her up, up and then down like a cascade, a fast-paced explosion of feeling. His name, just his name. Then other words came, another torrent of love murmured into his shoulder as he groaned her name, harsh and guttural, and shuddered against her.

She lay in his arms, beneath him still, holding him there as he kissed her face, her hair. Feeling the candle glow of exquisite happiness, reveling in being a woman with her man.

"I know it sounds trite, but—are you okay?" he murmured once he had his breathing under control.

She smiled up at him. "What do you think? I didn't exactly hide my feelings."

He rolled off her, but kept her in his arms. He was flushed, his body glistening with a fine coat of sweat, his hair damp and tousled from her fingers. His smile was bright as sunshine after clouds, rich and strong and free. "Does it hurt at all?"

She bit his neck softly. "I liked it, even the pain. It made me belong to you."

He groaned, lifted her face and kissed her, long and slow and hot, and the lovely tingling started again, the anticipation of more loving to come. "Hold that thought." Another kiss, soft and clinging, took her higher, damp and whimpering and *needing*. "I can't believe you waited this long," he murmured, his voice filled with wonder. "You waited for *me*."

She shrugged, smiling. "I told you, *amado*. We de Souzas love like that. Even when you were gone, I couldn't make myself want to, even when I knew it was dangerous to remain a virgin with Falcone so obsessed with the virginal Delia. And after Dan was, well, I couldn't allow myself to trust any man, or want them. I haven't looked seriously at a man since you left me, *meu amado*." She stretched against him. "It feels so good to call you that, to be able to speak in my own language again. I've worked so hard on my accent. I couldn't even let myself think in Portuguese."

He nuzzled her neck. "You want to talk about it, or play some more first? Do you need time to recover? It's your call."

He was ready again, and her body, already tingling, began the climb upward, the delicious pounding and languid heat.

She arched against him, then tangled her hands in his hair. ''Guess,'' she whispered as her mouth met his.

This time he was even more gentle, the tenderness beyond anything she'd ever known. Her big, dark Gypsy held himself in, touching and kissing every part of her, taking the time to give her slow-boiling pleasure so intense that she had to plead with him to take her…and oh, he did, just as slow and delicious and burning-bright. She turned and twisted beneath him, kissing and touching and filling herself with him, shadows and light, secrets and truth, bad boy and good guy and tortured hero. Loving every single part of him, McCall and team commander and her Brendan.

And after, she slid into sleep. A gentle, drifting sleep of peace and tiredness and trust, lying sprawled over him, her head on his chest, over his heart. ''I love you,'' was the last thing she said, a sweet whisper as she fell like rose petals into the first deep sleep she'd known in a decade.

And the man holding her, the man of shadows and secrets, moved one hand slowly toward his pager. *Subject took bait. Has confirmed ID Delia de Souza. Son with Skydancer and Countrygirl. Subject did not run. Location, Nighthawk training facility in Breckerville. Repeat, ID Delia de Souza. Will interrogate ASAP.*

Moments later, he saw the screen light up. *Roger that. ETA 1945 with team. Heidi okay. Good work, Flipper.*

His face twisted as he shoved the pager in a drawer. *Yeah, the complete career man,* he thought ironically, and gathered her dreaming form close to him in the closing light of day. He watched the sun go down through the west windows, just looking at her face; and he wondered if he'd ever hold her again, when she knew what he'd done.

Chapter 19

"No! Ana, don't be stupid, he's not following us. He doesn't know you've gone. He won't take Robbie! Ana, stop it! No! *Ana!*"

McCall, who'd jerked awake only moments before from his own dark dreams, gathered her close, soothing and caressing her until she fell back into quieter dreams.

So that's why she never sleeps a whole night through.

Yeah, they were kindred spirits, even more than he'd known. Her past walked the night with her just as it did with him, haunting them like ghosts unseen, darkening dreams, allowing no rest, no peace or freedom. Challenging every waking moment, shaping them as people. Keeping them in chains.

And with those few words, she'd just confirmed what he'd believed to be true from the moment he took her virginity.

Ana de Souza was the one who'd married Falcone. Beth had gone to save her, even after Ana had, it seemed, stolen Beth's identity and married Falcone under her name; and Beth had been in the accident that took Ana's life. She'd saved Danny, given him a life free of Falcone's filth, even if it meant sacrificing her own wants and needs.

And it wasn't Beth who'd ignored my calls, who'd refused to see me. It was Ana—Ana, who didn't have a clue who I was.

Freedom…sweet, beautiful liberty. Delia—Beth—had loved him then. She'd remained faithful to his memory, even while believing that he'd betrayed his country. She'd come with him today, made love with him, given him the priceless gift of her love and trust and virginity, still not knowing who he was, or whether he would betray her.

And I did.

And as fast as that, the walls slammed between them, even as he held her naked body in his arms, sated from their loving. There was no way back. He'd chosen the path he'd walked the past decade, the road of shadows and lies…and in doing so, he'd destroyed any hope of forgiveness. He'd tricked her into marriage, let her perform her innocent seduction, made love to her twice, all the while knowing he had betrayed her, and would again. He would take every piece of knowledge she'd given him and hand it to the relevant authorities, knowing she'd hate him for that.

Two roads. One betrayed her, Danny, and even himself, everything he'd ever wanted or dreamed of in life; the other destroyed every code he'd lived by since he'd joined the SEALs and the Nighthawks. Honor. Courage. Commitment. The greater good, the bigger picture—the faceless innocents who needed him to walk in the shadows, to not exist as a person, to kill if he had to, so that their daily survival was ensured.

The needs and hopes of three people, as against the thousands who would face Falcone's guns and bombs and drugs. There wasn't a choice. If he had to do it again he would, without hesitation.

That didn't mean he was proud of it; but self-hate was no stranger to his life. Neither was being alone.

He was what he was. A sealed juvenile file, courtesy of the navy, only locked the truth inside his heart. Yeah, he'd turned his back on his world, clawed his way through college and became a SEAL, then a Nighthawk; but he was still that kid beneath. The man only had a thin veneer of decency, honor and courage. He was the son of a dirty drunk, birth to death, the kid not even good enough for his own mom to love. He had to earn his place in the sun, had to fight every day to remain a man of integrity, and if that meant sacrificing the dream of home and love and family he still craved in his heart every day and night, so be it. He couldn't allow himself to hope that Beth, the original earth mother and fierce warrior-goddess for her son, would understand the bigger picture.

The guttersnipe eternally in love with the princess was a fairy tale with no chance of a happy ending. One day of happiness with her was all he was ever going to get, despite what he'd said about her being his woman—and he'd taken it.

And as soon as Beth awoke, it would be time to pay the piper.

Beth felt bubbles of happiness seeping through her soul as she came back from sleep, joy coming directly from the heartbeat beneath her ear, and the strong arms holding her close. And from feeling absolutely and thoroughly loved…

She sighed, feeling more content than she could have believed under the circumstances. For she knew what was coming. It might have been Brendan who'd taken her to bed today, but McCall the operative was always there, a part of him he wouldn't leave behind for long—not even for her sake. His sense of duty was too great a part of his makeup to submerge for love. It was intrinsic, undeniable, and she wouldn't love him so much if he didn't have such a strong code of honor, even if it meant he'd hand her over to his boss tonight. She had to trust in that sense of honor, to know he would never betray her.

"Mmm…" She stretched catlike over him, smiling at his body's immediate reaction, and knew he was awake. "I haven't slept that well in years." She allowed him to see the smile now, sweet and languorous, asking blatantly for more loving.

He didn't smile in return. "I gathered that, from your dream about Ana's death before."

She stilled. "All right. I was expecting the inquisition to start soon, anyway. Fire away. I'll tell you everything I can."

"No, baby," he growled with a brief, hard kiss. "You'll tell me everything. Period. We're out of time. Falcone's left his island, Beth—he's coming for you personally. We have to do this now, or not at all."

Beth sighed and nodded. "All right." Feeling oddly shy, she pulled the sheet against her bare breasts. "Can I get dressed first? I don't think this is your standard procedure to interrogate someone."

His mouth quirked a little. "I don't remember seeing it in the manual, or hearing it in Interrogation 101. James Bond might favor the approach, but it's too distracting." He walked into the living room to gather their clothes, naked and beautiful and mussed, musky with the loving they'd shared.

Beth ached, watching every step, wanting him so badly. *Thank you, God, for sending this man to me once again. Thank you for giving me the man I love to be my husband, and Danny's father...*

He came back dressed in his jeans and tossed her clothes over to her, turning his back while she dressed. When she made a soft coughing sound, he turned, a small tape recorder in one hand. He pressed "record" and spoke into the machine, his dark, musical voice cool and clipped, standing about six feet from her—the requisite distance in that damn manual, no doubt. Team Commander McCall had returned, the ultimate professional, and even expecting this from him, it hurt her in a way she couldn't explain. "Nighthawk Team Commander One, on Operation Falcon. This is a voluntary interview given by Delia de Souza Falcone—"

"No." Her interruption was sharp-edged. "That is not my name. I never married Robert Falcone. My cousin Anabella did, using my name, my birth certificate and my forged signature."

"Interview with subject Delia de Souza. Do you, Delia de Souza, give this information of your own free will?" he went on, relentless, but dropping the Falcone, at least.

She lifted her chin, sitting on the still-mussed bed with quiet defiance. "Yes, I do."

"Please answer the questions for the record." He moved the small microphone between them, but keeping his distance. "You confirm that you are Delia Isabella de Souza, the only child of the late Brazilian ambassador to the U.S.A., Eduardo de Souza, and his wife, Cristabel de Souza?"

"Yes, I do."

"You now live by the name Elizabeth Anne Silver?"

"Yes."

"State your last known address for the tape, please?"

"Lot 66, Parkfield Way, Renegade River, New Zealand."

"Were you living there legally?"

"No."

"For the record, are you the Delia Isabella de Souza who married Robert Falcone?"

"No, sir, I am not."

"Are you the Delia de Souza Falcone who is the natural mother of Robert Falcone's only known child, Roberto?"

Beth felt the blood drain from her face so fast she swayed. "Brendan, don't ask me that," she whispered. If he knew the consequences of what he'd asked…the possible consequences to Danny's life…

"Please address me for the tape as Team Commander McCall. Are you the birth mother of Robert Falcone's child, Roberto?" His beloved voice was cold, relentless—the voice of duty.

She squeezed her eyes shut, feeling the stinging tears trickle from between her lids. "No, I am not the birth mother of the child. My cousin, Anabella de Souza Falcone, who married Robert Falcone under my name, gave birth to Roberto."

"This is the child you now call by the name Daniel Silver?"

Agony gripped her. "Yes."

"Please speak up for the tape."

"Yes," she growled from between gritted teeth.

"For how many years did Anabella de Souza Falcone pass herself off as you, Miss de Souza?"

With a violent struggle, she regained control. She'd always

known this interview would be hard, but with the man she loved, her tender lover being the cold-faced interrogator, she felt violated—humiliated. "Just over three years."

"Was this substitution of lives done with your permission, Miss de Souza?"

"At first," she replied, now calm and cold. "My parents had just died. I wanted time to recover, and my work commitments didn't allow for that. I was under contract, so I had little choice...but Ana wanted to try my life. She'd just finished her final rounds of therapy for scoliosis—and she'd had a nose job that made her look almost exactly like me. I agreed to let her try modeling for a few weeks, and if anyone in the business knew about the switch, they didn't make a fuss. Maybe because I'd made it evident that I was no longer happy modeling. But Ana had always hungered for attention and reveled in the life, so much so, she wouldn't swap back. She ruined my reputation, made men think I'd sleep with anyone. I foresaw consequences I wasn't prepared to face. So I retired from public life, gave her my identity and took hers. I lived quietly in England for three years as Anabella de Souza, then after I took Danny I spent two years in England as Christina Le Mons, and for the last five years in New Zealand as Elizabeth Murray, then Beth Silver."

"Did Anabella Falcone marry Robert Falcone under your name with your knowledge and consent?"

She sat up straight, glaring at him. "I didn't know about the marriage until I read about it in the papers, and by then, Ana had convinced herself she had the right to marry Falcone as me, because she *was* Delia. She wanted the fame, and I didn't. I'd given up that life, and she'd done the hard work, increased my profile, made Delia de Souza someone apart from me. She'd met Falcone while she was fulfilling *my* contract."

"Why did you move from England to New Zealand and take the illegal identity of Elizabeth Anne Silver?"

She moistened her lips with her tongue. "When I first moved to England, I became the boarder of a man who'd worked for the Special Operations Executive, Churchill's spy network in Europe during World War II. A man who knew the business inside out, and he liked to talk to me about what he called 'the game'. He was demobbed after the war along with the entire division, tossed aside with another twenty operatives. Those people banded together and created their own post-spy group, men and women who liked to keep their skills sharp by seeking out peoples' secrets in their local areas and sharing their knowledge, in a room where the knowledge would never leave, so it hurt no one. Anyone they suspected of felonies, of course, they reported to the police.'' She smiled. ''Much to the annoyance of the local police at times. But it was basically harmless.''

She sighed and tucked a lock of hair behind her ear.

''Do you need anything…a drink of water?''

His voice was softer—not enough to be noticeable to many. Just to his lover. ''Yes, please.''

She accepted the water with quiet thanks, and gulped it down. Then she squared her shoulders and kept speaking. ''Dan Cassell was his name. He took me in as a boarder, showed me the area, and took me to the local evening college to learn pottery. I mimicked his accent, trying to sound English so that I would distance myself from all the baggage of Delia, and he never questioned it. And—and when I returned from Amalza with a baby, ten million dollars and enough evidence to send Falcone to the electric chair, he found me a new place to live, taught me to fly—he was a pilot with SOE. He also sent me to learn martial arts and to handle all kinds of weapons. He made all the necessary precautions to keep us safe.''

''Then what happened?''

The intrigued note in his voice would have made her smile at any other time. ''Ana had never been all that stable. She'd been in and out of hospitals all her life, and my aunt and uncle died when she was only six. She came to live with us, but she always had a love-hate relationship with me. I didn't have scoliosis, so in her mind, I was the pretty one. And when I got the modeling contract, and she only got more operations, she grew resentful.'' She sighed again. ''Falcone wasn't a kind husband, and his infatuation with her didn't last much past the honeymoon. He kept saying that she wasn't at all like the Delia he'd wanted. One day, after the baby's birth, she got tired of the gibes, and told him she'd duped him—she was Ana, and I, the real Delia, was living in England. He started searching for me that day. Thank God I'd been too angry with Ana to give her my address, and she burned her copy of my number once she overheard his plan.'' Her voice sounded flat, dead even in her own ears as she told him the rest of her unbelievable tale. "He planned to kill Ana and replace her with me. In his eyes, *I* was his real wife. He'd married the dream, Delia de Souza, and that was who he wanted, not some pathetic, overemotional substitute, as he called Ana.''

The silence lasted all of six seconds. "Go on.''

She nodded. "Ana called me and told me everything. She begged me to help her leave him, to get the baby away safe. She told me that Falcone let his hitmen play with the baby…that his men took recreational drugs near the baby, and people had liaisons openly in the house. She was desperate to get Robbie away from that kind of corruption, and I believed her. My parents brought us up very strictly, and though I understood why she'd gone wild when she first took my life, and made stupid mistakes, I knew she wouldn't want that life for her baby.'' She looked down, fiddling with her fingers. "I loved Ana, despite her problems—she was all I had. I promised to help. So I told Dan everything. He called in his people, and Hazel—she worked in the SOE, too—roped her son in. He was a fighter pilot in Vietnam and had his own charter business. I flew in to Amalza illegally with Ron and a few of Dan's friends to get Ana and Danny out.''

"What happened that night?''

She pressed her lips together and closed her eyes. Oh, dear God, she wanted to hold her hands to her ears, but nothing ever blocked out the agonized screams. They were wired in her head with amplified speakers covered in golden lettering: *guilt.* "Falcone couldn't kill Ana until I was installed in the house, but he kept her under guard, she and the baby and the nanny. We were in despair. I decided to show myself on Amalza, to distract him. I made a formal complaint to the police on the island as Ana de Souza, claiming he was abusing my cousin. Falcone couldn't let me believe that he was a wife abuser, not until he had me under lock and key as his 'legal' wife.'' She frowned down at her hands, watching them twisting, turning around each other.

"Go on," he prompted her gently.

"I called his house, demanding to talk to Falcone. I didn't give away too much—I came across as furious, suspicious of his motives, ready to press charges unless I saw evidence that Ana was being treated kindly. Falcone was smooth as cream, trying to charm me. I played Delia to the hilt for him. I said coldly that a man who locked my cousin in a cage like an animal was of no interest to me, beyond notifying his acts to the police. I said I had no desire to meet such a piece of filth, that I would remain in hiding until I saw for myself that Ana was well and happy. He was furious, I could tell, but he dared not take it out on Ana. He let her out, walking on the grounds every day while he grew obsessed with finding my hideout. And he grew more careless as I called him less and less, as I grew colder and more imperious—exactly the way he'd fantasized Delia to be. He became so careless that Ana collected the money and the evidence on him without his noticing. One night we went for broke. I kept him on the phone with me, and got him to deploy almost all his men to the other side of the island with an 'accidental' hint of where I was. When they left, I hinted at my sexual fantasies to keep Falcone riveted on the call—and Ana and the nanny snuck out of the house with the baby strapped to Ana's back. They made it to the trees Falcone kept by the walls. Ron climbed a tree and took Danny from Ana, and handed him to me.'' She felt the tender smile radiate from her face. Oh, that moment of pure joy, when she'd seen the child who would become her Danny for the first time…when she'd held him in her arms…

"Yes?"

She started. "Ron got Ana over the wall, then Lynette, the nanny. Then he and Lynette went in one car, and Ana, the baby and I in another. The plan was that we'd divide to confuse pursuers if necessary, but they didn't come." She shuddered. "But nothing I could say convinced Ana of that. She went off the rails, crying and screaming, accusing me of endangering her life to get mine back. She wouldn't shut up, and when I lost it and yelled at her that if she didn't like it I could take her back to her husband now, she panicked and grabbed at the wheel—and we hit a tree by the cliff face." A slow, shaking hand covered her mouth as the scene played over again in her mind, as it did almost every night, in vivid life-and-death color. "She screamed as we headed for the tree, and as we hit it, screamed in agony. But she didn't make a sound after that. She just looked at me, and then she died."

The silence grew. "I'm sorry for your loss." The stiff, formal words that eventually came from his mouth in no way conveyed the emotion in his eyes. The black, soulless eyes of a man who knew how it felt to watch someone die. The guilt of being left to go on, too tortured by the silent reproach to truly live and love and learn while they were cold in the grave.

Unwilling to give in, to share the emotion with him right now, while she had more to tell, she merely nodded.

"How did the car get down to the base of the ravine?"

"We—we pushed it over, Ron and Lynette and me. Ron—Ron said it was best to burn all the evidence possible. He wanted Falcone to think one of us was dead, maybe all three of us, if he'd believe that two bodies washed out on the tide. I had to do it," she said, her voice filled with quiet torture. "I had to help push my cousin off the cliff, watch the car explode on impact and incinerate her body, all to save her son. We took the suitcase with the money and the tape Ana stole, got into the other car, drove to the plane and flew back to England."

"Why did you leave England for New Zealand?"

She shuddered again. "Falcone kept looking for me. I was sure he knew who I was, that I had Danny. Old Dan—I named Danny after him, since he saved our lives—said it was too dangerous for me to live with him anymore. I moved in with Ron's brother's daughter, Ruby, a single mother in Newcastle. But one night Butch called—he was Dan's ex-gunner. He said Falcone's men were on to me...and they'd killed Dan, execution style through the head. He was eighty-five.'' She frowned, losing the thread of her story in the guilt that still drowned her every time she thought of Dan with a bullet hole in his forehead...

''You're bleeding, Miss de Souza.''

She tasted the metallic tang of blood in her mouth, and released the corner of her lip her teeth had unconsciously attacked. ''Butch didn't know what Falcone's men had found out, but I had to run. He booked me an e-ticket for Sydney to pick up at Heathrow—and he left a suitcase there for me with about five disguises in it for us, plus fresh passports I had to ditch in Auckland. He said I had to get to New Zealand without trace, and get to a given address in the Bay of Islands when I was certain my trail had grown cold. I rented a house for two months in Auckland until I was sure no one was looking for me in New Zealand. Then after I called to make sure he was still alive, I went to the address Butch gave me. Harry Silver was Dan's copilot, who moved out of England after the war, and he took us in as his granddaughter and greatgrandson. He created Beth, a single mother on the run from a violent ex-lover, and Danny Silver, her son, and the Bay people accepted us and protected us from prying questions, and warned us when anyone asked about us. Harry got us legallooking birth certificates from Dunedin, taught me how to fly a seaplane and drive boats. We settled in here, I opened my business, and our lives were quiet and happy. Harry died of a heart attack two years ago, but our identities were established in the Bay, and an escape route thoroughly practiced and assured. For the first time in years, I felt safe.''

''Where is the tape that Ana Falcone stole? The taped conversation that implicates him in the murder of U.S. Senator Bernard Colsten?''

She blew out a sigh. This was it, then—the final leverage she had to stay safe, given into the hands of these mysterious Nighthawks. She just prayed to God she'd made the right decision. ''Dan, Ron and I put it in a safe-deposit box in Zurich, along with Falcone's money, two days after I got back from Amalza. Only Ron or I can get it out now, and only together, to stop any chance of paid corruption. Both our handprints must be verified to get to the box. If Ron dies, a signed copy of his written permission, along with a legible handprint for verification, will come to me via three independent lawyers, two of whose names I don't know. And if I don't check in with the bank every Monday night—10 a.m., their time—and verify that I am alive, the tape, as well as two copies we made, goes to Britain, then on to the United States. One to the director of the FBI, another to the CIA, and one directly to the president of the United States via John Roth, one of the assistant directors of special ops in MI5.''

Silence, long and stunned. "Is this a joke?"

She lifted a eyebrow. "You've had people checking everything of mine, right? Have you found any money or tapes anywhere?"

"Answer the question for the tape. Is this the truth?"

At that, she got to her feet, looking hard into his eyes. "Yes. The tapes, and the money, are in Zurich. John Roth only knows what he has to do, not what's in the box. He's Butch's nephew, and assumes it's another spy game his uncle is playing.''

"You mentioned earlier that a man attacked you at the house in Renegade River." When she sighed an affirmative, he asked, "How do you know it was a male?"

Through gritted teeth, she growled, "Unless the woman in question had a problem with facial hair, and had rolled something hard down the front of her jeans, the person holding me was male, and turned on by trying to kill me. He was aroused.''

McCall nodded. "Thank you, Miss de Souza. This concludes my interview with the subject." He turned off the tape recorder.

Furious now, she decided to go for broke. "If I may be permitted to ask *you* a question, was our marriage today a joke, a plot to gain the evidence you're so desperate to get? Do operatives usually marry their subjects? Or does this show me how far you will go to—''

"Let's not do this. Keeping you safe—"

"Stop lying to me! I've put my damn life on the line here, and my six-year-old son's! Will you give me nothing in return—nothing but a piece of paper and a few hours in bed? Is *that* common practice for your operatives too?"

McCall swore to himself. He'd pushed her too far. He'd known it, even as he pushed; Beth had been through too much today. But the perfect SEAL and Nighthawk operative just kept going, relying on the inner strength that had kept her alive the past decade through a life worthy of a soap opera. "Beth…"

She gritted her teeth. "It's Miss de Souza to you, Team Commander McCall. Put the tape back on if you're going to incriminate yourself—or is it only me that risks it all here? Are you that much of a coward that you won't reveal what you've done to me for posterity? Is your damn career worth more to you than my life, or Danny's?"

He didn't answer; he couldn't. For Beth's words hit him like another land mine, blowing all his self-delusions up in his face. She was half-right, and that half made him feel like a piece of crap she'd just ground beneath her heel. Until this week, his career had meant everything to him.

Until this week, it had been all he had.

And after this day, it would be all he had once again. So he'd turned the tape off on instinct, sheltering his life and career as she risked everything on a throw, giving it all to him, body, heart and security, when he hadn't even given her any proof that he wasn't on the side of the devils.

She turned her back on him when he didn't speak. "When does your team arrive—including, I would guess, the lady who was apparently dead this morning—and where do we go after Zurich? Assuming, of course, that the offer of protective custody for us lasts beyond my giving you the tapes and the money? Assuming that your group will even remember me a week from now."

Yeah, she had it all down pat, including her assumption that Anson would conveniently forget about her once her part in world peace was played and their safety seemed assured. Hell, how did he answer her? "I'll personally ensure your safety,

Beth, yours and Danny's, for as long as you need it. You have my word on that."

She didn't laugh, as he'd half expected; a mere "Thank you" came from a throat that sounded choked with anything but derision. Then she turned back to him, her eyes burning bright, playing the star-queen once again—or was she? "I meant it when I said I love you. Did you know that? But you're going to leave me again. The white knight beds the girl, saves the world and rides off into the sunset."

A tiny droplet of blood appeared at the side of her mouth, showing how hard she was biting the inside of her lip. "You think I'm going to leave you, don't you, that I'll want my old life again? The truth is, it will be you walking away from me, just like the last time. I waited, I *waited* for you to call, but you never called to tell me that you were all right, that you were innocent or that you still loved me!"

"I did call, Beth," he growled. "I got your assistant, your manager, never you. I was told you refused to talk to me."

"You had my private cell number," she retorted. "You were almost the only person alive who had it. I was at home, even after Mama and Papa died, waiting for one word to prove that Papa was wrong about you!"

He couldn't look at her anymore. She was right—he'd been too much of a damn coward to call her at home, even after her parents died. Her last words as her father's men hauled her away had been *I love you. Call me.* And for all these years, he'd blamed her. She'd lost her family, and he hadn't even bothered to call the girl he loved at home to see if she was all right. Lost in his own sense of inadequacy, he'd taken the rejection he'd expected and disappeared, believing the worst.

Her parents had died. She'd been told he was a traitor. She'd had more than ample reason not to call him, yet she'd still waited for him. He had no excuse now, nowhere to hide. He'd caused them both a decade of loneliness. He'd left her alone when she'd needed him the most, because he was too damn scared to try and reach her. What a jerk. He didn't even deserve the honor of breaking the princess's heart.

What was there to say? She'd given him her heart twice,

and both times he couldn't explain that he was forced to walk away. He was a Nighthawk with a commitment to honor, duty and courage under fire that could never take second place to home and love and family.

Beth wasn't a second place woman. She *deserved* security, safety and a guy with a nice safe job who came home to her every night. Not someone like him, who put his life on the line every day.

"Is that girl alive—the one made up to look like me? Was this whole thing a scam to confirm my ID and get the tapes?"

Again, all he could do was nod.

She nodded, biting that poor lip again, abusing it so badly that he ached to kiss it better. She was so pale he had to shove his fists in his pockets to stop himself reaching for her. "Did— did you set up the whole plan?"

All he wanted to do now was close his eyes, but he made himself face her, looking into her eyes without flinching. "Yes."

"I see," she whispered, and fell silent for a minute—a quiet he dared not break. "Just give me one thing," she said eventually, her voice clogged with pain-filled hope. "Tell me that you'd still have wanted to marry me if I'd been Beth Silver. Tell me you'd really have let me go if I wanted to run. Tell me you didn't arrange this marriage solely because I am Delia, and all the stuff about caring about Danny and me wasn't a way to convince me to give you the evidence. Tell me you made love to me today because I was Beth...that part of you married Beth."

He knew the silence was too long; he saw the pain begin in those haunting eyes before he spoke, and he knew it would haunt his rare moments of sleep until the day he died. "I wish to God I could," he finally said, in a slow, hurting voice. "But I can't."

Chapter 20

She hadn't spoken. Not in the hour since he'd said those fateful words.

He'd only spoken the truth. He'd love nothing more than to give her the reassurance she craved, that he truly cared about her, but her questions had been too specific, and to only tell her that he loved her would mean lying to her again. His sad story about taking the fall for her if she wanted to run had been a fairy tale designed to break down her barriers, and the spectacular success of his plan left him feeling lower than he'd ever felt in his life.

I'm crazy about you, Beth. I swear to God, you took my heart the moment I saw you ten years ago, and it's tearing strips off me to leave you behind like this...

But the words couldn't be spoken, much as he ached for them to come out. She had to believe his lies. He knew her courage, her defiant, loving heart. If she believed for a moment the truth—that she was the only woman he'd ever love, and that she held his heart in her hand, and always would—she'd go to the ends of the earth, fight the world to stay with him.

And she'd live to regret it. In days, weeks, months—maybe

a year or two if he got lucky—she'd grow tired of the life he
led, the person that he was, and she'd want to leave him. And
the cycle of life would repeat: the flaming rows, the accusa-
tions, the cold silence his parents had endured before his
mother finally left. He might've only been eight, but the years
of screaming hatred before she left with Meg were burned into
his brain.

Danny deserved a better family life than the one he'd suf-
fered for so long and, like his mother with his father, Beth
deserved far better. She was too high above him, too pure,
strong and beautiful and—and *classy* for a guy like him. Pal-
aces had gutters, but only to get rid of the trash it didn't want.
Servants had their uses, but their own entrances and exits.
They had a job: to serve. And that was the way it should be.
He'd serve her now—keep her safe from Falcone—and he'd
already had more reward than he'd ever expected. Her words
of love as she'd worshipped his body would live inside his
heart until the day he died. *Which could be any day—and she
deserves better than that, too.*

In the velvety purple of evening, she stood in the shadows
of the veranda, a frozen wraith who held up her hand when
he tried to talk to her, or make some half-assed explanation
even he knew was lame. She shrugged on the jacket he put
on her when he couldn't stand watching her shiver anymore,
but she didn't give him a word of thanks, or even acknowledge
that he was there.

And he just kept standing in the fuzzy light behind the door,
leaning against the doorjamb, watching her. Hating himself for
not having the strength to walk away.

Anson and the team arrived right on time. As they spilled
out of the choppers, the lethal force, she didn't move, didn't
speak, didn't acknowledge anyone—not even Heidi, who shot
a half-apologetic glance her way as the two women stood par-
allel.

But when Anson passed her, not bothering to speak to her,
she spoke seven quiet, bitter words. "Congratulate McCall.
You've got what you want." She stepped off the veranda and

walked into the night, letting it enfold her like a cold lover's touch.

Yeah. Nice irony, McCall.

Anson's face was as close to jubilant as it would ever be. "She gave you what we need?"

McCall nodded, pushing past him. "Tape recorder's in the bedroom." He ran down the stairs.

"Flipper, don't do it," Anson said quietly. "She doesn't want you, obviously. I'll send Braveheart to find her. He's always good with the women in distress."

"Maybe, but this is *my* woman," McCall snapped, "and I caused her distress by putting duty first and getting the evidence. Go listen to it, boss. It's all you care about. I'll clean up the mess my brilliant plan left behind."

"Best to end this now, Flipper, before it goes any further—there's always collateral damage in a war."

McCall stalked back up the stairs and shoved his face right in front of his regional commander, the man he'd admired beyond any other—until tonight. And for once he didn't give a damn if his career went up in smoke. "No man knows about collateral damage better than me—but this 'damage' happens to be my wife, and the boy who is now my son. Did you think of that when I set this scam up? I did—I knew I'd be committing myself to them today. I'm responsible for their lives and happiness from this day on. I want to be there for them when they need help, or when their safety and security are in question. They're my family now."

Anson sighed. "I guess I don't know you as well as I thought I did. This is the job, Flipper. Whatever gets the job done is worth the cost. Give them a safe place to live, enough money to be comfortable and a certificate of divorce when she's ready to move on. You did your duty. No—more, you've done a top-class job today, and I'll be recommending you for a—"

McCall let Anson know what he thought of his recommendations with a few crude words. "You know, I didn't believe Irish when he said you'd let Beth and Danny drop as soon as you got the evidence. I didn't believe Skydancer when he said saving the world means more to you than the life of a real, living child in front of you. But they were right—about me as well as you. Too long on the job has made us inhuman. Do you care about *anyone*, Anson? Do you love anyone, or do you hide behind your desk every day, go home to an empty house and pretend that saving the world is enough to make you a better man than the snot-nosed punk you were on the streets of New Orleans?''

His boss flinched—literally flinched. "Go." The word was harsh, flintlike. "If it makes you feel better, find your woman, make things right. Get involved, McCall—and then you'll see how damn far it gets you." His face was white and strained, his eyes dark with ancient pain, buried deep and rotting from within. "Love her, give her and that kid all you've got, and watch as it all explodes in your face like one of Falcone's dirty bombs.''

McCall didn't even hesitate. He turned and vanished into the cold night, calling, "Beth! Beth!" Too late, he knew how wrong he'd been in choosing duty over love. He hadn't realized until he'd looked at how inhuman he'd become in the past ten years, living only for the job. He'd treated individual people as pawns, as unfortunate victims, acts to avenge or criminals to capture—or that dirty term he hated now, *collateral damage.*

Beth had made him care again. Danny had made him see just who it was that he was fighting for. They'd brought him back to life, made him a better man. Beth had given him back his heart—because she'd always had it, from the day they'd met, and having her heart in return made him complete. Without her, he'd return to the silent, isolated half barbarian he'd been all his life.

Tonight, looking in Anson's hollow, bitter eyes, he acknowledged a simple truth—he wasn't meant to be alone, as he'd always thought. He needed that one special, wonderful woman wandering in this darkness somewhere, the woman he loved with all his heart and soul and body and mind.

He didn't want to end up soulless and alone, like Anson. He didn't want to be a hero, with only the satisfaction of a job well done, memories and a pension when he grew old. He wanted to be an ordinary guy with a home and a dog and people to love, who loved him. He needed Beth, to become that man. He needed Danny in his life, to keep reminding him of what he fought for every day, to remind him that he was neither human refuse, nor the center of a save-the-world universe. He loved them—both of them—with an awe-inspiring, protective ferocity he wouldn't have believed just two weeks ago. Beth was his woman—Danny was his son—and he really would fight the whole damn world…even kill whoever he had to—to keep them by his side.

Now he just had to convince her of that.

How did she face him?

Beth stood shivering near the boundary fence by the McCluskey farm, fighting the temptation to get Danny and run. To find somewhere quiet—preferably without any spies—and lick her wounds.

How far would we get, anyway? Mitch and Lissa would report it before I got Danny out of bed, and he'd *be here, blocking my way.*

No, staying here was better.

Yes, standing shivering in the dark makes a lot of sense, her inner voice mocked her. *Making a fool of myself one way or the other, but at least this way he doesn't see me cry.*

It was really sad—pitiful, actually. But it was the ugly truth. She'd taken on another identity and crossed the world to escape the life she'd wanted to leave behind, but the voice of yesterday had overtaken her anyway. Delia de Souza, the stunning waif who'd had men around the world at her feet…who'd had *Brendan* at her feet…had tasted her first sexual rejection, the first rejection of her heart at the ripe old age of twenty-eight…and maybe she wasn't as mature or humble as she'd thought.

Realizing that she'd bought into the Delia legend as much as people like Falcone wasn't an epiphany she relished. Maybe she hadn't enjoyed modeling, but it had sheltered her from some of life's harsher realities. In her glittering world, *she* was the one who'd rejected men. *She* was the one who'd kept her distance. *She* was probably the one who'd hurt countless people the way Brendan had hurt her today.

Dear God—have I always been this self-centered?

"Beth! Beth!"

He'd been calling her for the past few minutes, and every time she'd moved somewhere else. Childish and stupid, considering all they'd been through today, but she hadn't been ready to see him. *Delia, the proud, immature child, strikes again.*

Beth lifted her chin and walked toward where she'd heard his voice last. "Is it time to go?" she asked in as calm a voice as she could manage.

"Beth." The growl was low, predatory—ragged. He appeared from the darkness, snatching her into his arms so fast she stumbled into him. "I thought you'd gone," he whispered in her ear, sending a hot shiver down her spine.

"Where would I go?" Her voice amazed her, cool and controlled, the exact opposite to the heated need and gladness she felt at being so close to him again, his passion for her driving the cold away. "This is a Nighthawk training facility, so I presume the whole perimeter's covered. I can't take Danny without you knowing. You told me I wouldn't get a mile if I ran. I believe you. Until you have the tapes, at least." As the sweet agony of being pressed against his body threatened to overwhelm her—oh, how she wanted to press her lips to his throat, his chest, his mouth and on down—she moved against him. "I told you, I won't run. You can let me go."

"No, I can't," he muttered, rough and hot. "I need you." His hand tipped up her chin and his mouth was on hers, conquering, demanding it all. He walked her backward until she was up against a tree, his hands hard on her body, claiming, branding her with a searing iron.

McCall's woman.

Somewhere in her hazy passion, she made an unconscious decision: *this is the last time.* But the pounding excitement took over. This was going to be wild—no bed, no gentle play.

He was going to take her standing up in the cold night, in a paddock against a tree…

And I'll take him, too, she thought in fierce gladness, seeing the raw man come to life from beneath the protective knight, hard and demanding and unapologetic. *This is me,* he seemed to say with every growl, every kiss and touch—even when he almost tore her jeans off, and her panties—and she loved every second of it.

My man. Mine. If he was going to leave her after tonight, she'd make absolutely sure he didn't forget her.

She claimed him with every hot, dragging touch over his skin, with nipping kisses on his throat and shoulders, pulling at his jeans. "Now, McCall. *Now,*" she demanded.

"Wrap your legs around me," he muttered against her ear, breathing harshly.

The excitement was unbearable, the loving fast and raw, slaking violent need. She climaxed within seconds, and to her shock, the taut spiral started again. She whimpered and writhed against him, desperate for more, and he responded with guttural sounds and moving in her even harder, deeper, and her body shook with the pleasure-pain gripping her entire body.

"That's it, let go," he whispered in her ear, gravel-edged, lush and dark and hot.

His words drove her over the edge. She gave a wild cry and let go, in beautiful, mind-disintegrating release. He followed her with a low growl and kisses to her mouth he couldn't seem to stop. He cradled her close against him, his hands protecting her from the roughness of the tree, as he'd done the whole time. He held her as if she was more than just a mission subject or a one-night stand, and though she tried so hard to remember why it was a bad idea, she couldn't fight her need to lay her head on his shoulder and whisper words of love in her native tongue.

"Flipper! Return stat!"

The call snapped her out of floating euphoria. She gasped, "They have flashlights. They'll see us!" He let her go, and she slid to the ground and scrabbled around in the dark, trying to find her clothes.

"Here!" he whispered.

She grabbed her jeans from him and pulled them on fast. She was still fumbling with the top button when a high-powered flashlight beam hit them. A woman's voice spoke. "Scarecrow cracked after interrogation—it was Scarecrow who attacked you in the hangar. Falcone bought him four months ago."

"Not long enough to be the rogue—and he's too new. He doesn't know enough," McCall muttered, sounding frustrated. "And how the hell did he get into the facility?"

"We don't know," the woman confirmed, "but we don't have time to investigate. Something's going down. He told us a shipment of arms is less than twelve hours from landing in Dilsemla, Commander. Suspected Iglas on board. We've been told to intercept the shipment. There're two navy ships ready to take control once we secure the ship, but the government wants us to confirm the reality of the arms on board before they get official."

"Let's go," McCall said briskly, heading for the house while Beth listened in. "What's the ETA?"

"Skydancer has a 35A Learjet in the hangar. ETA six hours if we push it."

"Who's piloting?"

"Skydancer, sir—you know he's magic with any kind of plane—with Panther copilot. You're needed to protect your subjects until you take point in the underwater mission."

Beth blinked, startled. "Am I going to this—Dilsemla?"

"No." McCall's voice was sharp as a honed knife. "I refuse to take a civilian—not to mention a child—into a damn war zone!"

"You have no choice, Flipper. Orders are direct from Virginia this time." McCall's boss stepped into the circle of light illuminating them as they headed for the house. "We're the closest team—there are two full teams here, including PJ and SEAL-capable operatives. We can't leave her here. We need her if we can't get a direct link from these weapons to Falcone.''

"They can use Malaysian SEAL team," McCall argued.

"They're deployed on a critical mission. We're the only team close enough to handle this without government interference.''

"Then we leave Beth and Danny with Countrygirl," McCall sounded so fierce, so protective.

"Yeah, that'll work," his boss retorted witheringly. "A woman who's outrun the CIA, MI5 and the Nighthawks in two continents—not to mention Falcone—will still be here in a week if we leave her with a woman with four kids, including a newborn baby.''

McCall snapped, "I'm not taking my wife and son into Dilsemla. It's not happening!''

My wife. My son. He was claiming her publicly—she and Danny both. What had changed his mind in the last hour? "Where's Dilsemla, and what's an Igla?" she asked to diffuse the fight.

They both turned to her, McCall scowling ferociously, his boss hesitating, his face closed. Yeah, he was a control freak, all right. "I think I have the right to know where I'm going, since it seems I *am* going," she argued, with a small, ironic smile. "I won't risk my son's life on your say-so, um, 'boss.' No offense, but I can't see you putting our welfare before your objective.''

The man's face softened with a grin, bringing forth dimples—things a man as hard-ass as he was shouldn't have. "None taken, Ms. Silver, and call me Ghost. Dilsemla is the capital of Tumah-ra, an island in the Arafura Sea, near Timor.''

"Ah." She nodded. "The oil fight? I gather Falcone sells his illegal arms to the rebel forces and warlords who are after control of the oil shelf? You have to stop a shipment now?''

"Yeah. Guns and bombs and Iglas," McCall said grimly before his boss could speak, "which are Russian-made portable one-man launch missiles, favored by terrorists worldwide to attack planes or army bases up to four miles away. It's too dangerous for civilians, Beth. It's no place for you and Danny.''

She turned on him in a flash, so appalled and offended that he still saw her as the pristine princess, she forgot her own fears and obsessive need to stay safe. "Oh? I can risk my life and safety for the sake of these people, but it's no place for me? How do you figure that, Team Commander?"

"You're great at stealth and hiding," McCall shot back, "not point-blank shooting at a kid holding a damn MP-5 in your face!"

"Excuse me," McCall's boss broke in tersely, "but since the shipment's less than twelve hours from Dilsemla, I think you two can keep the argument for the jet."

"She's not going, boss. I won't let it happen!"

"She and the boy are going to Makanra, Flipper. It's been a safe zone the past two months, held by the Australian SAS and the Tumah-ra government. A full team will be in situ to protect them while you're on point, as well as an SAS team within a ten-minute radius. We need you to take point on this—it has to be a SEAL-type mission, and the Malaysian-based SEALs can't do it. Damn it, Flipper," he growled as McCall planted his feet, his face dark, "think about it. If the rebels get their hands on some Iglas—"

Beth saw the tiny shudder rock McCall's frame. "A full team to protect Beth and Danny?"

"Eight, fully armed, and right near the jet if they need it."

Slowly, he nodded. "We'll leave the puppy with Country-girl."

As if it were a signal, the Nighthawks dispersed, including Ghost. McCall put his hands on her shoulders. For her comfort, or his? She didn't know—she had no idea what was going on in his mind. But one thing she had no doubt about now: however he denied it, whatever he said or did to push her away, he cared about her.

"You might as well say it," she said quietly. "You can't do any more damage to my illusions of self-determination after that display of control over my life."

He sighed, and pulled her close. "I'm not trying to control

you, Beth, I'm worried about yours and Danny's safety on the island. And that worry will transfer to my concentration on the job, and that will put the entire team at risk.''

The bald, stark words stopped her mid-stride. ''Oh.''

''It's a war zone, with the full show—soldiers, rebels, sniper rifles and bombs. Men who'd sell their grandmother for another bullet to pump into the enemy. There's no guarantee of your safety, or of Danny's, even in Makanra,'' he said quietly.

She looked up at him. His bronzed face was pale in the ring of light from the veranda, his eyes black as onyx. Resisting the need to wrap her arms around him, she said what needed to be spoken. ''Can you give me an ironclad guarantee that I'll be safe here, that nothing can happen to me if I stay here with Lissa, or if I go home to New Zealand? Tell me Falcone's men can't find us here, and I'll stay behind, and promise to be here when you come back.''

His eyes burned into hers for a full minute, blazing hot with fury; then his shoulders slumped. ''I hate this whole situation. I just need you to be safe,'' he muttered, pushing a lock of stray hair back from his face.

She couldn't weaken now; too much hinged on this. So she stood straight and still, watching him. ''I need Danny to be safe and free. And I believe our best chance of achieving it is with you and your team rather than alone here. They know too much, and I couldn't put Lissa and her kids at risk.'' She sighed. ''The truth is, I can't do this alone anymore. I'm exhausted. I have nothing left. I need your protection.''

McCall's head snapped up at her words. His eyes searched hers with intense question.

Beth shrugged. ''Whatever you've done to me personally, our best chance of safety is with you. Your people will protect us with their lives—at least until they have the tapes. And a war zone is the last place Falcone will expect us to go.'' She held out a hand to him. ''So, can we compromise?''

Before she could react, he pulled her flush against him. ''Meeting halfway,'' he murmured against her mouth, and in front of the entire team now exiting the house, he kissed her, long and hard, leaving no one in doubt that they were together.

"Flipper. To the van. Stat." Ghost tossed him a bag, which McCall turned and caught with ease. "Heidi has your bag, Beth. Danny's at the jet with Skydancer."

The pretty Asian woman tossed Beth her backpack. "There's a change of clothes, and a shower on the jet," she whispered as she passed Beth, moving on so that she missed Beth's vivid blush.

"What's going on?" she asked quietly, as they ran for the jet. "You made your feelings clear a few hours ago, yet now you're claiming us, as if we really are married."

"I am. We are."

Beth's head spun with all that had happened to her today. She couldn't work any of this out. "Why did you change your mind?"

"Isn't it enough to know that I did?" McCall led her down the stairs, toward the van that would take them to the local runway.

She wanted to scream, to hit him. And he'd accused her of playing games with him? "No, it's not enough. You're controlling my life again, and I won't let you without knowing why."

He shrugged and kept walking, holding her arm to help her over divots in the long dirt driveway. "You told me you love me, Beth. You want to be with me."

She bit her lip, but refused to lie to him; she'd done with lying. "Yes, I do love you. But so does Danny, and he's an innocent little boy who'll thinks he's getting a daddy forever. And I'm not willing to risk you disappearing again, and breaking his heart. Mine I can cope with. Not my baby's."

He led her over the cattle grid to the road. "I wouldn't hurt Danny." He sounded amazed she'd even think it. "I'm crazy about that kid. Do you think I'd leave him to the life I went through?"

"Not intentionally." She stumbled along beside him, speaking without rancor. She was too tired for anything but bald facts. "But a child needs the stability of parents who also love each other, and while I love you, you don't love me."

They reached the dark, oversize van. She climbed in, finding a space beside Heidi, but one click of his fingers and Heidi, with an apologetic smile, moved to the back. Beth sighed and looked out the window as he moved in beside her, close but not crowding her.

Not physically, anyway, she thought, scrubbing at her burning eyes with a fist.

"No, baby. I didn't make my feelings clear. I didn't tell you the truth." His voice was a gentle growl in her ear. "I did set up the op—the escape, and the marriage, even telling you I'd let you disappear—to make you tell us who you are, and get the tape. But I didn't tell you how I feel about you."

"Then don't now," she said wearily. "I don't know what's lie or truth with you anymore." When he moved his mouth to her ear, she held up a hand. "People can hear us, I'm too tired for an argument, and I have to explain to Danny yet again why he isn't getting this sleepover with his friends."

She felt him move away, but the reluctance hit her in waves. "This isn't over."

Tell me something I don't know, she wanted to retort. If she knew one thing, it was that it wasn't over with McCall. It never would be, until she could forget him. And from her experience in the past decade, that wasn't going to be an option.

Chapter 21

"Second recon of island's perimeter before landing, boss?"

"Affirmative, Skydancer," Ghost replied, his voice taut with the same exhaustion affecting them all. They'd all caught naps except Skydancer and Panther, who would be remaining behind to guard the jet; but it was sleep fraught with expectation, of preparation for the job ahead.

McCall had something on the table before him that looked like an oversize laptop but Beth suspected was not. "Falcone's ship is about 27.4 nautical miles out of the northern port. Two midsize boats are 2.6 nautical miles from port, heading toward the ship—customized Stingray cruisers with full defensive measures." He speared a quick glance at Beth, with a sleeping Danny in her arms. "This is gonna be ugly, boss—and we have less than two hours to get this done."

Beth couldn't answer. Ever since dawn began breaking ten minutes before, her gaze had been glued to a screen in front of her and she couldn't make her mouth work.

This Learjet had high-powered video cameras built into the underwings, relaying images to the TV screens inside. Satellites gave up-to-date information on movements of troops and rebels below. Beth kept Danny's face turned away from the screen, muttering fervent prayers that he would sleep until the jet landed, and he wouldn't have to see—

Carnage.

Horrified, nauseated and with a half-unwilling, *this-can't-be-real* fascination, she watched image after image flash up on the screens as the jet rode high over the island's perimeters. Bodies, hanging on trees or hacked apart by machetes, left to rot or be eaten by wild creatures, or piled high in open-pit graves. People running for their lives from boys who looked no older than fifteen, carrying assault rifles. Girls dragged away by the hair. People begging for their lives, shot without hesitation or mercy. Buildings torched and burning. And every few moments, the silver flash of bullets from automatic weapons, and people fell down...

And Danny's father sells these weapons to terrorist groups.

But for once Beth couldn't feel personal horror, or adopt her ever-ready defense mechanism of *anything to protect Danny.* For she'd finally seen the bigger picture McCall tried to paint—she and Danny were not the only ones in desperate need of protection from the conscienceless abomination that was Robert Falcone.

If I'd gone to the CIA years ago with the tape, those people down there would be alive right now.

In her frantic need to keep Danny safe—to keep herself free of Falcone's obsession with her—she'd been responsible for those deaths, and countless others in war zones and under dictatorships around the world.

"Don't blame yourself," McCall murmured for her ears alone. "You had a hell of a decision to make, and a baby to care for."

Too lost in the horrors happening right below her to be surprised by his acumen, she whispered, "But they're Falcone's weapons. Weapons he wouldn't have been free to sell but for me!"

A warm, strong hand cupped her shoulder. "If not Falcone, someone else. There's always another piece of scum ready to sell weapons to anyone. That's the harsh reality of life here."

"No." Her voice was scratchy, her eyes growing wider as the nausea threatened to overcome her. "The reality is that I am, by my decision to save myself and Danny alone, responsible for those people who just died. Oh, dear God, and I called Falcone a monster. I go to church. I hear the priest talk about loving your neighbor as yourself, but I never once thought of the people who would die while I stayed hiding in the shadows, believing I was the only victim. All the time I fought you, hating you for not leaving us alone or appreciating my sacrifices, I never once realized what you said—that others could die for my inaction." Her stomach heaved; she made a distressed sound.

McCall took Danny from her. "Beth—" With his free hand, he reached out to her.

She shrank away. "No! Don't touch me. God forgive me…" She lurched to her feet and stumbled to the bathroom.

"Right," Anson said quietly into the feed mike. "Flipper will take point from here."

In the gentle light of morning, fourteen nautical miles out to sea from Tumah-ra, McCall cursed the sunshine peeping out from behind the cloud cover he'd hoped would last. The navy ships and choppers were out of unaided sight, but even with the four RIBs—the rigid inflatable boats heli-cast from the choppers, specially made to look as inconspicuous as possible—they could be visible to anyone with strong binoculars. "Our objective is to intercept and take control of the Stingray cruisers six nautical miles from meeting point. They've disguised the ship as a fishing hull, but they'll have sophisticated radar as well as Falcone's weapons. We have to get in fast, take control, find the weapons and let the navy move in. Disable and disarm attack. Take all possible prisoners."

Irish and Songbird, here as medical backup, were lying flat at the back of two of the RIBs, scanning the ocean back toward the war-torn island with high-powered binoculars. Both murmured at once, "Cruisers coming into sight."

McCall nodded. "Roger that. Prelim team, mask up."

Wildman, Heidi, Nightshift, Braveheart, Phantom and

McCall covered their last inches of exposed skin, to protect them from the lethal box jellyfish common to the area. With a nod, he sent them all quietly splashing into the water. With closed-circuit communication McCall spoke to the team as they swam full bore four feet underwater toward the cruisers. "RIB team, set it up."

Those left behind in the RIBs got out mock fishing gear to divert any watchers in the cruisers, and give the underwater team as much time as possible.

"Underwater teams, divide in two," McCall uttered tersely when the churning of the water let him know the targets were in range and they'd taken the bait. They'd switched direction to check out the RIBs more thoroughly before meeting the ship.

All six prepared their spearlike grappling hooks for deployment. Heidi, Wildman and Braveheart detached from the other three, heading toward the second cruiser.

"Prepare hooks. Submerge, and wait for the signal."

The six swam deeper underwater, and waited for the cruisers to pass them.

Beneath, McCall waited. *Three. Two. One.*

The boats came over their heads at medium speed, slowing to approach the RIBs. *They're not in full throttle,* he thought. And wondered why. "Deploy."

"Where are we going, Mummy?" Danny asked as Beth led him away from the safety of the jet.

Beth gave a quick, fearful glance backward. The sight of Mitch, whom she now knew was Skydancer, following them, his weapons hidden with an understanding smile while Panther and another three Nighthawks—she'd forgotten their code names—guarded the jet, reassured her.

Mitch said this area was as secure as any in Tumah-ra could be. The government controlled the village, and she and Danny were completely safe so long as they didn't leave its boundaries, and always had a Nighthawk with them. But if she'd learned anything in the past week, it was that safety and con-

trol were as shifting as sand in wind, illusory terms that meant
nothing when faced by true strength, or real evil.

This morning, Beth had felt a terrible, crying need for
help—for forgiveness. Brendan and his teams were about to
risk their lives to rectify her mistakes. To intercept a shipment
of arms that wouldn't be on its way here if she'd had the
courage to speak out. To save people she hadn't even consid-
ered in her fears for only herself and Danny. And as the jet
circled the village of Makanra just on sunrise, preparing to
land, she'd seen the sign.

Its denomination was uncertain, its western roof and wall
partly burned, its bell tower bordering on decrepit, looking as
if it had been ransacked more than once, but it was still a
church. And when they got news that Brendan and his aquatic
team was about to board the boats of the gunrunners, Beth felt
anxiety bordering on panic. She needed strength and peace
now.

"We're going to church, sweetie," she whispered back to
Danny. "We're going to pray for Brendan and his friends,
okay? But you have to be very quiet, stick close to me and
watch where you're going. There are some bad people around
here."

Danny, who was as sensitive to her feelings as he was to
the atmosphere, merely nodded and said softly, "Okay,
Mummy." He walked subdued at her side instead of in his
usual hop-skip fashion, smiling with open uncertainty at the
people staring at his fair skin and round eyes. "Brendan said
to call him daddy since you guys got married," he remarked,
his little voice shaking.

Yes, he felt it as much as she did, felt what was coming to
them. She could smell it even. *Danger....*

God bless him, her baby was trying to distract her, to make
her think happy thoughts. "Really, sweetie? Wow, huh?"
Though she tried to follow Danny's lead, she kept casting
worried looks right and left, clutching his hand. She scurried
toward the church, her apprehension growing with every step
she took. Seeing shadows moving where none should be. Find-

ing specters in silence, evil inside the stares of children who were only fascinated by her blue eyes.

They'd passed the strange-looking Irish pub—what a crazy place for it—past a school that looked long closed, and had almost reached the tiny church; but suddenly her knees shook, her stomach seized and the hair at the back of her neck lifted. She wheeled back, making Danny yelp as she yanked him around. "Hurry up, sweetie, we've got to get to the church…"

Then the shadows beyond the trees at the end of the village gelled into human forms—forms bearing guns. The villagers scattered without a word, and she didn't need Mitch's sudden presence right behind her, or his quiet whisper of, "Run for the church," to know that they were all in grave danger.

The SAR-21S amphibious assault rifles he'd specially modified acted as one when the team hit the release buttons. Six spearlike objects shot out from above the sights, blossoming into four-clawed grappling hooks with a steel-tip center, laser sharp and magnetic. Even if the shots weren't high enough, hitting the boat ensured grip. Four seconds later, the synchronized thuds told the cruisers' crews that they were under attack. "Seven seconds to deck," McCall said tersely as he heard shouts from the bow of their cruiser.

Seven seconds later, the teams were on deck. Twelve seconds, fins off and hooks detached from the SAR-21s, up and ready to intimidate—to shoot if necessary. "RIB teams, U-Teams One and Two successful. Board cruisers at will."

"Roger that," Anson and Irish reported back. "Seems quiet."

Yeah—too quiet. McCall frowned. His fighter's instincts were up and screaming at the continued silence. Gunrunners and their buyers were notoriously paranoid; crews of up to twenty should be here by now, fully armed and ready to fight. Yet no one had arrived on the stern, thirty seconds after they'd hit deck…

McCall was a man who listened to that gut instinct; it had saved his ass too many times not to. "This stinks, boss. Sniffing a setup here. Call in the navy, stat. Send them to the mother lode with all firepower.''

"Roger that.''

"Go, teams," he said, feeling as if they'd walked into a trap.

"Get down, Beth. Keep out of sight, but check the back for possible points of entry and barricade them, any way you can.''

Beth nodded to Mitch, dropping to her hands and knees. "Danny, there are bad men out there. I want you to hide," she whispered. She couldn't chance Danny's safety on the bet that the threat wasn't Falcone. "Come with me toward the back, and when I tell you, climb the bell tower. I'll join you as soon as I can, but I need to help Mitch now.''

Danny, wide-eyed but well trained in his fear of bad men, nodded and crawled beside her toward the ragged altar.

"Nighthawk Team Three, Skydancer needs urgent assistance at Mankara village church. I repeat, urgent assistance, stat, with all available firepower. Request SAS backup!''

"Roger that, Skydancer," Panther snapped. "ETA two minutes.''

Beth, crouched over, ran with all speed toward the presbytery and nave at the back of the long-abandoned church. Peering over the edge of the broken windows, she saw young men, dressed in secondhand-store army fatigues, belly-crawling toward the door. They looked like kids playing dress-up, barely older than Danny, except for the assault rifles in their hands…

"Danny, go," she whispered. And with one terrified look, Danny took off running for the bell-tower stairs. Grabbing the half-blackened but sturdy chair, she shoved it against the doors, then slammed the partly rotten wooden bar into place between the old-fashioned twist-up handles.

It might hold them for a minute or two. She pulled out the Glock that Brendan had given to her before he'd headed out. "Just in case," he'd said with a short, serious look and a hard kiss.

Right now, she'd give anything to be able to have that moment back, forget her guilt and return his kiss.

Mitch started firing his rifle through a hole he'd punched into the locked front doors. Turning to her, seeing the gun in her hand, he yelled, "Hold them off until backup arrives!"

She nodded, her stomach roiling. *Brendan, I need you now! What do I do?*

And then, as the belly-crawling kids came closer, she whispered a brief prayer, took careful aim and started firing out the hole in the nave window.

Oh, yeah, baby, this *reeked* of setup...

Only two people on board each cruiser, and only the most basic of handguns for defense? And hell, they'd given up in two minutes flat without more than a shot or two fired. If these guys were in the arms trade, he was a raw recruit. So what did that make the people on the ship? *What was really on that ship?*

As they neared the small ship, more like a barge than anything else, he knew he was about to find out, but he had a gut feeling that he was going to hate the answer.

"What's the status on the *Hardwicke,* boss?"

For answer, Anson cocked his head toward the eastern horizon. "Two, three miles max. Keeping out of sight, but ready to go full steam. Can get its choppers there within two minutes."

Not close enough. His gut was churning, the pain behind his eyes like a fire; his every instinct screamed *danger.* "Call in the choppers from the *Hardwicke,* boss," he said softly.

Anson only glanced at him for a moment, then he nodded. "I already prepped them to coincide with our arrival. This stinks. I feel it in my gut." He pressed send on his paging device.

McCall smiled grimly. He hadn't realized how much he depended on Anson's having the same deep-gut reaction and forethought.

As the two cruisers approached the ship, McCall saw fifty men on deck, but among them was a face he recognized. Nobody important, just a lackey, a beefy no-brain brawler—but a faithful one. Two choppers lifted off from the back of the ship—big, shiny Apaches, built for speed, heading for the island.

Suddenly he wanted to puke. For he knew who was behind

this elaborate scheme, including ordering Skydancer to fly a convenient jet. He'd been had—all of the Nighthawks had been taken for a ride. Big-time. The rogue had struck again.

"There are no arms in that ship—it's Falcone, boss. He's after Beth and Danny—and our jet to get them all back to Minca bel Sol. Get that ship here fast, and every chopper—and clear two of all but the crew. I need them," he yelled. "We have to get back to Makanra—now!"

Beth felt like the painted red bull's-eye on a dartboard. A ring of furious kids with assault rifles surrounded them. All four of the Nighthawks and a single SAS team tried confusing them, to draw their fire. Mark time until the rest of the team returned. "We need to find out what the hell's going on," Mitch yelled grimly.

So Beth kept shooting, one careful bullet at a time, aimed just before or beside one soldier, to stop their advance toward the church. Yet closer they came. And while Mitch and the others had to dodge bullets everywhere, none came near Beth. No one attempted to burn the church to smoke them out. As if they'd been told to keep the people inside safe.

Dread pooled in the pit of her stomach. *There are no arms on that ship. It was a decoy to get me where he could take me.*

As if in answer, the soft *whump-whump* of rotor blades came to her, growing louder as they came closer. A chopper…no, two of them…and bile rose in her throat. Her deepest instincts told her it wasn't Brendan. *Falcone was here.*

And the boy-soldiers moved a little closer.

Time to stop playing. And she used all her skills to shoot now. Stifled screams came from the kids one after the other as she shot rifles out of their hands, or hit their fingers when she couldn't manage to hit the weapons. She couldn't make herself kill, or even seriously hurt these kids, even if it meant—

She shuddered and kept firing to disable, to disarm as many as she could, and prayed desperately for Brendan and his team of angel-rescuers to come back to her.

Chapter 22

"Nighthawk Teams One and Two, we are under attack. I repeat—we are under attack at the Makanra church!"

"We're on the way, Skydancer. Repeat—five teams on our way to you!" Chafing, McCall sat with his team in one of four S-70B Seahawks on its way to Makanra, the fastest the Australian Navy had and, thank God, the equivalent of Falcone's sleek, fast Apaches. They hadn't lost sight of Falcone. The navy pilot pushed the Seahawk to its limit of a hundred and eighty knots; the engine screamed and every green light on the futuristic black console had hit max.

Not fast enough!

But the pilot knew what he was doing. The objective was to take Falcone alive, not engage in an exchange of firepower with their machine guns or torpedoes. The gunners crouched behind their armaments, ready to go, but held off. The tactical coordinator beside the captain checked for deployment from the Apache constantly, ready for evasive action.

The Apache began descending, and as they followed it down, McCall saw the tower of a ruined church...and an advantage. "Secure and drop lines! Prepare to enter by way of the bell tower!"

Nightshift secured a line to the chopper and tossed it to him. "How many?" he yelled back.

"Full team. Nighthawk Team Two, secure the jet. Navy Teams One, Two and Three, join the outer perimeter of the church and take Falcone. NH Team One rescue subjects by way of tower."

After a quick-fire set of affirmatives, he spoke over the headset to the captain. "Captain Davies, hover over the bell tower as long as possible. Gunners to cover us!"

"Aye, Commander!" Davies bore right, to the rickety wooden tower. McCall prayed fervently that Beth and Danny were okay—

And then he heard the bell ringing!

As they reached the bell tower, to the deadly, whining symphony of constant bullets, McCall slithered down the rope with trained agility, and his heart almost burst with pride. For, all alone in that unsteady bell tower, jumping up and down to reach the bell, and whacking it with a ripped-up piece of flooring, was his little boy. "Help!" he was screaming between thuds to the brass bell. "Daddy, come back! Help us!"

"Danny-boy!" he yelled as he slid the last few feet and swung into the massive hole on one side. "Danny!"

"Daddy!" Danny screamed, and threw his skinny, shaking little body at McCall. McCall hugged him close. "Good boy, Danny. You did good—you did great! Now get down behind the bell, pal—there are bad men firing bullets. I'm going down to get your mom and Mitch, and we're all going for a ride in a helicopter, okay?"

"Okay, Daddy." Danny, still shaking with the valiant effort not to cry, dropped to the floor.

When the final man dropped into the bell tower and hit the ground running downstairs to support Skydancer, McCall shouted, "Rig a harness to a second line, Heidi."

"Yes, sir!"

"I'll be sending Danny up on it. Stay there to take care of him when he reaches the chopper."

"Yes, sir." Heidi's voice soured a little.

McCall didn't have time to care about Heidi's nonexistent maternal instincts. He raced down the stairs, leaping three at a time when they were uncertain or rotting. "Beth!" he roared.

"Brendan!" she screamed from the direction of the nave, and he bolted there. She stood in the shadows of a shattered stained-glass window. On either window beside her, Wildman and Braveheart were shooting lines in the dirt, creating dust clouds so thick it choked the kids outside and they couldn't see to shoot straight.

McCall hauled Beth so close she felt like an extension of him, part of his skin. "I'm sorry, so sorry to put you through this. We should have known, should have seen the setup!"

"It's my fault. He's after me," she cried fiercely, and dragged his mouth down to hers for a fast, hard kiss. "Now let's get to Danny, and out of here!"

He nodded. "Braveheart, Wildman, go ahead into the chopper. Remaining Nighthawks, block all exits and prepare to evacuate!"

They split into two groups—one man covered them as the others blocked the exits. Within a minute, all eight men would be in the bell tower.

McCall led Beth up the stairs as quickly as safety allowed.

Confused shouting reigned outside as dust clouds from more chopper blades sent dirt into unprotected eyes, throats and lungs. With deadly intent, Falcone's Apaches closed in on the outer ring of Nighthawk/SAS fighters, but the navy teams had landed, and men poured out to reinforce the rescue efforts.

The ragtag army of teenagers screamed and started to run.

And the second Nighthawk chopper remained hovering on the other side of the bell tower, covering the rescue operation in the church, facing off against Falcone's hovering Apache. Firepower against firepower, a bare three hundred feet apart: mutually assured destruction. It would just take one button.

But the Nighthawks inside never faltered. If that was what it took to stop Falcone's men moving in with relentless purpose on their mission subject, so be it. If they could take Falcone alive, kudos for them—if not, they would get Beth and Danny away safely, whatever the cost.

In the tower, the wind blasted around McCall and Beth as they tried to get Danny, squirming and crying, into the harness. "No! I can't! Mummy, I'll fall down and the bad men will get me!"

"No, baby, it's all rigged up to make you safe," Beth soothed frantically. "Come on, sweetie."

"No! No! The bad man will get me! I want Daddy!"

"He'll follow us. Come on, sweetie, you're such a big, brave boy. It's just a little ride—"

"No!" Danny screamed, wrenching out of her hold. "I want to go with Daddy. *I want to go with Daddy!*"

"Danny, sweetie—"

"Stop coddling him, Beth! No one's gonna shoot him when Falcone wants him safe!" McCall picked up Danny's wriggling body and dumped him in the triple-locking harness, strapping him up safely. "Danny-boy, you can't fall out of this, and the only way someone will get you is if you don't go now! If you want Mummy and Daddy up there with you, *stop fighting us.* Now make me proud of you, son, stop crying *and go!*"

Danny stopped crying with a savage hiccup and stared at McCall for a long moment. Then he nodded. "Y-yes, D-daddy."

"Good boy. Go!" he screamed into his two-way. Braveheart and Wildman, who'd swarmed up into the chopper ready to lift Danny, hiked him up and into the chopper while the gunners kept the Apache in their sights. Beth watched in open terror.

Not a single shot fired while Danny was in the harness; but as soon as he was inside safely, the Apache started moving in.

"Team One! Remain on ground and make your way to the other choppers or the jet. Rendezvous on board the *Hardwicke* for debriefing ASAP."

"Affirmative, sir!"

As soon as the harness fell again, McCall started shoving

Beth into it, to the violent whirring wind of two choppers' rotors too close together. "Send a line for me, stat!"

"Affirmative, sir!"

A line fell. He wrapped it around his waist, then looped its midsection around one wrist. "Let's go," he yelled into the two-way. "Take Beth up, stat. I'll haul myself, and cover her."

"Yes, sir!"

"No!" Beth screamed as her line yanked up, and he lifted himself on his line at the same time, forming a human shield for her. "No, Brendan, I'll go alone!"

"Don't go against the Team Commander's orders in an op," he yelled back. "This suit's double-lined. I'm SEAL-trained, Beth, I can protect myself." *And God forgive me for lying to you.* "Now go!"

She rose another foot, her lip bitten down hard, her eyes filled with fear and love as he matched her, motion for motion. He smiled at her. Her hand reached out to him, then fell. She looked so helpless. "Don't die, *amado,*" she mouthed. "Please don't die."

He smiled again, but didn't answer, and the terror in her eyes grew, knowing as well as he did that he was unable to lie in the last words he might ever speak to her. "I love you," he mouthed back. "I always loved you, Beth. I always will."

Her eyes closed, and tears dripped down, splashing over him as her body jerked and swayed with the movement of the lifting harness and he kept perfect pace, jump and hold.

They made it out of the bell tower, out of the possible dangers from broken tiles and splintered wood. She harnessed helplessly, he using all the strength he had to lift himself up, hand over hand, with palms and fingers he'd roughened with dirt from the floor to gain better grip. Even with his arm aching from the recent stitches, he kept pace with her. He gave her a cheeky wink. "Halfway up and all's well—" Another hand, another—

Thwack.

He jerked on the rope as the pain smacked into his side through the thick, padded wet suit he still wore. He'd known all along. *Of course Falcone would bring a sniper with him to take out Beth's bodyguards.* He'd take Beth someplace where some of his cronies would see him kill her, slowly. He couldn't let it happen. He had to keep climbing…if only he could *breathe.*

"Oh, my God!" Beth cried, as Brendan's body snapped backward, and he roared in agony but kept climbing, kept her covered with his body. "Brendan! Brendan's been hit!" *Thwack.*

Another hit. Oh, no, she couldn't see where, but she could see his hands, slipping just a fraction, and he fell a foot, two— oh, God, they were killing him.

"Take me down!" she screamed, making frantic hand movements in case those in the chopper couldn't hear her.

An inch down, two…and she twisted her totally-harnessed body around, reached down to him. "Brendan!"

Slowly, his face lifted. It was ashen-white. "Go." She couldn't hear the word, only read his lips. "Too close. They'll hit you." His right hand, above the left, gripped another foot higher on the rope.

He was still climbing in an effort to cover her, to save her.

"No! Damn it, McCall, *no!*" She threw her entire body into the reach and got a hold of his right wrist, still with the rope wrapped around it. "Damn you, *help me!*" she screamed.

Again, he said something she couldn't hear, but three she could read clearly. *Falcone catch you.*

She strained with her free hand, panicking as her left, gripping his right, began to slip. "I don't care! I won't live without you, McCall. Now *give me your hand!*"

He gazed at her one last time, his tortured eyes searching her face. Then, with agonizing slowness, as if his body fought his will, his left hand came up, gripped her right.

The chopper took off, racing for the sea and the safety of the waiting ship. Even in his agony, Brendan swung his body right and left, making them both a moving target as the bullets kept flying, flying around the fight going on below them, and at them.

Thwack. She felt another small, sickening thud, and the horrifying jerk of his beloved body. Three shots…and he was losing strength to hold on…

She'd never blessed her tough potter's hands more than now. Her rough skin gave grip that nicely moisturized model's hands never would. But oh, how she wished she'd wrapped the rope around her wrists first for strength. She was losing more every moment.

Thank God, they were out of range of the bullets, it seemed. *Hang on, Brendan, meu amado! Hang on! Fight!*

Falcone's Apache was chasing them! Thank God, it was held up by returning fire to the Navy chopper behind it, but it was coming after her, after Danny. Was Falcone that insane, that obsessed with his so-called honor, with killing her and taking Danny that he'd chase them all the way to a navy fighter ship?

She couldn't look up, or cry out, or think. All her strength was focused on holding Brendan, on trying to ignore the agonizing burn of pain in her wrists and shoulders, elbows and every muscle in her upper body, stopping that sickening fall to earth—

She fought it with all the desperation she had, but Brendan could no longer help—he was unconscious and a dead weight, too heavy for her to hold. Another twenty seconds, and her left wrist snapped, her right shoulder popped—and he fell from her useless hands. "No! *No!*" she screamed in despair. "Brendan! *Brendan!*"

He fell only twenty feet, jerking with a *snap* against the rope tied against his waist—the snap of a fraying rope…

"Get him in! Get him inside!" she screeched. The chopper swayed and rocked as it dashed frantically toward the ship. And inch by agonizing inch, McCall was lifted up, up—

The Apache was gaining on them, less than half a mile behind.

Four feet to the chopper, and safety—three—

Snap.

His body hurtled past her helpless, useless arms, and she couldn't do a thing to save him. "Brendan!"

Three. Two. One… *Splash.* Her eyes snapped open. They'd

reached the ocean before he fell. They were actually past the beach, the bay and were in open seas. Protected by that double-thick, strong wet suit, maybe he could have survived the fall, but she was trapped inside this damn stupid *harness* with two busted arms—

Another body hurtled past her—a big, male body attached to two lines. He dived like an Olympian, straight and graceful and *fast,* over sixty feet down into the ocean.

The chopper dropped altitude until it was only about twenty feet above ocean level. And slowly, slowly Beth felt her harness jerk and lift, until at last she'd made it inside the chopper.

As the big, bearlike Nighthawk pulled her in, and Danny, not understanding the gravity of the situation, had swarmed on her before she was fully standing, Heidi dropped a rescue stretcher-harness attached to six lines leading into two, right and left.

With a neat splash, the diver entered the ocean about eight feet from where Brendan floated facedown in the water. In seconds he'd flipped the body over and onto the stretcher-harness and hooked both himself and Brendan securely onto it. He signaled up to the chopper, and began CPR as they lifted up, up—

A strange *honk, honk* noise came from the chopper, like something from a Hollywood thriller, but Beth barely registered. Her world had shrunk to two people, and for once, one wasn't her son, cuddled safely on her lap. The two men on the stretcher held all her attention—Brendan and the tall, bronzed man with the dark hair… *Wildman*—who was struggling to keep Brendan alive.

The *honk, honk* sounds were piercing; she heard the captain yelling, but it all seemed far off, surreal. She only noticed the Apache swinging away in her peripheral vision, noting it with the same sense of distance that she'd accept a news item on TV.

Then four choppers seemed to burst into existence all around them, rotor blades filling the air with sound and furious whirring. The navy choppers from the second warship passed their chopper. The cavalry had finally arrived, and were chasing off Falcone's Apache. It was over. Falcone couldn't escape.

Then Braveheart, Heidi and the gunners brought Brendan and Wildman into the chopper. "He's alive but losing blood beneath the suit," Wildman reported. "Captain, apprise Team Commander Two of the situation and tell him to set up the O.R. with the ship's surgeon. And get to the ship, stat!"

"Aye, sir. ETA four minutes."

The race was on to save the man she loved.

Chapter 23

"Nine hours. It's been almost nine hours!" Even bound by two slings and plaster on one arm, and in obvious pain, Beth paced the room like a caged tigress. Anson almost felt the lashing of her tail, she was so wound up. "What could be taking so long?"

"He has three bullets lodged in him," he replied on a sigh. "It takes hours to stabilize a man, and the wet suits are real hard to get off without hurting him. They'd have to cut it off with razors to avoid further injury."

"But what if they found something pierced...an artery? What if infection set in, and he hasn't got the strength to fight it—"

"That's some imagination." He tried to smile, hating the picture she'd painted. "You should try your hand at writing."

"A spy novel," Wildman suggested, grinning. "You could write a blockbuster, based on your life story."

But the woman wasn't diverted—nope, not a bit. She didn't even acknowledge the news of Falcone's capture, or his sitting in the brig below, awaiting immediate extradition to the States. He doubted a nuke dropping in front of her would get her interest. "What if one bullet's lodged too deeply to reach? And if—"

Braveheart stepped in front of her, not touching her—the woman had Keep Off signs posted all over her. "He'll pull through—he has a lot to live for. He has a family."

"But—but I—" She worried at her lip, clearly on a negative and fearful trip, despite the nonresponse of the team.

Skydancer took over the job that Braveheart had, for once, failed to get right. He smiled at Beth with the understanding of a family man. "Beth, I've seen Flipper pull through impossible situations and heal from wounds in weeks that would take most guys months. You know him, he's one tough nut to crack—"

"That he is." She gave a short, bitter laugh, and like a torrent bursting from banked-up clouds, she broke. "He told me about his past, you know, but only when it suited the mission. He gives me so much, but he doesn't *share* unless it helps his job. It's as if my knowing anything about him as a man is a breach of international security!"

The men all shared wry looks. Yeah, that sounded familiar. Adrenalin junkies, they could respond to an SOS in seconds, but when it came to love they were as dysfunctional as a fourteen-year-old boy suddenly meeting Elle Macpherson or Cameron Diaz.

Even Heidi had that look on her face. The comprehension none of them wanted to face: how their lives and personas squared up to civilian expectations, and their complete inability to live up to that one word none of them could handle. *Sharing.*

But Anson had seen the look on Flipper's face when he looked at this woman and the kid curled up on a cot in the corner. After ten years of the most faithful life-and-death service he could ask for in a commander, McCall needed—and deserved—a bit of help here. But what to do he didn't know, apart from handing over Flipper's file, which was classified information. Right this moment he was almost tempted if it would keep the damn woman quiet for half an hour and let them worry for Flipper without imagining him bleeding to death on the table.

Before he could do more than toy with an idea he knew he'd never give in to, the O.R. doors swung open and she forgot everything else. Her gaze fixed on Irish, blazing with hope and need and *terror*. It was obvious that Beth Silver didn't just love Flipper—she'd handed him her soul. Anson felt another tug of crazy wistfulness—the kind he'd felt too often lately.

No. It was irritation. Losing his best, always-on-call operatives to love. Evoking damnable, irremovable *memories*.

"Well?" he barked, to cover his weakness.

Irish looked hollow-eyed and gray with exhaustion, but he and Songbird had radiant smiles on their faces. "He's lost a lot of blood and his spleen's gone, but he'll make it. He's awake."

While the Nighthawks celebrated with grins and back-slapping and jokes, McCall's woman fell to her knees, her face incandescent with gratitude and love. And though she spoke in Portuguese, almost everyone could translate her words. "Thank you, Father, oh thank you for saving the man I love. I will keep my promise to you. I will make him happy for the rest of his life."

Damn grit in his eyes. He wasn't the kind of guy who indulged in emotion. Hell, no. He had a life, and it was best lived alone. It had been that way since he was eighteen and made the one decision that set his life in stone.

But that grit in his eyes was damn annoying.

Anson shook his head to clear it, and stalked into the O.R. to apprise his Commander of the outcome of the mission, before he let love have its way with the most committed and courageous commanding operative he'd ever had.

Fairy kisses wakened him from the exhausted doze he'd fallen into when Anson finally finished the debriefing of the mission.

They were featherlight, sweet, tickling sensations shooting through his nerve endings. Each and every one was a healing of body and spirit. Each whispered word a balm on his wounded soul.

"Amo-o," she whispered, over and over as she kissed his face with ultimate tenderness, in pure love. "Minha alegria, faz me viver, meu amado, meu Brendan." *I love you. You are my joy, you make me live, my love, my Brendan.*

"You have to get well," she whispered between kisses. "I can't live without you. I need you so much. I love you so much!"

He turned his face, meeting her petal-soft kiss with one of his own. "I know," he whispered back in Portuguese. And the miracle was, he *did* know. He finally felt her love in all his damaged heart and soul. He'd had nowhere to hide from the moment she'd risked her life to save him. The thought of what she'd done for him unlocked the dark vault holding his trust captive. His terrified cynicism could no longer override the faith in her that had begun the night she'd given him her name, and her heart. She *loved* him. She'd held him up for miles before she'd had to let him fall. Beth, his wonderful, incredible Beth, truly loved him, a one-in-a-lifetime love. It wasn't like the brief infatuation Mom had had with his handsome, wild father, easily won, just as quickly destroyed. "I love you, too," he said, still in her native tongue.

She kissed him again, then again. Her eyes, those amazing, unforgettable eyes were shining with happiness. "I know."

He grinned. "Love in two languages. This is fun." Then he truly looked at her. She was beyond exhausted, still clad in the grubby gear from the church, arms bound in slings and plaster, but her smile was radiant, lighting her eyes from within.

She leaned into him, nuzzled his unshaven cheek, his jaw, his lips. "I've been so scared, Brendan. Life without you…" She shuddered, but her kiss was filled with sweet relief.

When the kiss ended, he touched her sling, her plastered arm. "You broke your arms, holding on to me until we reached water."

Her lovely eyes, red-rimmed with exhaustion, filled with tears. "I had to. My life is empty without you, meu amado, *minha alegria,*" she said simply. "Don't make me live another ten years without you."

My love, my joy. To Beth, that's what he was—what he'd always been. After long years of wandering in the darkness alone, Brendan McCall found home, and love and the courage to give her his complete heart. "Not even ten minutes. We're getting married—properly this time—and we'll never be apart again."

She shone and glowed like the sun, but shook her head. "Don't make promises you can't keep. You'll always have to go away on missions. Just make sure you come home to us," she whispered, and kissed him. "I can't do what you do, but I'm proud that you help make life safer for so many people. You keep making a difference. I'll be at home with our children, waiting for you."

Moved beyond words by her love and pride in him, not trying to change him, he drew her down for a long, deep kiss. "You'll never have cause to regret it. I'll make sure of it."

"So long as I have your love, and our family, I'll have all I ever wanted," she whispered, kissing him over and over. "I want babies, Brendan. I want lovely fat babies with forest-green eyes and smiles that melt my heart, just like their daddy."

His own heart melted at her words. "We'll start on that as soon as we're both healed," he murmured huskily.

"Daddy?"

The doors had swung open while they'd been wrapped up in each other, but at the quavering little voice, McCall looked around. "Hey, Danny boy. I could use a glass of water, if you've got one on you," he joked, to lighten the worry on his son's face.

His son. Man, it felt good to think of this adorable, giving child as his own son and to be a part of a family as beautiful as the one that had claimed him. To know that, for the rest of his life, they'd be there for him as he'd be for them, loving him as much as he loved them.

A family. He had a *family*…

Danny was beside him before McCall had finished his sentence, patting his bandaged chest with a shaking little hand, as if needing to reassure his baby mind that his newfound father was still alive. "I love you, Daddy. I love you."

McCall grinned fatalistically as he hugged the boy. Knowing his Beth, she'd said something to Danny about telling people you love them in case they die. He'd have to keep that woman so busy in the future, she wouldn't have time to scare the hell out of their kids with her fearful pronouncements. But words of love had been rare in his life, and they crept inside his heart with bone-warming sweetness. "I'm fine, Danny boy. I'll be up and out of this bed by tomorrow."

Danny's anxious dark eyes scanned McCall's. "Really?"

"Really-really," he vowed solemnly. "We'll be playing ball in a few weeks. Got to get you off that reserves bench."

Danny's face broke into a smile—a big, wide-open grin of disbelieving joy. "We're going home? You're coming with us?"

"You betcha, kid." McCall winked at him, ignoring the pulling twinges of pain in about a million different areas of his body. Pain meds must be starting to wear off.

Danny sniffed and wiped at his eyes with his sleeve. "I thought you'd be angry, and not want to be with us no more…I was such a bad boy. I'm sorry, Daddy…"

The déjà-vu slammed into him and with it, a revelation that Danny—and he as a child—couldn't know. Beth made a tiny sound of distress, but McCall spoke before she could. He'd been there—man, had he been there—and only he, McCall, could stop Danny's fear from turning into damage. "Danny, I don't have any experience at this dad thing, so I'm going to say and do things that hurt you sometimes, but you could *never* make me so angry that I'd leave you. If I'm ever so stupid as to leave, it won't be your fault, it will be mine. Kids don't make adults so mad they'd go away. Grown-ups are just taller kids, Danny, they make mistakes, too."

"Huh?" Danny's head tilted in puzzled inquiry.

McCall was too lost in a stunned kind of newfound freedom to answer. He finally saw his mother with the clarity of adult perspective; he knew why she'd taken only Meg, and left him behind. Meg, quiet, artistic and playing with her dolls, had been *easy*. She'd made Mom feel good about her limited child-rearing skills and low tolerance for any trouble. He'd been a difficult child, always into everything and aggressive—but that wasn't why she'd left. It was *her* problem. He'd been a little kid in need of patient guidance, not her tears, condemnation and comparisons to Meg. Mom hadn't run away from him, she'd run from reminders of what she liked least about herself.

He'd brought himself up, with help on the way, but all in all, he'd done a pretty good job. He'd dragged himself out of his sordid world and created a better one. A man who defined success by what he gave to others. He was a man who could raise a son in pride, who could have love and family, yeah, even a picket fence.

Looking at the anxious face of his little boy, he smiled. "I guess what it boils down to, is that I love you and your mom, so you're stuck with me from now on."

He winced as Danny almost jumped on him, snuggling his head almost flush against a bullet wound, but he didn't complain. He didn't think he'd ever feel like griping at the inconveniences of being so thoroughly loved. "It's all right, son," he murmured, caressing Danny's spiky mop of dark hair as the boy held on to him, afraid to let go.

"Yes, sweetie, it is all right. It's all going to be fine," Beth caressed Danny's back as she spoke, her voice holding a confidence, a security McCall had never heard in her before, but it was McCall she looked at, her eyes filled with absolute trust and total love. "Daddy's coming home with us, and we'll be a family. Daddy will help you play football, and with homework, and we'll give you brothers and sisters. How does that sound?"

Danny lifted his face. McCall gulped at the look of utter joy there, but the responsibility fell gently onto his shoulders with a rightness, a pure feeling of happiness he'd never known before. Having a family would be hard work, but he'd never faced the unknown with such eager anticipation. He nodded and winked at Danny. "It's true, pal. I'm your dad from now on. Now where's that water I asked for, son?" He added with a grin, "Lesson one in having a dad—you obey him when he wants water. Off you go."

Laughing, Danny dashed off, and McCall turned to Beth with a smile. "So when will we set the wedding date for? I'd like Mitch and Lissa and the kids to come. We can ask them about it when we pick up Bark."

It didn't even surprise him that he felt no fear, expected no rejection. Looking into Beth's eyes, he felt absolutely bathed in her love. Beth knew all about his sordid past, and she still loved him with all her fierce loyalty and pride, loved both the boy he'd been and the man he'd become.

After years in black, rusted chains, he walked free of his past, and faced the future with the sun on his face.

"It had better be soon, I think," Beth replied, with more butterfly kisses. "Or I'll be walking down the aisle with a big fat tummy."

He frowned. "But you can't know already if—" Yet the thought thrilled him. Beth, rounded with his child.

"I know," she sighed. "No, I'm planning ahead." She smiled down at him and whispered, "You'd better get well soon, *amado*. You have a very bad girl on your hands. Here I am with two broken arms, you with bullet wounds and almost died last night, and all I can think about is when I can jump you."

He burst out laughing. It felt damn good, healing even, despite the twinges of pain it caused his wounds. "My tigress."

"You'd better believe it, McCall." Her brows wiggled in naughty provocation, so unlike the reserved woman of last week. Happiness had changed her, given her wings, and man, she was flying. "And when you're well, I'll prove it—thoroughly. Now that I don't have to keep my hands off you, they're going to be a permanent fixture on your body."

He grinned. "Hold that thought for the next forty years."

"Here it is, Daddy. I got your water." Danny returned at that moment, proudly carrying a dripping glass.

"Thanks, pal." But though he drank it, right now he wanted something other than water. Putting down the glass, he held out his arms to them, holding them close against his heart, and felt true peace for the first time. "I have a son. A wife. Babies to come." He shook his head. "Six months ago, I was alone."

Beth turned his face to hers and kissed him, deep, soft and loving. "You never will be again." Then she grinned. "Get used to it, family man. You're going to be surrounded by your wife and children. I want at least three more kids, and after years of being a single mother, I believe in the benefits of shared parenting, diaper changes, cleaning spit-ups and all."

"Yes, ma'am." McCall laughed in the sheer joy of it. Brendan McCall, The Untouchable, The Ice Man, complete career Nighthawk would never be the same man again. A harassed dad, diaper changer, part-time football coach, helping out with her church fetes, cooking and cleaning and taking out the garbage. Helping his adoring son with homework, crazy in love with a fiercely loyal, sensual tigress who did whatever it took to make his life right, and who thought the sun shone only when he was near her.

Nope, life didn't get any better than this.

* * * * *

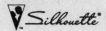

If you enjoyed what you just read,
then we've got an offer you can't resist!

Take 2 bestselling
love stories FREE!
Plus get a FREE surprise gift!

Clip this page and mail it to Silhouette Reader Service™

IN U.S.A.
3010 Walden Ave.
P.O. Box 1867
Buffalo, N.Y. 14240-1867

IN CANADA
P.O. Box 609
Fort Erie, Ontario
L2A 5X3

YES! Please send me 2 free Silhouette Intimate Moments® novels and my free surprise gift. After receiving them, if I don't wish to receive anymore, I can return the shipping statement marked cancel. If I don't cancel, I will receive 6 brand-new novels every month, before they're available in stores! In the U.S.A., bill me at the bargain price of $3.99 plus 25¢ shipping and handling per book and applicable sales tax, if any*. In Canada, bill me at the bargain price of $4.74 plus 25¢ shipping and handling per book and applicable taxes**. That's the complete price and a savings of at least 10% off the cover prices—what a great deal! I understand that accepting the 2 free books and gift places me under no obligation ever to buy any books. I can always return a shipment and cancel at any time. Even if I never buy another book from Silhouette, the 2 free books and gift are mine to keep forever.

245 SDN DNUV
345 SDN DNUW

Name	(PLEASE PRINT)	
Address	Apt.#	
City	State/Prov.	Zip/Postal Code

* Terms and prices subject to change without notice. Sales tax applicable in N.Y.
** Canadian residents will be charged applicable provincial taxes and GST.
  All orders subject to approval. Offer limited to one per household and not valid to
  current Silhouette Intimate Moments® subscribers.
  ® are registered trademarks of Harlequin Books S.A., used under license.

INMOM02   ©1998 Harlequin Enterprises Limited

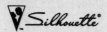
INTIMATE MOMENTS™

An Order of Protection
(Silhouette Intimate Moments #1292)
by
KATHLEEN CREIGHTON

A brand-new book in her bestselling series

STARRS OF THE WEST

Jo Lynn Starr's best friend is missing but no one will believe her. No one except police officer Scott Cavanaugh—and even he has his doubts. But as they work together to unravel the mystery, one thing becomes perilously clear—their growing attraction for each other!

Available May 2004 at your favorite retail outlet.

COMING NEXT MONTH

SIMCNM0404